T0246893

SHOW GAME

STEVE ANDERSON

OPEN ROAD
INTEGRATED MEDIA
NEW YORK

ISBN: 978-1-5040-8677-6

Published in 2024 by Open Road Integrated Media, Inc.
180 Maiden Lane
New York, NY 10038
www.openroadmedia.com

SHOW
GAME

TUESDAY, OCTOBER 17
ALEX

I have the bastard, finally, I got him. Target number one. He's cowering on the high-backed chair before me, in the near dark. We keep a single harsh light on him, a bare caged bulb hanging from one of the rafters, just above his eyes, still swinging a little. He'd tried standing twice and bumped into the bulb before my hard eyes made him drop right down again.

It was so easy. We have duct tape and various tools of the trade in a tactical backpack and are more than happy to use them. But he doesn't even need taping up. He's clenching the chair's cracked leather so hard his knuckles are whiter than those pricey snow-white crowns of his. It can't help that his seat resembles a dentist chair.

"You tricked me," he keeps repeating. "I trusted you."

"Sound familiar?" I say and let the question hang in the air a good minute. To see how he likes it done to him. I'll let him fill in the rest, going back decades.

Oh, before we get too far—I will be known as "Alex." It's my vigilante name, for my first-ever job. I'm speaking to my target in a lower, rougher voice to help cover myself.

Dwayne Specklin, forty-nine and quivering before us, is the founder and head pastor of one of the largest megachurches in southern California, let alone the country. But before that, before he was "ordained," he was a scoutmaster and Scout unit chaplain for many, many years. So many boys had put their trust in him.

You might see where this is going. But I'll let Dwayne Specklin tell you, and soon.

We're in a warehouse in San Diego. It's only minutes from the surf and the palms and so many retired admirals' young grandsons, but inside here it's cold enough to be the Pacific Northwest. Up north, I'd found out, was where Dwayne had escaped justice after molesting his first ten-year-old, a lowly Cub Scout. All Dwayne had to do back then was abscond for college.

On one side of Dwayne is an aluminum briefcase, silver and dinged up, displayed upright on an old music stand. It holds video of him with boys, ready to roll on an old and unregistered iPad. Sick and vile footage. I won't tell you what Dwayne was doing to those boys. After months of trying, I'd gotten the video from one of his accomplices—a junior pastor.

Dwayne has to know what's inside the briefcase. It's bathed in a red glow from the color lens of the military-grade LED flashlight mounted to our tripod.

He keeps glaring at the metal case like it's a bomb ticking down to one.

Then I raise the handheld voice changer to my mouth. He recoils at the sight.

"Are you ready?" I say in my newly digitally warped tone.

He releases a little yelp.

"Ah, now . . ." I come in close and lean down to him, just like he as Scout chaplain might have done while visiting another troubled boy at home, in a time of such dire need and defense-lessness. I even stroke his plump knee gently. A heat of disgust swells in my throat.

"Are you ready?" I repeat. "It's time to play the Show Game."

"The wha? . . ." Dwayne's eyes widen.

I don't answer. In my planning, I decided to reverse the wording of "Game Show." Let him figure it out. It's barely after-noon. We've got all day and night.

I let Dwayne squint around a few moments, first at the brief-case again, then around the whole room. All he is going to find, if his bleary, puffy eyes can adjust enough, is our dim corner of an old machine shop, its only windows opening to a fully dark former manufacturing hall, both now gutted. Then there's a cavernous warehouse surrounding that, and on and on, like some Russian doll of those abandoned factory locations from the season finales of thriller shows. I look around along with Dwayne, following his eyes and scrunched-up nose. We see corrugated metal walls, busted windows, jagged exposed bolts sawed off, and gaping holes and hatches to who knows where. Grease stains, oily puddles left from somewhere, something.

I flinch inside a moment, wondering what might have first activated my target's depraved mind. Maybe a Scout leader or priest had committed the same abuse on Dwayne, or even his own father? Maybe Dwayne, deep down, has the same develop-mental age as the ones he deceives and abuses.

Who knows. Screw him.

Dwayne is looking up now, as you do, probably seeking that megachurch god he justified his crimes to—if he even bothered. But all he can probably see is the white glare of that bare bulb, and he sniffs and snorts, and his nostrils surely fill with the tang of stale oil and dead insects and the boozy metallic fear breath of his own bastard self.

Target number one is ready to play. My first contestant! I have to admit, I feel a little swell of happy warmth in my chest. I cannot reiterate how easy this has been, especially for my first. To help ease Dwayne's stage jitters, we have a bottle of Old Taylor, ten bucks plus tax at the nearby Vons. We had offered him a paper cup, but he drank straight from the bottle despite claiming to be a lifelong teetotaler. And I was all too happy to corrupt him. The booze had made him gasp and emit a wheezing trill that left him breathing heavy and drooling. Then the tears started running down his cheeks. I was expecting vomit soon. I'd remembered to wear my waterproof boots just in case.

Talk about drinking to forget. It was far too late for that, though. Because I'm here to make Dwayno remember. Total recall.

Time to play.

"Dwayne?"

"Yes. No," he says. "I'm not ready. I don't get it! Who are you? What do you want?"

"I want you to tell me what you did."

"Did?"

"You know. All of it. And do not lie. Because we will know."

His eyes go dead a moment. Silence ensues. He stares at his white knuckles. His face flashes green. I see it coming so I move back with a quick little two-step and the stream of hot vomit gushes out straight for the industrial floor drain we'd conveniently placed the chair near. He misses himself but it splatters, then it dribbles down the front of his pearlescent, still tucked-in golf shirt. Thank god he wipes at his chin because I'm not going to keep staring at that in this harsh downward light.

It's such a contrast to the public Dwayne Specklin, a rotund if not fleshy fellow with pale pink skin that you never would've guessed spent much of its adult life in sunny California. His full head of hair somehow still more blond than gray, and a little spiky. His look reminds me of a jokey football coach, capable of either great care or extreme pressure within seconds.

He always had this little upturned grin in all those official photos and videos I researched, just one side of his mouth, but without that grin he truly does look like the eternally enabled child molester that he is. I wonder if he'd trained himself in the mirror at some point. He's still wearing the pricey kangaroo leather sandals he had on when we'd approached him, his feet and toes soft and pedicured with a nearly white gloss.

He squints at me, and at the metal case again, then around. Squints, case, around. This repeats for like a minute.

"Who sent you?" he says finally.

Nobody sent me. I sent myself. Let him wonder why. This should be for all the victims. Let Dwayne Specklin mine his foul and barbed memory until blind.

"Someone from the congregation?" He releases another snort. "It was them, wasn't it?"

My eyebrows raise behind the dark glasses I use for my disguise. But I don't say anything.

He releases a little grumble that makes the vomit on the rolls of his golf shirt vibrate. "She put you up to this," he wheezes. "She did, didn't she?"

He must be talking about his wife. Brenda. Her very own father founded the megachurch. My research shows that she hates Dwayne's guts from stomach to sphincter, but they're both too far into this scam now. She's been committing her own crimes—embezzlement and coke and multiple threesome affairs to name a few—but who's counting? Screw her, too, what a cliché. Let's just say I'm doing his better half a big favor.

"Does this mean it's been happening at the church, too," I say, "and not just in the Scouts? Gee, what a surprise." I look out around the empty warehouse as if a studio audience were here to share my amazement. His congregation maybe. The family members of so many Scouts. The boys.

"Well, this is going to be quite a show," I add, but I growl it because the hot disgust in my throat is now filling my chest and fists with full boiling anger. Hearing me makes Dwayne squeeze his eyes shut so hard you'd think I was squirting a fire hose at them.

He eventually gets that there's no fire hose and, after a couple false starts that sound like hiccups, he says:

"So that's what this is all about."

He says it with surprising resolve, as if announcing the start of one of his annoyingly popular sermons that are more like folksy skits, complete with live backing music. Recalling this only makes me angrier. He plays all the characters in his sermons himself—except, that is, when he needs a little boy character onstage. And there's always such huge applause, a nice pat on the head. I'm guessing those boys are also Cub Scouts. And why not? If anything, current times have shown us that the real crimes are always found right in front of us.

"It is," I say. "And we're going all the way back to your first time."

He takes a moment. He mumbles to himself, staring down at his hands now in his lap, and I wonder if it's his way of praying. Then he reaches down for the bottle next to the chair and takes a steady and measured swig as if it were Gatorade. As if he had drunk booze his whole life.

On the tripod next to me is an unregistered, no-SIM-card iPhone with the video set to record.

"You're not going to kill me, are you?" he says.

"Nope. Not me. But maybe the truth will, with any luck."

He nods a couple times, but to himself.

"So here's how this works," I say. "See that metal case—"

"What's in it?" he blurts, one shoulder up in defense. "What's in that thing?"

"Excellent question. For some, it's clear proof of their horrible deeds. A photo or video. Someone confessing. A victim exposing. For others, it's hearing that the only person or thing they ever loved will be horribly destroyed. For still others, maybe it's their worst phobia, which they'll now have to face. Who knows. Pandemic's over, but why couldn't it be some new virus worse than COVID?"

Of course I'm not going to tell him. Let him shiver. Then Dwayne actually shudders. The peach fuzz on his forearms stands up in the light.

"If you don't answer? We open it."

It's a major goal of mine never to use violence. The temptation is real, and I don't like how warm it makes me feel inside just imagining it. But I don't want to become just like my targets. It's enough just to make Dwayne's fears run wild and dark and deadly. That's what he did to his victims' fears. And it devastated them.

I'm betting that my contestants will want to win so badly, to tell the truth their own way, in a manner that they themselves can own, that they will prefer to confess rather than have that case opened.

"And when we open it? That is how you lose the game," I add.

Dwayne's blinking at the case glowing red, then at me, then at the case.

"To win, you have to earn a hundred fifty points!" I say, still using the voice changer. "You get fifty for admitting that you did it. You get another fifty for saying who helped you directly. Then, you get that final fifty for saying that you are sorry. To the world. To all those who you hurt, who you devastated, who you let die thinking they were worthless. If you do all that, you win—you're set free!"

I so want him to win. He may think he's free. He may be deceiving himself into thinking that everything's all right, that he still won. But it won't work. He will be destroyed, since all that he covets so much will be taken from him for good. I want him to be humiliated. I want people to look at him the wrong way or, better yet, to turn away from him. I want his self-worth shot. I want him so deprived of self that he even considers killing himself.

Just like too many of his victims.

Dwayne's eyes are wide again. His mouth has parted slightly, unable to speak.

"Ah, you're wondering what comes after?" I say. "What people will think? How you'll sleep at night, maybe? You'll be all right, really you will."

See how I did that? I'm lying to him, giving him solace just like he did to others.

"I mean, you apparently slept fine before," I add.

"This is not fair," he says.

I shrug. "Welcome," I say. "Welcome to the world of all of us who get screwed over by the likes of you every single day."

"Jesus," he mutters. "Why? Why now?"

"I told you. Because it's time to tell the truth. It's time to say who, and what, you really are. For justice. For healing." I take a deep breath, poised to speak from my diaphragm like a game show announcer. I tighten my grip around the voice changer. "Now. Are . . . you . . . ready?"

Dwayne doesn't answer. He just stares, his eyes dimming.

I take that as a yes. I push the red button. Recording . . .

WEDNESDAY, OCTOBER 18
OWEN

Owen Tanaka of *AltaVista News* deleted one sentence, then another, cutting that whole lovely lede he'd polished so many times in anticipation of this very day, and then he cut whole paragraphs, even that crucial nut graph he'd massaged one last time early this morning, cursing under his breath now. He abandoned all his allegations and proof, and the truth. He moved the whole document to the trash, then emptied it with a digital clunk, lowering his index finger to the return key like a heavy guided missile from on high. Dork that he was, he even made a cartoon bomb sound.

His big story was over. Annihilated, beyond saving.

"Disturbing Questions Emerge About Church Leader," his headline had read.

Owen had thought trashing the draft would ease the tightening in his chest, but it only moved the feeling lower, into his gut.

"For what?" he muttered, slouching inside his cubicle, his old chair creaking.

Out in the open newsroom, computer and TV screens still had the already infamous online video playing, as if on a loop. Other screens showed countless news stories covering it.

Everyone will remember this day, he thought. But to him it would be the anniversary of losing his biggest story so far.

In his agitation he picked up his mobile phone aimlessly, something he rarely did, and couldn't help clicking on the video yet again. It started with a simple black screen, then a scrolling title that read "Contestant #1: Dwayne Specklin." The rules of the "game" followed. You "won" by reaching 150 points, but if you didn't get there? You lost, which meant opening "the case." The black screen then dissolved to reveal a video of Dwayne Specklin in a chair, under a harsh light, sitting next to a metal briefcase on a pedestal in a red glow, Dwayne Specklin stealing shocked glances at the case like it was a sleeping pit bull without a leash. He had something pale brown and clumpy running down the front of him like baby food. There was no sign of a gun, but who knew what they had pointed on him off camera.

Dwayne Specklin didn't fight it much. He even cleared his throat. Looked down the lens of the camera. "I admit," he began, "to molesting hundreds, maybe thousands of boys over decades if you take into account my accomplices. It started up in the Northwest, yes. I thought it would end when I left. It only got worse when I rose up the Scouts. I certainly did not let up after I was ordained and named leader of my church. Some of the boys' names include . . ." He named names, which seemed unfair as well as unethical, until it was confirmed over the course of the morning that he was only naming those few who had tried to sue him. Who were willing to talk. The rumors had followed him for years, but he had fended off all attacks. The Scouts had lawyers, and his own church surely did. Fending off, Dwayne Specklin now admitted, had included buying off victims, and settlements, and even intimidation if required.

A *ding!* was heard, and a red light flashed along with it. Dwayne Specklin had his first fifty points.

He proceeded to name more names, including all those he knew who were doing the same inside the Scouts, inside the megachurch, and all those they'd hired to shut people up and keep it a secret. "The Catholic Church can't hold a candle to us," he added with a sickly grin, just one side of his mouth turned down, his teeth tainted red from the glowing case. "Some of my victims, though? Some joined me in doing it. One is a junior pastor. His name is . . ."

Ding ding! One hundred points . . .

Dwayne Specklin took a moment. He stared nearly straight at the screen, at someone next to the camera. His brow seemed to double in size in the harsh downlight. He stared at the floor a moment. His head shot up.

"I'm sorry. All right? I apologize to everyone. I hurt so many. They can never have their lives back. I'm so sorry . . ." He let the words trail off.

Ding ding ding!

"We have a winner," said the digitally altered voice. It was automatically subtitled, which helped because the voice sounded like Darth Vader as a child.

Dwayne Specklin's face scrunched up like he wanted to spit, and that downturned, lopsided sneer returned. This gave the impression that Dwayne Specklin was actually not sorry, not yet, but that he might be soon enough, and dearly so. The video faded out as Dwayne Specklin bowed his head, his head bobbing a little, possibly from sobbing.

The sensational video ran three minutes, forty seconds.

Owen stared at the blank black screen, recapping what happened afterward as if covering the story himself.

Dwayne Specklin had been found a few hours ago in an abandoned warehouse in San Diego not far from his ministry. He was asleep on the floor, covered in his own vomit. The police found him after an anonymous call was placed—likely from an untraceable pay phone, it was already being reported. He had been there all night, didn't even bother to leave after his captor was long gone. Owen guessed Dwayne didn't want to face his real self out in the world. His destroyed self. The perpetrators, or whistleblower, or vigilante, or hero, depending on your angle, had left Dwayne a pillow that he took down to the floor. The old leather chair still stood there along with the music pedestal that had held the metal briefcase. A nearly empty bottle of whiskey. The video had been posted to FreeChain, YouTube, Vimeo, TikTok, and other sites by an otherwise anonymous user named "Alex." It had gone so viral, was copied and reposted so many times, that it was pointless to take it down. Meanwhile, Alex had also alerted the authorities and major media.

That was this morning. It was now one p.m. Owen tried tuning out the noise in the open newsroom around him, the whoops and whistles and excited talk and the voice of Dwayne Specklin telling the whole damning truth replayed and replayed.

Owen shook and shook his head. What was left for him to uncover now? The Specklin article had been by far his best piece. He'd been working on it for a year. He had been in such a rut after coming to *AltaVista* and had been searching for that perfect story encompassing all-American hypocrisy and abuse of power—that one bitter yet perfect truth. Because he never wanted to make the mistake he'd once made. He could never be wrong again. People had gotten hurt. If he got the story wrong, then he was just part of the problem—he was only abetting those abusing truth.

He was thirty-nine already. With the Dwayne Specklin story, he had let himself dream a little again. Maybe he could truly change some minds with this one. No one had talked a Pulitzer, of course, not at that early stage, but who knew? He had long dreamed of fronting a bold news venture, with nonprofit status to keep the monied interests out of it. All it took was backing, and this story would have helped cement his true credentials.

Then "Alex" swept in and took it all away.

Owen had wanted to run the Specklin piece as an investigative series earlier, or maybe even a podcast, but his editor had ruled it out, claiming that he needed more corroboration. Today would've been the first in that series. Owen sighed at the thought. He now also understood, from this video just released, that his own reporting hadn't gone nearly far enough. He only knew about a few victims and possible abettors. Many victims' lawyers had never talked.

Owen heard another laugh out in the newsroom, and it snapped him out of his funk. The mood seemed lighter around him. In the world outside Owen's head, a major asshole had finally gotten his comeuppance—it was such a wondrous thing in this era, that rarest of birds. Owen now wrung his hands as if choking that bird, but he snapped himself out of that too. He imagined strumming his ukulele instead, as taught to him by his Japanese-Hawaiian grandmother. He used to play it—softly—in the newsroom, but HR had asked him to stop on behalf of certain disgruntled staffers. During the pandemic he'd played it even more, and he still played it at home sometimes to calm down.

He had to consider his next move. The clock was ticking. A couple years ago he, Owen Tanaka, formerly of the *Denver Post* and most recently the Associated Press, was brought in to revive the investigative side of newsgathering at *AltaVista*

News. Progress was too damn slow. Then *AltaVista News* had been bought—by none other than tech billionaire Mason Snead, the charismatic founder of the social media behemoth FreeChain, which had beaten Facebook at its own game. Snead and FreeChain had made a vow to its users: they would never ban a post or a feed before its time. Except porn. Snead was adamant about that. Snead was also the brains behind a "sharing economy humanitarian start-up," #AllGood (always with hashtag as per brand guidelines). #AllGood was FreeChain and Twitter and Mercy Corps and LifeForce and Kickstarter all rolled into one, but with a relentlessly open yet positive bent. #AllGood inspired people to share and support good causes. Speculation had run rampant as to what Mason Snead was going to do with a news operation. After the shock wore off, nothing happened. But everyone knew this was the calm before the storm, possibly the calmest period *AltaVista News* had ever seen. Before Mason Snead, this all-digital news arm of *AltaVista* once had grandiose ideas. Yet it still lumbered on, still the news org of the future. Its newsroom even looked like that of a hundred-year-old print daily that was still struggling to go digital-first. While other digital operations and even newspapers now had open layouts that resembled the lobbies of pricey hotels or start-ups, they were still working in the former space of a New York tabloid that had given up the ghost. The big plans for renovating never happened. Stuff was piled everywhere, and Owen wondered if it was the same stuff the former daily had simply left behind and no one was the wiser. All around him, the stacks of books and manuals, files, boxes, and actual trunks and the aging desks and computer displays stood in the way of collaboration. He'd even spotted two stout yellow electric typewriters providing the foundation for a tower of fading bankers' boxes. Many reporters simply used their own laptops, having worked from home for so long during the pandemic. It might as well have been the hometown paper he first worked at in Colorado. It even smelled like the to-go lunches of reporters long retired, a permeating staleness of rancid pastrami and spilled Fresca. The light was insufficient, too, not helped by the low ceilings, forcing people to squint all the time. The only natural light was blocked by the surrounding cramped conference rooms and editors' offices that always seemed to be closing in around their maze of cubicles like the walls of a trash compactor. Here he was. He had finally made it to New York City, to the epicenter of storied journalism, but it was the 1978 version.

Owen knew he would still have to report on Dwayne Specklin and what came next. He knew the background better than anyone. But now he was chasing the story instead of breaking it. Dwayne Specklin's life was clearly destroyed, if not his sense of self, and Owen's contribution would only be like writing an obituary.

None of Owen's surrounding colleagues had yet mentioned his sudden and utter undoing from the Alex video. He couldn't look at them. He'd stayed in his cubicle since the morning. Most of them had some idea of what he'd been working on. The grapevine knew. Some probably took pleasure in his getting screwed. He was the odd one, as the investigative guy, like the soldier in a war movie who just won't die and it's bad luck to be standing next to because the odds weren't with you. They used to have the investigative teams in the basement, but it had been Owen's idea to bring them up here for better collaboration. How he wished he could now be down there staring at a cinderblock wall in fluorescent light.

He scratched at his mop of dark hair that never seemed to grow longer or lose thickness, which he appreciated because it hid his large ears that everyone used to make fun of. With this video release, he couldn't help thinking that he might very well be the worst investigative reporter around, and he winced at the notion. But he knew he wasn't. He had won awards, regional ones, certainly none that journalists in NYC had heard of. He'd helped put bad guys in jail. He'd made others resort to draining their ill-gotten savings to hire lawyers. He had even made a few admit it, eventually.

Alex, he thought. *Just who was this Alex anyway?*

Owen's next thought was that things were getting a little too quiet in the newsroom. He checked chats, checked emails, texts. Too little interaction. Something was going down, his instincts told him. He sprang up from inside his cubicle like a meerkat standing sentry, peering around. He smiled at those watching him. His smile was hardly a grin, nor was it a baring of teeth, but it was automatic and a little old-fashioned, like a man tipping his hat. Something inside him needed to show others that all was okay. This helped him in his work, with his interview targets and his sources.

A message popped up from his editor: *Come see me.*

Owen the meerkat tried taking a couple deep breaths, but they came out as sighs. His editor never requested a face-to-face.

He marched through the cubicle maze, shifting his hips and minding his toes so he didn't stub them on this or that stack or protrusion, like a gifted soccer player with an imaginary ball. He felt more eyes on him, the heads turning.

He marched into her glass office—Managing Editor Anne Blade. Anne was typing. The wonder of the Midtown skyline beyond awed Owen a moment, stopping him in his tracks. Anne Blade didn't look up, just kept tap-tapping away. He imagined her having to explain his now squandered story budget to some higher-up bean counter, and his heart sunk into his pit of a stomach. Anne was the same editor who, when first arriving to major fanfare, had stood on a chair with her sleeves rolled up like Ben Bradlee and told them all that their new mission from this day forward was to "go viral." The layoffs started the next day.

Now it was his turn.

The thought came to him that he'd simply quit first.

Anne held up a hand as if reading his mind, but needing to finish her thought. Owen stepped in place with anticipation. He looked around for a chair to stand on, maybe that would work.

"Maybe let one of the new ones take Specklin from here?" he blurted finally. "They can have all my notes. It's not me anymore. It's an obit."

Anne tapped out a couple more words, pounded a period, and pushed back her straightened auburn hair behind one ear. Looked up. "True. Fine."

"Really?"

"Really." Anne pushed hair behind her other ear, and her face opened up. She stood and grabbed her phone and her purse and stuffed a couple things from a drawer into it that Owen couldn't see. She came around the desk to him, then passed him by.

"Where are you going?" Owen said.

"To get a drink," Anne Blade said from the door. "I just got laid off, Owen. It's started, finally. I'm thinking Old Town Bar on the way home, nice and dark. Fuck it. Good riddance."

She was oddly pale, even for a redhead, and Owen wondered what else was going on, his eyes narrowing, focusing. He needed to get clarity on himself.

"What about me?" he asked her.

Anne's eyes widened. Then she laughed, and it sounded like the rattle of a rusty chain. "You? Why, you have an appointment with none other than Mason Snead."

ALEX

It worked! I actually did it, finally, after so many months—years—dreaming, planning, taking actions.

I was never sure the Show Game was actually going to work until Dwayne Specklin was winning those first fifty points. He'd barely resisted when we first came for him. But then again, we were in disguise when we picked him up in that parking garage. I had been wearing my simulated FBI getup—big drab windbreaker, wig, baggy clothes, those wraparound dark glasses like I just got back from target practice. N95 mask on, a blast from our pandemic past just to creep him out. Fake FBI ID. My holstered gun is a fake, too, because the truth is that I hate any gun stronger than a BB shooter. I'm adamant about the no-violence part, I can tell you. Maybe it's a pipe dream, but I have to stick to it.

Anyway, Dwayne Specklin bought the trusted authority ruse, and of course he did because he'd manipulated that same kind of misdirected respect and fear for his victims. Next thing he knew, we were cuffing him and taping his mouth and pulling a black hood over his head while hauling him into a van, all in one fluid movement, almost a ballet.

Part of me had hoped we could open the briefcase, to show the world in graphic video just what Dwayno had done. But he'd caved instead, and naturally he'd thrown his junior pastor accomplice under the bus. Still, he's done me a huge, huge favor. Because the next contestants will now assume that I have the goods and am not just playing on fears, not just using psychology to turn the tables. They can assume I have clear and unvarnished and unspun proof of their misdeeds. Dwayne Specklin had a no-win choice. He chose, as always, to assert control and power over the message one last time, and in his narcissism and delusions of grandeur probably still thinks it might be working, if even just a little.

The last thing I told Dwayno before clearing out was that he could never reveal who or what I was—if he'd even been able to tell, that is, through my disorienting disguise, handheld voice changer, the fetid darkness, and his fog of fear and numbing drink. But if he did, I would reveal what was in that case anyway. Specklin had nodded to that, solemnly, as if concluding one of his exhausting sermons.

By the time his confession uploaded to FreeChain and other platforms and to the media, we were long gone. I smashed the unregistered iPhone to bits afterward. VPN and location cloaking had obscured its connection. I'm already back home. It's now afternoon. I'd slipped back inside early this morning through the back door. My actual vehicle had been sitting in the driveway the whole time I was gone. The last time a neighbor might've seen me go in or out the front was two days ago. None of them have a clue. None of us are close. I chose my little house carefully. It doesn't stick out, it's close to an airport. The best part is, no one would ever think it was me. How could they? There were so many victims and so many possible avengers. Tracking them all would take years. Sure, I'd talked to many victims over the years. But owing to my job, to my past, it was easy to make it look routine and certainly not preparation for the Show Game. Plus, I had an alibi, watertight. By all accounts, I wasn't near enough to San Diego. Besides, who would want to know or even stop me? I'd just exposed one of the biggest hypocrite abusers in the country outside of the Catholic Church.

Now Dwayne Specklin is all over the news. It's breaking wide open, that media beast that now must be fed. I do feel bad, though, for that intrepid investigative reporter from *AltaVista News*, Owen Tanaka. He was digging deeper than anyone, I'd heard, so all the more reason for me to get it done before he found out too much and blew it for me. Now, postmortem, I see that *AltaVista* already has a couple young reporters, instead of Tanaka, covering the aftermath. Meanwhile Dwayne Specklin is in custody, where he's probably happy to be, since many more victims are already coming forward. Brenda's daddy's megachurch has disowned him in a statement. They're shocked, shocked, I tell you! That video of him with the boys will come out at some point. And the junior pastor will talk. There will be lawsuits soon, accomplices arrested. Hopefully the Scouts and the megachurch will have to pay for this too. Though I highly doubt it.

Recently, another victim killed himself, another hanging, and that was my final catalyst to do this before that Tanaka guy got his story out. When I spoke to this victim before, he told me that he never thought anyone would believe him, not over the word of the powerful. *They own the truth forever*, he told me, and he wasn't crying, wasn't even distraught. He might as well have been telling me the scientifically proven distance to the moon.

Getting at the truth wasn't enough, I realized. I had to undo the accepted truth.

Hearing Dwayne Specklin finally sing like he did, I felt such a weight lift off me, like I'd been wearing a motor home for a backpack. My target number one was so pathetic, so simple, so banal, so little developed mentally and intellectually that you could imagine him relating to the boys he molested on a certain level. So I think that a part of me, deep down, again wondered if maybe it wasn't really true. That maybe I was exaggerating. That I was lashing out in too much anger. That the likes of Dwayne Specklin didn't deserve it.

Well, you know what? He did.

I emerged from the pandemic even more steeled to do this. Things can never go back to the way they were in the Before Time, as I like to call it. Not if I can help it.

I was even humming to the rental car radio on the long drive back, something I hadn't recalled doing since forever. And yet, here's the thing: I thought it would be so damn satisfying, that it would bring some closure seeing Dwayne Specklin destroy himself like he'd destroyed so many. No. All it did was make me even more determined, because there is still so much more to do. Soon I'd turned off the radio and was making encrypted voice memos in my phone for what came next.

Bye-bye, Dwayne Specklin. Thanks so much for playing, Contestant #1. I'm already aiming for my next target; the Show Game will return. You better believe it! But next time will not be easy, and it's only going to get harder from there. And the worst part is? Now they know that I exist.

OWEN

After Owen Tanaka left Anne Blade's now former office, the excitement and dread tumbled around in his head and in his stomach like a stacked washer-dryer, both on high speed. He returned to his cubicle to find a message on his company Slack from someone named Viktoria.

Mason Snead will meet with you tomorrow morning at 5:30 a.m. Be outside your building at that time.

Then the washer-dryer slowed, leaving only puzzlement. Mason Snead himself—the new owner of *AltaVista*? Because of the spelling, this Viktoria could only be Viktoria Jett, Mason

Snead's enigmatic right-hand woman. Her wording made it sound as if Owen had requested the meeting, but he'd done no such thing—which in essence made this an order. Owen released an incredulous chuckle. He did his meerkat routine to make sure no one was playing a joke on him, but the usual suspects were now rising from their cubicles with ashen expressions, angry mugs, or happy faces. Most had boxes of their belongings. He watched them exit. He stuck around the newsroom a little while, to monitor the increasingly feverish mood if nothing else, since the news of the layoffs had meanwhile made it online. Twitter was all outrage, FreeChain all tears and conspiracies and no feed too sensational. The Show Game video was a new, different level. Exposing bad guys only proved Snead's point in being so stubborn about FreeChain's lenient content policy, Owen surmised.

He soon saw little else to do but go home, owing to his early appointment. He lived in a five-hundred-square-foot place just north of the West Village, not far from a great little bar called Johnny's that he always told himself he'd hit every Friday after work for the great camaraderie he'd experienced the one time he'd actually gone there. But he hadn't ever been able to re-create that in his five years in New York City. He was too busy, and now after the pandemic the city was too busy remaking itself into every other city that wanted to become, ironically, its own idea of NYC. Gentrified monotony. The top-producing speculators meanwhile snatching up the COVID-cheapened real estate. The nearby Google headquarters loomed, unleashing a steady treadmill stream of tech dudes interchangeable with San Francisco or Seattle and on and on, probably making jokes now about the fate of the once-vaunted *AltaVista*. Then there was the long-subdued Meatpacking District all scrubbed and polished and now known for the High Line and Chelsea

Market. The area used be, or so he'd heard, prostitutes in drag and dime bags and actual graffiti and illegal after-hours clubs. He never knew. All he knew was his work. *AltaVista* had gotten him the apartment, on the ground floor luckily so he could be that much closer to work.

Now it was eight p.m. on the evening of the first full day of Alex, and of the *AltaVista* layoffs. Dwayne Specklin, according to updates, was already on suicide watch, which Owen doubted was a ploy at such an early stage. If it was Alex's plan to destroy Dwayne Specklin just like he had his so many victims, then Mission Accomplished. The whole truth, which had been Owen's goal, was just a tool for Alex, it seemed. Mason Snead's *AltaVista News*, meanwhile, had cut over two-thirds of its editorial staff and more were quitting. Anne Blade had probably been typing the staffwide layoff email when Owen entered her office.

The Specklin Show Game seemed so right, yet the layoffs so wrong. Owen had a strong sense of right and wrong but it was often too simplified for his own good: whatever was not yet known was "wrong" and what was known was "right." Discovered, good; undiscovered, bad. He knew this about himself. He couldn't help it, never could. A professor mentor once told him that sometimes certain things are better left unknown. But that very same professor, a journalism expert, had ended up getting convicted for fraud. Owen figured he could've become anything hard-core, from a platoon sergeant to a priest. Investigative journalism was his religion. He was disciplined about it, like a top mountain climber, leaving nothing to chance, always knowing the exact contents of each and every pack, pouch, pocket. He was not sloppy like the cliché. His desk was like a clear-cut island among the aging newsroom clutter and his apartment neater than a nun's chamber.

Owen normally used his rare downtime at home to sleep or play the ukulele, and do laundry. While his laundry now finished drying down the hall, Owen sat at his home desk and pondered writing the letter. He appreciated the slower, calming process of writing a letter this way, the mechanical pencil lead dragging slightly on pulp paper, his thoughts having to slow down for his fingers that sometimes cramped even though he took research and interview notes in longhand all the time. His IKEA desk was too small and facing a bare wall, and he imagined his counterpart writing him back from a similar position, though he doubted IKEA supplied prisons.

He imagined how it would go down. *Dear Shane*, he would write, always the same, loving the outdated formality of it. The letter was meant to right that wrong he had done. In his first big story for *AltaVista News*, Owen had been investigating the mob getting embezzled. He'd believed the caper involved a certain janitor for the mob, who was skimming. This was Shane. Something had seemed fishy to Owen. Shane Bagley had too much education for a janitor, including a degree in accounting and a master's in English, not to mention an online criminology course, so it looked as if he'd been planning this for a long time. But Owen had gotten his reporting wrong. He'd been sure it had been Shane because Shane had a brother who was killed by the mob (though not the same mob). The truth was, all that poor Shane had done was skim a tiny bit from the money-filled backroom of just one little mob fence. Those who had done the actual embezzling were only too happy to let Shane take the blame. The mob's crafty expensive lawyers soon went after Shane, too, since Owen had reported enough for prosecutors to find a way to convict Shane for far more than he was guilty of. By that point Owen had realized, to his horror, that the mob was covering up its own money trails, using Shane as a perfect diversion and, in turn, making Owen the ultimate dupe. The mob didn't bother threatening Owen or even suing him. They should've *made* him, truth be told, since the damage he'd done handed them a watertight case. After the story had died and Shane was in jail, Owen did more discreet digging and confirmed the sick truth. All he had done was fuck over Shane Bagley. And all his degrees? Shane was simply a smart guy, his plight an old tragedy: He'd been attempting to write a novel, and his janitor job gave him the time to do it. He'd been running out of money and had simply gotten desperate one time.

Owen didn't write the letter. He couldn't bring himself to. He had destroyed a man's life with his errant reporting. He'd been too eager, too arrogant. He'd thought it was one of those little guy-gets-revenge, David-versus-Goliath pieces that sold TV and film rights. Now there was nothing he could do, and he would be the last person Shane Bagley ever wanted to hear from. He recalled, again: "Nice try—dumbshit" had been the only quote Shane had ever given to a reporter about Owen.

He opened his laptop instead and searched the news for any mentions of Shane's status in prison. Nothing, of course. He'd kept in touch with Shane's lawyer but there was nothing new there either. Same old same old, lawyer said. Shane had learned to avoid physical altercations. He'd gotten a job in the prison library and was hoping for parole. The only good thing was that he had more time to work on his novel.

Owen wanted to write Shane that his worst fear was doing exactly what he'd done to Shane—getting the truth wrong again. And worse yet, everyone would believe it forever. *I'm scared I'll die getting it wrong*, he wanted to tell Shane. Someday, he would write to him: *I'm so sorry. But I am working on making it right.*

"You're only as good as your last play," he muttered, closing his laptop.

His last play? Who was he kidding? He hadn't even gotten far enough to be wrong about Dwayne Specklin. And the person he really should be mad at was this vigilante. *Just who was this Alex anyway?* he again thought. The whole country was wondering now. It was already the mystery of an era.

His phone beeped. A text.

It read: *Banging your head against the wall again?*

It was from his wife, Molly—correction: ex-wife. Strike that; that wasn't yet confirmed. Estranged? That sounded, too, well, strange, as if one of them were nuts. No, they had simply drifted their separate ways. Molly had tired of his all-in reporter routine, especially when he brought it home to move in with them for good during the height of the pandemic, and he couldn't blame her. She now lived with her sister in Seattle, where she was working as a teacher's assistant in an elementary school like she'd always wanted to. He was happy for her. Anyway, he guessed that made them separated. It had been three months now since she'd left. The bizarre part was they probably got along better now than they ever had.

Banging his head against the wall about losing his big story, Molly meant. She'd seen all the news of course. He'd told her what he'd been working on. He'd texted her earlier that he'd survived the layoffs and joked that poor Anne Blade never did get the chance to take them viral.

I am, he texted back, but after a few minutes. He always waited at least a few minutes. Let her think he was busy. He added, *Dwayne Specklin was all mine.*

I meant about Shane Bagley, she texted back. *Screw that Specklin guy. He deserved it. Sucks that you lost the story. But, bravo, Alex.*

I guess. You okay?

Sure. You?

He gave that one another few minutes. Let her think he had a life. *I'll let you know*, he added eventually, but with a smiley face.

THURSDAY, OCTOBER 19
OWEN

The next morning, at 5:25 a.m., Owen stood outside his building on Eighth Avenue between West Fourteenth and Fifteenth. All was dark, those first hints of the coming dawn not quite glowing just beyond the horizon. And it was colder, covering the exposed skin of his face and hands like a chilled gel. In the shadows the early fall leaves were making their way down to the pavement between the walls of buildings despite no trees in sight, like stray ticker tape from some ghost parade—fickle things, these bright leaves, shifting back and forth with the breeze and passing vehicles. Or were they trying to find their way back to their home branches? As if they were too early and too cold to have left for good and were now regretting their enthusiasm. But it was too late to turn back, for them or for him. He had a meeting with Mason Snead.

All Owen's excitement and dread and puzzlement surrounded him, and he took deep breaths to keep the creeping feelings at arm's length. He wished he knew how to meditate. Instead, like so often in his profession when he really had no idea what was about to happen, he focused on his gear. He carried his high-end laptop backpack holding his regular MacBook bootable in Windows and Linux with all the apps and resources for quick notetaking, deep researching, and secure sending and receiving; a small, cheap air-gapped laptop not connected to the internet in any way, for opening sensitive files; a second phone with the Hushed app for calls and texts using disposable encrypted phone numbers like a burner phone; a trusty digital voice recorder in case his regular phone with recorder app died; not to mention an array of old-school analog tools, including a narrow, flip-style reporter's notebook, various pens and pencils, lozenges, Emergen-C, Airborne, hand sanitizer, the one face mask that didn't fog his reading glasses, plus a N95 mask. All of it was arranged in ultraorderly fashion, not out of any neatness fixation but out of pure necessity if it was all going to fit. Any new mother or budding helicopter parent would have been highly impressed. The high-end backpack was disguised inside a cheap one, too, because you never knew. Needless to say, his small, wiry shoulders were as strong as a Sherpa porter's. Still, he reminded himself yet again, none of all that mattered if his instincts were wrong. And he really hoped this meeting was leading to coffee because, out of respect, he wasn't holding a full hot thermos like he'd usually be.

A couple people passed with heads down, aiming for the subway stairs. Owen was watching the street, glancing at the delivery trucks and cabs passing, expecting a limo to pull up or even a helicopter or a drone to land in the middle of Eighth Ave. Who knew, really? Mason Snead, despite his penchant for changing the world for the better with #AllGood, was rumored to be just as much an iconoclast as every other tech economy tycoon.

A woman was walking his way looking like something out of a low-budget new wave video from the early '80s, her black suit complete with exaggerated shoulder pads, cropped jacket, skirt no bigger than short shorts, and fishnet stockings. She even wore platform Doc Martens boots. Her hair was black, too, a severe bob cut that came to two sharp points like pincers, and all of it highlighted with platinum streaks. The only concession to modern times was her nose ring. She kept coming straight at him, her dark eyes hard and seeming to widen in a wild way. He couldn't stop staring and she appeared not to care, to want it even. He was about to tell her he didn't have a cigarette, but she smiled before he could, a surprisingly warm smile, her hard-set jaw and cheeks opening up to round it out.

"Morning, Owen," she said. "Come with me." Then she kept going.

"Good morning," Owen said, his eyebrows rising, and followed. "So you're Viktoria?"

"Yup," she shot back over a shoulder.

And Owen didn't know if he was in a Billy Wilder comedy or a Hitchcock thriller. Maybe both. She turned on Fourteenth and strode on a few blocks, taking rights and lefts, and Owen didn't bother making small talk. Viktoria's next obvious concessions to the here and now were her Apple Watch and earbuds that consulted her repeatedly, and to which she barked, "Yes" or "No," "Fuck you" and "Hell yeah." If only he could hear what was coming through the other end.

Viktoria strode up to an aging coffee joint with the shutter rolled down. Owen had been there once or twice but never needed to go back. She pulled up the shutter, opened the door, and gestured Owen to enter when his eyebrows rose again.

"He'd prefer a public and definitely better coffee shop," Viktoria said, a tone of disgust curling one corner of her mouth, "but people are always pitching him, selfies, all that shit."

"Right," Owen said. So he bought himself a coffee shop for a meeting? Owen wouldn't have been surprised.

It was dark apart from a dim light behind the counter. Owen could smell coffee and feel its warmth, to which he gave silent thanks.

The bathroom door swung open and a man came out. Owen, still adjusting to the dim light, had to squint. The man had longish hair. It took a second for Owen to realize that this was none other than Mason Snead.

"Good morning," Owen said.

"Isn't it, though?" Mason Snead said, adding a thin smile that bared no teeth. He shook Owen's hand despite just coming out of the bathroom, yet didn't mention it like many people do. It was a firm though bony shake, his eyes on Owen's the whole time.

Viktoria found a light switch.

"Ah, thanks, Vik," Snead said, and it occurred to Owen that Mason Snead had likely been waiting for him in the near dark this whole time, what with the shutters down. Like a vampire now come to life. This was an optimistic vampire, though—like a vampire about to give a TED Talk maybe.

"Someone needs coffee, am I right?" Snead said to Owen, adding a second smile.

"Please. Thanks."

Snead asked Owen how he liked it (black) and fetched the coffee himself from behind the counter, which gave Owen a chance to steal glances at the man while Viktoria scanned the still-dead street. Owen had never seen Snead in person, let alone up close. He was still young, thirty-five, Owen believed. "Millennial from hell," someone once joked in the newsroom. He didn't have a boyish face though. It was bony, and a little gaunt, like a mask, making him look older than he was judging

33

from face alone, reminding Owen of one of those old black-and-white photos where the men are supposedly in their early thirties but look to be in their forties at least. His skin was pale and a little shiny. He wore a simple outfit, grayish crewneck top and over that a chambray button-down, unbuttoned, and olive pants with no discernible hem, the tones making Owen think of the sky and the earth and new growth, all of it so simple and monotone that the pieces could've been sweats at a glance but so perfectly fit that this outfit alone probably cost more than Owen's rent. Snead was accordingly slender. His longer, sandy-blond hair was parted down the middle, severely, and snipped at a perfect right angle—a less severe bob than Viktoria's, basically. He wore flip-flops despite the time of year.

Owen, ignoring his now oddly racing pulse and weak feeling in his muscles, made mental note after mental note to write all this down once he was in the clear, just in case he'd ever do a profile of Snead. At a near distance Snead appeared unkempt, but if close, everything was neat and perfect. Jeff Spicoli from afar, Wes Anderson up close. Not one strand of that long-bob hair was out of place, as if he (or Viktoria) ironed it. His nails looked like a woman's right after a visit to the salon, though with a clear gloss coat, and his long toenails were the same. His skin was smooth and clean, nearly fake, like a wax figure come to life—though it was one of the figures the wax museum hadn't gotten quite right and you had to check the sign to know for sure.

Considering all this, Owen was expecting a Howard Hughes vibe from Snead, a California guy excited to pitch you his next film project.

"Sit, man, sit." Snead beckoned him to the table in the middle of the room, a four-top but with two chairs only, clearly meant for them since the rest of the chairs were upside-down on the other tables. Owen glanced at Viktoria to see if she'd join them, but she stood back to let Snead get things going, as if she were the one who was the head of a massive tech economy operation and Snead the executive assistant, or whatever Viktoria was. She kept stealing glances outside, her back never to the windows and door, and it now occurred to Owen that maybe she was also his security in addition to whatever else she may be. She had the earbuds and smartwatch and surely a phone somewhere inside her structured uniform, and Owen recalled reading somewhere that the mysterious Viktoria had possibly—though he'd never confirmed it—served in the marines in a former life. It was also said that Viktoria might be a man, but Owen was seeing no sign of that; she had hips and no Adam's apple, though he supposed anything could be changed. He fought the urge to reach into his bag for his notepad, his arm practically shaking for it like your leg does in bed wanting you to turn over. He wondered if she had a weapon somewhere too.

"So, thanks for coming," Snead said, leaning forward on the table, his eyes sparkling now, a bright gray blue.

Owen had to admit he was feeling engaged, and the good coffee wasn't hurting. "My pleasure," he said. "And thanks for the coffee. It's better than I expected from this place, I have to say. Last time I was here, wasn't so great."

"That's because we brought our own."

"Oh."

"You really like it?" Snead leaned forward. "You really do?"

Owen now wondered if he was being tested for some new crop Mason Snead was developing for a coffee plantation he'd bought, but Snead didn't elaborate.

He tugged at the end of his nose instead, the second or third time he'd done so.

"And thanks for coming at such an early hour," he then added, keeping those glittering eyes on him.

"Sure, sure," Owen said. It was all so unnecessarily secretive, and yet not really. He felt more like he was meeting a source for a discreet interview, off-the-record. Yet anyone could spot them here if they wanted. He figured there was more security outside somewhere, but he really couldn't be sure.

"It was the only slot," Viktoria said from her observation post near the window.

Owen nodded at her and confirmed how very different her dress was to Mason Snead's. Together they looked like two grad students dressed up for Halloween or a costume party: she the singer of a 1981 Neue Deutsche Welle band, he the kooky dormitory sidekick on some '90s sitcom.

When Owen turned back around, Snead was still directing that thin, closed-mouth smile at him, and those eyes. He looked like a fan who really wanted to ask Owen a question but was too excited to ask. But Owen wasn't famous. He hadn't even landed so much as a hint of a book deal from one of his investigative pieces.

He's engaging, Owen noted. *Looks you in the eye. Has that way of zeroing in on what you want to hear. He won't promise you anything; he'll make you make a promise to yourself.* Owen was thinking this already even though Snead hadn't even proposed anything. What was going on here? *It's called charisma*, Owen added to his mental note. *Though the way he sometimes tugs at his nose threatens to spoil it, like he's adjusting a mask.*

"I just go, go, go all the time," Snead added, expounding on Viktoria's comment.

Owen didn't have a response to that. He drank his coffee, nodding along.

"Sucks what happened to you," Snead said, his voice harder now. His eyelids had drooped, and his eyes took on a gloss. Sympathy.

"Uh . . ." Owen said, prompting him for more.

"This Dwayne Specklin story."

"Ah. But how did you know?"

"I had Anne Blade report on any promising projects. You were doing great, she said."

"She did?"

"Yep. I want to know every aspect of my operation."

"Not a great feeling to lose a big story," Owen said, now sensing his eyes drooping and glossing over like Snead's.

"I bet you have it out for this 'Alex' person," Snead said, his smile returning, but this time with teeth. His were surprisingly narrow, and small, like little spikes. Owen tried not to stare.

"I'm not happy about it," he said, "but what can I do? A vigilante, a whistleblower, when they release the whole truth? They must have good reason."

"Maybe."

Viktoria snorted somewhere behind Owen.

"You do have it out," Snead said. "You just don't realize it. This Alex really fucked you. Deep down you know it."

"I won't deny it," Owen said, surprising himself.

"Good." Mason Snead sat up. "I'm not letting you go like the rest. I'm going to rebuild *AltaVista News* from the ground up. I promised I'd never change the name. But we all know how that works." He grinned. Owen expected a laugh to follow, but Snead only held the grin a little too long. "Though what I'd really like to do is just keep the name—just to show those bumbling fucks who buy these companies and ruin them what could really be accomplished if you're farsighted enough."

Mason Snead left a pause here, most likely for Owen to comment.

"That happens a lot," Owen said, and he felt surprisingly talky, wanting to tell Snead what he wanted to hear but not quite sure knowing why. He continued, "Take, for example—"

"You'll have a new position," Snead said, cutting him off.

"Oh?"

"Head investigative reporter," Snead said, sounding out each syllable as if discovering a new word in a foreign language.

Owen's current title was lead investigative reporter. He wasn't about to edit Snead though. "That sounds great," was all he said.

"And . . ." Snead sat up even taller, though he already looked ramrod straight. "Are you ready?"

Owen felt Viktoria's Doc Martens turn his way, a slight grinding on the linoleum.

"I'm ready," Owen said.

"You," Snead said, "are going to go after this Alex yourself. You, my man, are going to uncover the Show Game."

MONDAY, OCTOBER 23
ALEX

I have my second target for the Show Game and, man, is this going to be good. I can tell you that this next bastard definitely deserves to be on it. He's a real winner, should get big ratings, just like the target himself would love. And the latest show's got a brand-new location: Washington, DC!

Conrad Holmes is an up-and-coming representative in the House. Holmes is missing an arm. He claims to have lost it serving his country in Iraq. Well, I got the goods on that. But the actual reason for choosing Conrad Holmes is that he's the ultimate hypocrite, if not a criminal sociopath. Stay tuned for more on that too. Let's just say he's been a sham the whole time. He slept in his meager DC office his first few months as a representative, but now, just two elections later, he already has a whole town house in Georgetown.

We're watching him right now. Tracking his movements, night and day. To sustain my alibi, combined with my industrial-grade GPS location cloaking app, I can only go at night. We have a van for surveilling, like in the movies, but without all the fancy equipment. It's only a two-way window, binoculars, burner phone cameras, handwritten logs, digital police scanner. It's just after midnight, which means time for a shift change. Using the darkness as cover, dressed in a jogging outfit, complete with hoodie over my head, and a mask on, I approach the van, a used Ford Econoline camper conversion we bought for cash in the suburbs.

I enter on the passenger side sliding door. My partner in so-called crime knows I'm coming. We can text with the burners.

"Hey," I say.

"Hey, Alex," Chip says back. "What up?"

Chip loves calling me Alex, kind of like a call sign. Chip likes call signs.

"Nothing new," I say and offer him an energy bar, which he declines. "How we looking?"

"Same. Been lights out for three hours."

We're parked across the street from a redbrick town house that must be a hundred fifty years old at least. We're a half block down, but we have a good line of sight as usual. It's not the nicest of the Georgetown town houses, but it's quite a move up in comparison. These old town houses are great for surveilling. This one stands alone, with a clear glass front door and all the windows stacked in the front. There's a small backyard and rear door, but the occupant still has to come along the side and to the front to exit.

I nod to Chip. Lights out for three hours—it fits the pattern, again. So this could be the day we do it.

"We'll have to do it sooner than later or my alibi runs out," I remind Chip.

He nods back to that. Chip and I are a team. Chip isn't his real name. He thought it was humorous because it sounds like such a white-guy call sign, and he's a Black guy. I tracked down Chip. He's a vet. Chip is perfect for this. He wants Conrad Holmes exposed; I want Conrad Holmes exposed. Chip has a personal reason, just like I had before. And in seeking his vengeance on Conrad, Chip has discovered something that Conrad Holmes did not want a soul to know.

While serving in Afghanistan, Chip was transferred to a CIA extraction team where he had to do some nasty stuff that Chip regrets. So Chip blames Holmes for that now, too, though he mostly blames himself because he took the bargain and is now paying for it. One day, Chip went to the States on leave—and never returned for duty. He's a deserter, technically. But I have my ways. He'd surfaced in various dark web online forums, basically begging for someone like me to come along and expose the Conrad Holmeses of this world. I sent him a private encrypted message, and now here we are, our own little private extraction team. Chip knows abduction, and he's taught me plenty already. He agreed to help me as long as we could target Conrad Holmes specifically.

So here we sit, looking out through the side windows, Chip in his swiveling captain chair, me in a fold-up. I glance at Chip, see how he's doing. To look at him, you'd never know he ended up an extraction guy. His face is rounded and boyish, with wide eyes, making him look naive. The glasses he often wears complete the look, something like a guileless young lawyer in a movie. His dress is understated and what some would call boring, with lots of fleece vests and hiking shoes and Dockers. He's a year younger than me, but dressed this way, he looks ten years older than my thirty-seven years. Go figure. Tonight he's wearing mostly dark gear, though, just in case.

"You want?" he says, gesturing at his captain chair.

"No, not till you're ready."

Chip, I should add, doesn't love leaving the van. He's been living in it, actually. He'll keep staring out a little longer with me, for the company, and then withdraw onto the built-in bed for a few hours. Luckily he sleeps silently, barely even moves. The first couple times I was expecting him to wear his nightmares on his sleeve, but it's been smooth sailing so far.

"All righty," he says.

And so we watch. Four black squares for windows, two to a floor, and the front door a slightly recessed rectangle. I keep glancing at Chip because I know that he's sometimes conflicted about this. In his lawbreaking (let's call it what it is), he doesn't want to become what he's trying to stop—yet another Conrad Holmes.

"Stop eyeing me. I'm fine," he says out of a corner of his mouth.

"We could've picked another one, you know. Work up to this."

"I know. No."

It was really tough to choose, let me tell you. There are so many candidates. There's the secretary of health and human services who, during one major pandemic wave certain to plummet the stock market, dumped all his stocks beforehand based on confidential info, all while reassuring the public and other investors that everything was fine, nothing to worry about. There's a certain philandering "thought leader" and huge backer of women's causes who's a closet misogynist. And on and on. The same old story. They're all guys. There could be a female out there who deserves it, sure, but I haven't located one so far who rises to this level. Mind you, these considerations are not political, not at all. They're simply a case of righting clear moral wrongs. While we do have our own personal selections, it also comes down to what's doable operationally. Many candidates are not doable, at least not yet. Plus, I'll only have so many chances until the authorities— and, worse yet, the powers that be—are on to me. At which point I—hopefully we—will have to make that one big play for my one big target.

But now, right here, we have our play. Many mornings at around 5:30 a.m., our target Conrad will exit his house alone and stroll through Georgetown, get a coffee and his usual raisin scone at the place that opens early, then take a cab or Uber. No bus or subway for this cat, oh no, not anymore. If he does his stroll, without any escort, we'll nab him. And it should be a snap. Because Chip not only knows the guy all too well—he has the goods on him.

OWEN

By October 23, the first Monday after meeting with Mason Snead four days before, Owen had moved into the future new headquarters for *AltaVista News*. The space was just blocks away from their old, decrepit, low-ceilinged cave and to Owen's utter amazement was ready to go, planned in advance in secret; Snead must've been developing it the whole time. City records showed Owen that Snead had bought the whole building for a steal at the end of NYC's pandemic exodus, and who knew how much other real estate. The whole operation was soon going to be renamed too. Mason Snead had hinted as much to Owen over the early morning coffee the man had made himself for their meeting in that aging shuttered coffee joint, confiding in Owen in that way he had that made you feel like you were the only one in the know—a maneuver that an investigative reporter like Owen certainly did appreciate.

Owen had his *own* office now, on a corner of the second of *AltaVista*'s two stories starting at the twenty-fifth floor. His glass partition facing the open-layout newsroom was frosted for privacy, thankfully, while his windows looking out over Midtown seemed as clear as if just wiped clean, which they probably had been, considering Mason Snead was behind this all. Owen didn't recognize some of the buildings around him, not from their tops and middles, anyway, so like a tourist he found himself checking his map app to pick out which was which. This was distracting enough, and then there were the offices. The contrast with the old newsroom couldn't be starker. His office was all shining white and silver, with actual matching file cabinets and a leather office chair that offered more positions than a pedicure shop massage recliner. The carpet was low but comfortable to stretch on, which he had done, but the leather love seat crossed the line. He had always wanted a neat and spare office, despite the clichés about his profession (to disprove them, if anything), but this was making him scratch at his mop of hair. He felt like an imposter here, as if camping out in the publisher's office to protest the newsroom's continuing layoffs and low pay. He wouldn't be the first reporter to do so, when they weren't quitting in protest. And to think that the press used to be called the Fourth Estate, with equal parts pride and awe. Then there was what Snead called the newsroom. It was so glossy and new and open. It looked more like the open office of some top public relations agency, all long, shared desks and laptop stands and couches and coffee stations everywhere, all of it matching, too, which now made Owen wince inside, since those agencies were the exact ones he trusted least in his line of work.

He was like some crazed salmon swimming in the opposite direction of the whole school. He was the only one here, in fact. The surviving rump of *AltaVista News* was still slaving away among stacks of folders probably predating the internet.

That gave him a sharper wince, deep in his gut. No one knew about him here, he realized—that made himself a guarded and unknown scoop in itself. He was now embargoed. The opposite of what he was always hunting. Owen could only shake his head at that. Luckily, he'd brought his ukulele. Why not? He was all alone here. As if all newsgathering had been beamed to some other planet—that or zapped into oblivion, which was an angle he didn't want to think about.

Owen spun around in his new chair, closing his eyes, trying to reboot himself. He should be so excited about this. And yet? Part of him had been hoping that he was going to be fired just like Anne Blade. And Snead's humane demeanor should've been raising the old red flags. Only afterward, for example, did Owen notice that Snead never actually drank his coffee, not one sip. He was like some alien approximating human form, not to mention his slightly shiny skin and outfit with no pockets, and gloss on his toenails—on toes, he now realized, that had no hairs on them. Who waxes his toes? Or maybe he doesn't have any hair at all. Just like an alien.

Snead certainly was from another world. Mason Snead's father had been one of the two founders of Ocsic Networks, which had more or less provided the underpinnings for the internet and still did, though now under different ownership. Snead's father, Myron, had died under mysterious circumstances. There were rumors, conspiracy theories. Myron supposedly had a heart attack, but the whispers were that it had been induced somehow. Myron and Mason had hated each other, which wasn't uncommon for such families, but the rest was only speculation. In any case, Myron left all he had to his only son, who immediately launched #AllGood with such zeal and determination and preplanning, it was if he'd long before received some sort of divine premonition regarding his bright future. *His concepts had greased the rails*, everyone in tech had said of the father, then they were claiming similar about the son. *His ideas illuminated whole stars*, wrote one fawning tech evangelist about Mason Snead. This only fueled more speculation. Was Mason Snead a true wunderkind? Just another silver-spoon lucky brat? The anti-Christ? Some feared he was all those combined, while others saw the Second Coming.

So what does that make me? Owen thought and sighed and grabbed his ukulele and played an old Frank Ferera tune, "Pinin' Hawaii for You." That calmed him down a bit. He could believe in Snead, he told himself. Someone had to mix things up. There really were two worlds of news now: the traditional and the new. He had thought he was joining the new before, but it was just another half-assed effort—here he was finally among the new news.

He could even admit that their ideas aligned somewhat. Like Snead, he believed that news did have to be more transparent, open, shared from the start. That way the ones trying to hide the truth would always know they wouldn't have a chance in the long run. The only problem was, where did the transparency end? At some point, if taken too far, having everything known all the time can mask a big lie. Just look at FreeChain. Transparency becomes a white noise that might as well be a true black of deceit. And yet, Snead had also been right about another thing, and the half smile Owen couldn't help showing Snead had confirmed it. He really did have it out for this "Alex." And then another thought hit him: if it were not for this Alex, he wouldn't even be sitting here.

He put his uke down on the desk, which he held on to because his spinnable chair felt like it was spinning again even though he hadn't prompted it. There was simply too much to think about. All he could do was go after the truth. So he opened his laptop, flipped open his notepad, and got back to work.

Following the money certainly wouldn't work for a situation like Dwayne Specklin's, not yet at least. Judging from the video, the job Alex did on Specklin looked like vengeance through and through. Owen started breaking it all down, perusing his various datasets, running his spreadsheets and visualizers, rechecking his fact-checking, and again realized he was looking at too many possible vigilantes out there, owing to all of Dwayne Specklin's victims. He would tackle that eventually. But first he needed an angle, a weakness in the operation that would lead him to Alex. And he quickly realized one thing.

Alex must have had at least one accomplice. And either Alex or that accomplice had passable abduction skills. That, in turn, meant that the authorities were likely drawing the same conclusion, and since the feds were now involved, this could surely be prosecuted as a kidnapping. Owen sighed again, reaching for his uke but not touching it. He didn't want to get scooped again, especially not in his new position.

"Better get after it," he said under his breath.

WEDNESDAY, OCTOBER 25
ALEX

It takes a couple more all-nighters for Conrad Holmes to exit his Georgetown town house early for his raisin scone, but he finally does it on Wednesday—the last possible day for my alibi.

It's 5:34 a.m. We're out of the van. I'm watching from the dark. Chip approaches Holmes on the nearest dim corner, one that we'd confirmed beforehand did not have CCTV, Chip looking all regular-guy-out-for-a-walk in his fleece and baseball cap.

"Hey, Con," Chip says, calling Conrad Holmes by his old nickname.

Conrad Holmes, not missing a beat, fakes a friendly smile and even adds a bro hug with one arm, even though he clearly doesn't know Chip.

But then he stiffens. Eyes bulging. "It's you?" Con says, and he calls Chip by his real name.

This makes Chip twist Con's one arm up behind his back.

This is where I come in. I rush over and poke my unloaded gun into Con's back. "Let's go," I grunt.

I'm speaking in that different voice again, lower, rougher, and I've got a stocking cap on, and those big wraparound glasses again, face mask, turtleneck, practically a mummy.

But old Con still has the balls to try smooth-talking Chip. "Hey, man, come on," he says.

"Do it," Chip says in a low and creepy voice I've never heard before, something like a Doberman able to mimic human speech.

That shuts up Conrad Holmes. We stuff him inside the van, duct-tape his mouth. Just like with Specklin, we frisk him and seize and turn off all his devices. It's weird at first patting down a one-armed man, but a person could joke that it's one less thing to worry about. We make him remove his clothes. We do a more thorough strip search for any obvious tracking devices, Tiles, AirTags, what have you. And on goes the black hood. Chip scrambles up through the front captains' seats and drives us away.

Then it's 6:30 a.m., right before day starts to break. We're on our "soundstage" for our very own second broadcast of the Show Game. It's a secluded basement apartment in an abandoned building near Brentwood. It doesn't smell great, a mix of stale urine and a small dead, decaying animal, but we weren't about to clean it up first. There's no electricity, and the two small windows are boarded up except for a crack we can peek through if we hear activity outside. It might as well be a cave, which is fine with me. I don't have to see the mangy carpet and moldy walls and pitted old metal kitchenette that's smothered with so much splashed grease and who knows what else that it's like someone tried slaughtering a goat in there. Hopefully good old Con caught a glimpse of that before we hung the battery-powered shop light above his head, which glares so brightly he might as well be under a stage light.

Same drill. We've got Con in a chair, this time duct-taped to the thing since he's putting up more of a fight than doughy

Dwayne Specklin. We've rendered both his legs and the one arm immovable. We pull the duct tape off his mouth. But Con's not speaking now. He just keeps peering through the bright light shining on him to try and locate Chip's silhouette. Chip told me that it was all right that Con recognizes him—it would only help the operation, and Chip had already gone to the mattresses, anyway, so he wasn't exactly exposing himself to legal danger.

Still, the first thing I tell Con when we rip off his duct tape is: "You reveal this man's identity at any time during what comes next, and you'll be dead before you can get his last name out. Got me?" It's a bluff, of course. Like I could kill him with this BB gun I have.

"Yeah, yeah, I got you," Con says, still defiant.

"That goes the same for me—no details about me, or else."

He practically rolls his eyes. But that hard and insubordinate big chin he's showing us ratchets down a little when I set up another old music stand and prop the metal briefcase on it. He's peering at it, too, and then at us until we shine the red light on it.

"Oh shit," he says. "It's you. You're the ones got that Specklin fucker," and he sounds excited for a second until he realizes, with a tightening of his jaw, that we view him on the same level as the power-hungry, pompous, double-dealing, and self-seeking child abusers of this world.

I give him a moment. Let it sink in.

Like with Dwayne Specklin, Con likely has his reasons. Horrible father? Screw you. Go home and tell it to the man. You think that's abuse? What else you got? Bad neighborhood, societal pressures, self-destructive addictions to power, to deceit? Try me, you bastard. Chip and me, we're here to break this chain.

I glance back at Chip in the dark. He nods for me to continue. I'd offered him the chance to run this broadcast, but he declined, telling me that I do such a good job, which did warm my heart a little, I have to say, since my ten-year-old self always did want to be a TV show host. Well, world, here I am!

I rub some hand sanitizer into my hands, hoping that will creep Conrad Holmes out a little. Or maybe it's my needing a shower after seeing him in person. He only glares at me. Guy like this probably never used sanitizer. That or he bought it up back when everyone needed it.

"I know all about you," I begin in my low, rough voice. "I know all that he over there knows."

"How many times do I have to tell you—I was cleared of that." A sickly smile forms on Con's face, and it swivels to face Chip.

"Not talking about that," Chip says in that human Doberman voice.

Indeed, we are not. Chip and Conrad Holmes both grew up on the same poor side of the tracks. While Chip got good grades, he still saw no future and definitely no way to pay tuition unless he got a leg up, so for that he enlisted in the military like many on that side of the tracks do. Conrad meanwhile had become a patrol cop and had entered a subset of that poor side of the tracks—the white authority brother-hood. Chip had an older brother, Wilson, who'd gotten into drugs and crime, but he had been cleaning himself up. Until Officer Holmes and his crew pulled Wilson over. Something happened, a misunderstanding. Officer Holmes fired, seven times, point-blank. Wilson dead before he hit the ground. This happened in the few weeks between Chip enlisting and reporting for boot camp. Chip almost didn't go. He was vowing to stay behind and exact his revenge. Some watching afar said that all Wilson had done was stand tall.

In the first month Chip was in boot camp, Officer Holmes was cleared of any wrongdoing despite clear evidence to the contrary. But Chip never gave up his vow. He couldn't get Conrad Holmes on what he did to Wilson, but he could get him on something. Conrad soon left the police force and got his college degree and enlisted himself, serving in Iraq. His rise was meteoric. But Chip never gave up.

Conrad's white eyes widen even more. "But you're the little brother. Right?"

Chip doesn't answer. I'm glad he doesn't, because I'm afraid his answer will involve a broken neck.

"This is about something else," I say. "Something you're not cleared of. Let's start with what my partner knows. Over there, in Iraq, you became a lieutenant with your fresh degree, not exactly from a silver spoon owing to your small-town roots, but you might as well have come from Kennebunkport and West Point compared to him. Then you lost your arm over there. You claimed you were attacked."

Con can't take his big bulging eyes off Chip. "We never crossed paths, units."

"Nope. I was hoping to. But I got to know folks. With intel. CID. JAG."

Con shifts back and forth. Soon he's wriggling and trying to topple his chair, but it ain't working. "That thing on?" he growls, pointing his chin at our many-faceted tripod.

"What, that? My little truth totem pole? No, it's not on yet. But soon!" I add. "You call yourself an officer? Here's the truth about your arm: You were stealing from an Iraqi man while doing a house search, taking all the money his family had. The man attacks you with a knife, but only gets as far as your arm. You kill him, hobble back to your unit down the road, and claim you were ambushed. The thing is, you'd been doing this before. The stealing. You learned enough Arabic to not need an interpreter, which would've been impressive, but you only used it to help keep your dealings secret, with fewer witnesses. You did it many times to this very family, who had nothing. Who were probably, ironically, saving that money to get to America, if America would even let them in. Meanwhile, you couldn't work alone. You had a team as your backup. You swore them to secrecy, with payoffs—"

"That's enough," Con says. He speaks to the dark corner where Chip has retreated, the sweat now rolling off Con's chin and glistening on the duct tape. "Dude, look, let's work this out."

All he gets is silence.

"Tell it to Wilson," Chip says eventually, in that same Doberman voice.

"My partner has his reasons, and they're more than valid alone," I say. "But I have a different one. It's about the bigger picture. It's because you are now a representative on the rise and you claim to be a big patriot and friend of the veteran even while you're cutting funds for the VA and other programs. The balls on you. But even that is only the start—"

"Wait, just wait." Conrad adds a show of teeth.

"Shut up," Chip barks at him from the darkness.

"What are you going to do? Seriously," Con says, his voice warping now, nearly pleading yet still defiant, and I realize we're finally getting to the real person.

"Any questions?" I say.

"Yeah," Con says, "you told me you have more on me."

"I do, and you're going to tell it. Follow me now? And if you do not comply? We have our lovely briefcase here."

Of course I don't tell him what's inside. As always. We have two confessions from Lt. Holmes's old team in Iraq, a corporal and a sergeant. Now respected in their communities, but ready to clear their consciences if need be. In the briefcase is the audio.

So let Conrad worry about whatever he fears the worst. It might be more of what Chip knows, maybe even something about Wilson. It might well be something I don't know. Maybe Con, say, raped a young and impressionable woman who thought he was someone to look up to. My game is psychological. It's one of the reasons, beyond any operational workability or security considerations, that I pick the ones I pick. My bet is that my targets are so narcissistic, so egotistical, they think they'll have a better chance spinning their version of the truth than anything I will introduce. It's worked throughout history and it sure as fuck is working these days in the world. So I turn it on its head. I'm betting that they'll want to win so badly, sure. But it's more than that. They will want to tell the real truth in their own twisted way so badly, in a voice that they themselves can own, that they will prefer to confess rather than have that metal case opened.

"You can't do this," Holmes says. "Me, I'm not the one. I'm just like your partner, see. Just a cog, a fucking tool . . ."

He lets the words trail off.

Chip makes a *tsk-tsk* sound at Holmes from the darkness.

Well, this is interesting. It's not what I was expecting from Conrad Holmes. Talking about turning things on their head, looking forward not back. The likes of Conrad Holmes, up-and-coming representative war hero, is saying that he's only a tool for the powerful? So much for the abusive background. So much for the Wilson angle, so much for the Iraq scam. Conrad Holmes is ready to take things much bigger. Maybe his party and his donors made his worst transgressions disappear, all for his enduring loyalty. So I'm going to go broad, see what sticks. Because the powerful bastards in this world always aim to suck others into their orbit, to do their dirty work so that they're implicated forever. Once implicated, even a little, the most moral-seeming soul can become a completely different nature of human being, if you can call them that. They in turn dig themselves a deeper and deeper hole, until they reach hell itself. I might've expected a play like this from someone who started out good, but for an egotistical bastard like Conrad Holmes to go there? All righty then. This should make for a good Show Game.

"Hot enough for ya?" I blurt at Con.

"What?"

"So you're fine. Good. Ready? Are you ready to play?"

Holmes is glaring at the case glowing red, then at me, then at the case.

I start explaining the rules of the game, practically singing it, actually, as I'm pretty excited. To win, a hundred fifty points: fifty for admitting you did it, another fifty for saying who helped you, then that final fifty for saying you're sorry. "If you do all that, you win—you're set free."

"I know, I've seen it," Holmes mutters to his lap. "Everyone's seen it."

"Now, just remember, we have proof of it all, plus we have that briefcase there as your handy reminder, so we'll just release it all, anyway, if you don't admit it, or say who helped you, or that you're sorry—"

"Fuck you."

I shrug at that. Close enough.

I raise the handheld voice changer. On the mounted phone, I push the red button, turning on video.

I leave a few beats of silence for my titles to appear on the screen as we fade into Conrad Holmes glaring at the camera.

"For fifty points, do you admit to the following?" I begin in my digitally altered voice that will again be subtitled, considering the fact that I sound like a baby robot. "You're an avid church-goer, every Sunday, always at the National Prayer Breakfast and the whole nine yards. Yet you cheat on your wife, and you claim to be pro-life while you actually—"

"Stop! No," Holmes blurts.

I pause here. I shake my head for him, make a big show of it, me the unhappy director. "Now we're going to have to redo the take, edit, et cetera. Let me finish before answering, please. All right? Good." I press record.

". . . and yet, you cheat on your wife. You also claim to be pro-life, yet you paid for your girlfriends' abortions. That's girlfriends as in plural, and abortions plural. At least three times. At the same time you're hitting stride as a representative, the big star war hero; suddenly you own tons of properties in the US and the world, and your bank accounts are filled with money. No need to deny. We even have your tax records." I'm lying about this last one, but, hey, it's show business. "Where's that money coming from? Corporations and foreign governments. Oh yes. You take their money all while claiming that America and Americans should be more self-reliant. And yet, your votes and your political attacks, while seeming maverick-y on the surface, actually line up with the corporations' and foreign governments' interests. So very maverick-y. Just what America expects from a war hero who lost an arm serving his country . . . Conrad? Hello? Look at me, the camera's right here. Thank you. . . . Where was I? Ah, right. Now, you claim to be a big patriot and friend of the regular Joe, and the veteran, and the family, yet you consistently oppose or cut funds for Veterans Affairs and other programs, including farming assistance and immigration—which our country was built on. Oh, and let's not forget health care. COVID relief bill, which you fought tooth and nail. Then you took full credit."

To my surprise, Conrad is now nodding along to it.

"This is a pattern of hypocrisy," I say. "I couldn't believe how many diverse injustices you perpetrate on people. You're doing it all, really, like there's some playbook for it that you've been keeping on your nightstand. It's evil in its precision, to damage the very thing you profess to support. Sociopathic, really."

Conrad Holmes sputters a laugh that makes his spittle shine in the glaring light. Not a good look for him, yet it fits the show.

"Conrad? Look at the camera. Good. Now, for the first fifty points. Do you admit it?"

Dramatic pause. Holmes keeps his head down. Then he glances at the metal briefcase. Good, this is good. Great TV.

"I do."

Ding! Okay, we'll throw that sound effect in soon after, but I like it.

"Now, for a hundred points: Who was helping you in this—"

"It's the ones with all the money, who you think? The billion-aires, the donors, corporations, corrupt governments. There really are only a few of them," Holmes blurts. "You were thinking I was going to say some senior politician type, or a lobbyist. Hell no. Lobbyists, us politicians, we're all just paid errand boys who are pushing and pulling levers for them with the votes we make." Holmes is sneering now. "And the people out there? They're so fucking stupid, thinking they ever have some kind of say at all. A say in this? Fuck you. If I'm a tool, you the people are just a fucking diseased ant, all over FreeChain and social media with your knee-jerk opinions, addicted to the aggro you're fed, thinking your vote counts. You vote for me, who votes only for them! Why in the hell do you think they pay zero taxes?" Holmes pauses, then takes a deep breath like he's diving back into a deep dark pool, his mouth hanging open, his face pale and stretched. This really will all go out into the world, he's now realizing.

"Time to name names," I say. "Time's almost up." There's no actual timer counting down but it's not a bad idea. Maybe in a future production.

Conrad Holmes is sitting up straight, shoulders squared. "I've said enough. I'm not going to name names. If I do, they will ruin me for sure, and it won't do any good anyway. They'll only buy the next tool for extracting the hard work of all you ants. That's what you are—ants."

This is good. He's doing my work for me.

"If you can't figure that out," he continues, "then you're as fucking stupid as the rest of them. I mean, just open your eyes!"

This is so good, I think I'm going to let it slide. I'm seeking justice but also the truth and he's delivering in spades.

"It's obvious who they are," he says now, "so why don't you go after them?"

I want to tell him my future plans, I really do. I am going to go after them—one of them at least. But I'm the one posing the questions here.

A pause has ensued where a commercial break might be. I lower my handheld voice changer. I let things sink in for the viewers. If anyone still has any sympathy for this guy now destroying himself in real time under this spotlight, hopefully they'll come to the realization that Conrad Holmes might've climbed so high he could've become president someday. We're all dodging a bullet, because of me, because of Chip.

"I just do what they pay me to do," Holmes adds. "And on down the line, all the way from the very top." He stares at the screen. "Maybe someone should start investigating that. Maybe someone should start exposing them. Like I said, it's obvious who they are."

"Tell us," I say.

Holmes shakes his head.

"Tell us!" I shout.

"Tell you? Tell me!" Holmes shouts back. "It's so obvious,

it's exactly who you think it is, and it's happening right in front of your face, like a junkie stealing that package right off your porch!"

We're not only witnessing self-destruction in real time, we might just be seeing a hint of rehabilitation. Such drama! I should be pressing him harder on names, corporations, but he's really giving us a show. I glance back at Chip. He nods.

Ding ding!

I open my mouth but catch myself—I've forgotten the voice changer. I take a quick breath, shake it off, and hold the voice changer to my lips, my fingers tight around it so they don't tremble.

"That's another fifty points!" my baby robot voice says. "Well done, Conrad Holmes."

Holmes's armless shoulder rises as if throwing up a hand in despair. He shakes his head.

"Okay, here we go," I say. "For that final fifty: It's time to say sorry. Let's recap. People suffer because of you. People die because of you. Regular people. Life savings, loved ones. A future. Directly because of your actions. Yet all you've cared about, as you've just admitted, is those five men in that clandestine boardroom pouring you scotch in a crystal glass and whispering sweet fucking nothings into your ear. Maybe they even tell you how much you're helping, how much you're making a difference. But it's actually only them you're helping, at the expense of all others. So, Conrad Holmes, to win it all, to be set free . . ."

"Don't you mean 'to be destroyed'?" he says.

Just like all those he destroyed? "It depends how you look at it," I say instead. "Besides, people at home need closure. So, now, for the full one hundred fifty points, will you—"

"Pssst!" Chip blurts. "Hey! Stop, turn it off."

I press pause.

Chip's over at the crack in the boarded window, peering out. It's daylight now.

"Listen," he says.

I do.

Sirens.

My heart starts racing, all pins and needles filling my chest. I nod at the digital scanner he's clutching like an unpinned grenade. He has an earphone in.

"Nothing on the scanner?" I whisper his way.

He only shakes his head, his eyes widening.

In the background, Conrad Holmes sputters a bitter chuckle. "Shut up, shut the fuck up!"

The sirens are nearing, and they're all police, no fire.

Then, silence. . . .

"Incoming," Chip says seconds later.

He doesn't have to tell me: sirens switch off once the vehicles are close, still speeding our way in silence, hoping to catch us flat-footed.

Chip and I grab the metal briefcase and our tripod with everything on it, no need to wipe anything down since we always wear gloves. I dump the gear right into an empty case. We move without speaking, following the plan, pulling out in seconds.

Chip leads me out. We scramble through the abandoned apartment complex. I'm following Chip's hard-charging yet careful military-style maneuvers—using cover, ducking, peering, hand signals. We only catch sight of the vehicles a couple times, just a blur of black silhouettes and a rush of accelerating engines and gripping rubber.

We abandon Chip's van, which is too bad, but he has all that he needs in a backpack. Once clear of our location, I dump my disguise and Chip pulls on his—just glasses and a modest Afro, and we hole up in a dingy café. Going over the possibilities.

"Were they even coming for us?" I whisper, trying not to still pant.

"Good question," Chip says, never having panted the whole time. "We had to assume so."

"Do you think that's why it wasn't on the scanner?"

Chip shrugs. "They could've been feds, all those black vehicles."

"We have to assume that too."

"Then again, city PD has tactical teams."

Chip adds another shrug and adjusts his Afro, then stares into his coffee.

"Half full," I say.

"Half full," Chip repeats, and he softly knocks on the wooden underside of the laminated table. Then we slam our coffees like Gatorade after a marathon and go our own ways—see you on the dark web, Chip.

Chip has his own plan B from here. Soon I get the hell out of Dodge, editing the video on the fly, adding the titles and "To be continued . . ."

THURSDAY, OCTOBER 26
OWEN

Owen still couldn't believe it. Late yesterday afternoon, a new Show Game video was released to FreeChain, YouTube, and elsewhere. The Alex video exposed an outspoken and up-and-coming representative in the US House, one Conrad Holmes, to be the exact opposite of the populist war hero and defender of the regular Joe he was so often promoted as, despite having once been cleared of being a violent racist cop. Same low-budget production, same game show concept, digitally altered voice. Holmes, too, had been abducted, obviously, as shown by the duct tape on his two ankles and one wrist. Somewhat surprisingly, possibly out of narcissistic delusion, possibly out of self-serving contrition, or both, Holmes ended up condemning the very powerful who used him as a blunt but shiny instrument with just enough glare to blind the public as to the actual threat—the very powerful themselves.

This Show Game had another twist, though. It cut off before Conrad Holmes could "win it all" by saying he was sorry. It was edited in a way that left open the reason for the cliffhanger, with a title reading "To be continued . . ." By leaving out the actual apology, was it supposed to get the audience thinking? Maybe there was a special final segment still to come, for just the apology? Or, as others were surmising, did the Alex crew suddenly have to break it off for some reason and split the scene? The authorities weren't talking, not yet. But Owen was able to confirm via his sources that Conrad Holmes was now in their safekeeping after having been left on the premises—an abandoned tenement apartment this time instead of a warehouse.

It was unclear, though already surmised many times over, whether Conrad Holmes would be charged with anything based on the Show Game. There was no specific crime exposed, yet multiple possible ones were mentioned, so investigators in both the media and law enforcement would certainly now be pursuing those. Conrad Holmes's meteoric rise was over. Some were even speculating that maybe the so-called war hero hadn't lost his arm in the manner so endlessly hyped. There was also that certain incident when Holmes was a young patrol cop.

In his pristine white open office environment, and still all alone there, Owen was meanwhile starting to feel even more frustrated than before his meeting with Mason Snead. He was supposed to be investigating "Alex" from the previous abduction, yet events were now spiraling faster than he could follow, everything snowballing exponentially. No one had expected a second Show Game. Owen had come into his personal unoccupied newsroom at 5:30 a.m. after barely sleeping all night, his mind racing as to how he could get ahead of this. It was now four in the afternoon, twenty-four hours past when the Show Game was posted. He'd been doing all he could to brainstorm new leads but Dwayne Specklin was already old news. He was going to need an investigative team and soon.

Owen picked up his ukulele but couldn't even strum a chord before the damning thoughts came roaring back. He just cradled his uke absently, thinking, *This is worse than getting scooped once. That terrible fear you have in the middle of the night might be coming true—that you just keep pursuing the wrong facts again and again.*

If that were not enough, Mason Snead had announced at ten a.m. this morning that *AltaVista News* was, as he'd told Owen, being rebuilt from the ground up. He'd done this without embargoing for major media, apparently, and certainly without informing Owen or anyone else, it seemed.

The new "brand," read the press release, would now be called *FreeChain News*.

"With this announcement, we're pivoting to focus on open-source, peer-to-peer, user-generated news items complemented by our own reporters' investigations. This groundbreaking augmentation puts us in an unmatched position to fulfill our laserlike mission, which is to give every user the ability to discover—and reveal—the full and actual truth from the news."

No one really knew what this meant. Reactions ran the gamut, hot takes abounded. It was communism for news. It was fascism of the people. It was a nightmare. It was a heavenly vision. It was just Twitter. No, it was like Wikipedia for newsgathering but without constraints and sure to be monetized by none other than Mason Snead. It threatened to demolish the Fourth Estate for good. It only emphasized the importance of the Fourth Estate and would compel all to report the news better.

Owen wasn't sure if he should feel horrified or emancipated. As the announcement hit, he started receiving texts from Viktoria detailing his role as dictated by Mason Snead. There would always be a "professional" component to *FreeChain*

News. Owen would remain in his position and be independent of peer-to-peer newsgathering, of course. He was still head investigative reporter, but also managing editor if he wanted it.

"Mason Snead says it will be open to everyone," one commentator was saying on the TV screen on the wall above Owen's head. "But then there's Mason Snead at the top. In theory, he could squash any story. Forget about outdoing Facebook. This is like doubling down on FreeChain—and a daggerlike threat to Truth."

Owen had winced right off the bat when hearing a news org called a brand, but he honestly didn't know what to make of the rest. And Mason Snead was not screwing around. This was a huge leap forward into unknown territory. Some were already comparing him to Ted Turner, to Steve Jobs, to Orson Welles, some to all three wrapped into one man. He wasn't getting lucky like Zuckerberg. He was creating a whole new definition of luck. By announcing it when he did, it was nearly as if Snead were trying to steal the spotlight from the breaking news of a new Show Game. It was strange timing, for sure, but Owen figured that he should somehow be grateful. Yet it also put more pressure on him. Rushing to conclusions, he knew, was the investigative reporter's worst friend. It made you release the wrong stories.

He couldn't help getting a bad feeling. Who wouldn't? And he was right to. Just ask Shane Bagley. A part of Owen had always wanted newsgathering to return to some sort of perfect past. He'd always pictured himself in the best scenes in *All the President's Men*. But he also knew there was no turning back. *FreeChain News* was happening, and it was better to be on the inside, at least for the time being. As such he might as well be an astronaut, just now landing on a planet never before discovered, let alone inhabited by earthlings.

His phone buzzed, a text from Molly: *He stole your idea.*

She was only partly right. Owen *had* been toying around with his own idea for a completely new newsgathering model. The peer-to-peer aspect was strikingly similar to Mason Snead's open news sharing idea. But his concept wasn't a top-down monetized model masquerading as free and liberating. His was to be like NPR, for the public good, funded by the taxpayers so that everyone truly did own the news. So was Amtrak, others were sure to joke, and look how that turned out. So let them.

Thoughts aren't copyrighted, he texted back.

Not yet, came her reply.

His estranged wife was nothing if not sharp as a pinprick. He'd always loved that about her. And he had to admit that it was almost as if Mason Snead had been reading his mind somehow. Something about that thought made him set his ukulele safely inside his drawer.

Touché, he texted her.

Even that name. FreeChain? Come on. A chain can't free you.

I said touché already.

Fucking scary. Sounds like open carry but for news.

Owen had no response to that, and luckily he didn't get a chance to. Something had startled him—he'd heard voices entering his slick new space station for the very first time. He tiptoed over to the doorway of his own office as if he'd been squatting in it and security was coming.

Young men and women were streaming in, about ten of them, all in their early twenties, with every race represented, like a clothing ad, with their outfits suitably crisp and casual and fun. Owen thought maybe it was a tour, or some fresh interns, or simply that good old postpandemic optimism. They looked so cheerful, they could have been working for any new economy start-up. It was a stock photo in motion.

Owen stepped out into the main newsroom. He tried a smile, not sure if he should ask if they needed help or just watch them pass.

A perky young woman with glasses spotted him first. She grabbed the nearest shoulder and turned it Owen's way, and they all stopped and turned as if that shoulder had been a lever.

"Hi, Owen!" they chirped in unison.

"Hello. Uh, can I help you?"

A young man with hair resembling Owen's smiled as if Owen were a GIF of a kitten. "Oh, you don't know? No one told you? He doesn't know."

The woman in glasses stepped forward. "Owen, we're your new investigative team."

Right then his phone beeped. *Ass, gas, or grass, nobody rides for free*, Molly was texting him as if now reading his mind too. And there was no smiley face.

SUNDAY, OCTOBER 29
ALEX

I've made it back home, finally. It's two and a half days later. Trains and planes and automobiles. Driving nonstop is no hoot at night, let me tell you. Along the way I'd texted my dad and my mom for cover. It's all part of my plan B. My alibi isn't completely covered, but it will have to do. Just before sunup, I'd slipped in the back door of my nondescript house. I'm in the bathtub now with my feet cooling up on the tiles and a whiskey rocks on the tub's edge.

It's now pushing five p.m. I'd tried sleeping through the day to catch up on sleep but I also had to wake periodically and do the usual emails and texts and activities that make it look like I'm having a regular day. I really want to go work out after sitting in a car (rented using an alias) so long, or maybe just go camping again, but I mostly just need to decompress. I'd like to take a drag or two off my vape as well but I have to make sure that things have calmed down first. So far I've seen no red flags among my usual sources online, but that only gives me the creeping feeling that things are just a little too quiet out there.

The only big news is that one Conrad Holmes is finally getting his due from the latest Show Game, hosted by Alex. Great news! But, fuck, man, was that a close one. My heart starts beating again like I'm still in that abandoned apartment complex in Brentwood. I take a sip of the whiskey, sucking it in between my gritting teeth.

Over the next couple days, I hole up mostly. Still, I don't see any clear sign that any law enforcement agencies are coming for us. We get a possible break when the media reports a leak that Holmes told authorities he didn't know who it was who'd nabbed him. There is also the chance that Holmes wouldn't reveal Wilson's younger brother, considering all that Chip knows and all that such associations might revisit. Chip and I had considered this. If Holmes tells about Chip, then he loses the last thing that might save him—if he's anticipating any kind of rehabilitation at all. His war hero status. A memoir. All gone, poof. But, then again, sometimes leaks are also for a reason. Anything could be a ruse.

October 31, Halloween. I'm back in the tub. I keep the lights off, don't answer the door, never get near the front windows. Anything could be a trick and no treat. That makes me reach for my trusty whiskey rocks there on the tub's edge as I pull my feet below the warm sudsy water. Talk about trick or treat. I was not expecting Conrad Holmes to go where he did, fingering his overlords like he did. I'd assumed he was just going to identify a few in his orbit, throw some fellow conspirators under the bus. Dwayne Specklin never accused the actual leaders and money boosters of the Scouts and his church who really owned him, for example. But this? Wowza. Holmes was apparently not quite as narcissistic as I thought. Though he might've just been scared as hell. Which in turn scares me a little, I have to admit. Either way, it was the truth, and that was my main goal. Plus it made for good TV.

I take a deep breath, considering my next move. Nothing's changed. I'd committed to this come hell or high water. You better believe it! First thing is to return to my daily routine, starting tomorrow. Then I'll check in with Chip provided the coast is still looking clear. Then we're back on track. Target #3, I am coming for you, and soon.

But you will not be the the last one. And that final contestant will reveal all.

WEDNESDAY, NOVEMBER 1
OWEN

Owen sat in a coffee shop in Portland, Oregon, not far from the Central Library. The place had the same clean lines and openness of *FreeChain News*'s brand-new open layout newsroom, all glistening white expanses, light wood furniture, and new gray tile, and surely a brand-new HVAC system. A social distancer's paragon. Yet it could be anywhere. Starbucks or any chain used to be interchangeable; now it seemed as if any indie coffee shop or bar were the interchangeable ones and the Starbucks individualized. He welcomed any shelter, though, since the combination of gray sky and frigid air, confining like a butcher's walk-in freezer, was giving him a worse chill than NYC despite the lack of that infamous Pacific Northwest rain. What did impress him about Portland were that the central city blocks were smaller than normal US scale, like some European movie-set notion of an American city. He could see another corner right now through the tall plate glass even though this coffee place was located in the middle of the block. Owen sat with his back to the white wall, facing out like he always did, and doing this gave him a little rush deep down like he was a spy in Cold War Berlin and not an investigative reporter so desperate for a lead he'd traveled all the way across the country.

Here he was to meet his latest contact. Her name was Lucy Holden, a private investigator. She'd told him she was busy juggling cases but could meet him downtown near the library.

Owen was early. He was always early. He honestly could not remember a time when he'd been late. It had never really helped him, though, because everyone and everything else was either just on time or late. He sipped his coffee, good stuff, and kept thinking about that flourless dark chocolate cookie up at the counter, and then his ukulele. Anything but Mason Snead, *FreeChain News*, and his new "investigative team." He had to admit he'd been desperate to get away from them, too, and a trip to the Left Coast definitely fit the bill. But the parade of Portlanders in their twenties coming and going here might as well have been from the *FreeChain News* team itself. The outfits had a little more lumberjack vibe for the men and nerdcore librarian for the women, but still.

Molly had texted him how it was in the urban Pacific Northwest, and now it was his turn. *Coffee shop I'm in might as well be Brooklyn*, he texted back, and they shared LOL emojis.

Five minutes later, Lucy Holden was officially late. Some women came and went but never stayed long, professional types or tourist moms, most grabbing coffees to go. Certainly not this Lucy Holden. A woman strode in wearing the workout gear that so many wore, tights and some slim but comfortably fitting top, and even a yoga mat under one arm. Owen looked away, scanning the street for a woman in her thirties who might look like a private investigator. What did that look like? He had no good idea.

"Hey, are you meeting someone here?"

Owen's head shot up. The woman in the workout gear had halted sideways midstep a couple feet from his table. Medium build, suitably amateur athletic. She had dark hair, an asymmetric cut close to a mullet, her bangs cut severely high and tight. Deep green eyes. Olive skin, but freckled. She spoke loudly, and slowly, and for a second he thought she might be one of those people who spoke like this to him because they assumed he didn't know English that well on account of his Asian-ish looks. Then he realized it was her. "Lucy, right? Lucy Holden."

"Correct. Hi."

"Want a coffee? My treat—"

"No, I'll get one, it's fine. Want anything?"

That cookie? "No, it's okay, thanks." There was always that awkward bit about getting the coffee. And now he realized that this Lucy always spoke that way, partly, he guessed, because she had a slight lisp. *But we all have something*, Owen thought. She'd probably already noticed that birthmark on his right temple that he hated, in the rough shape of Texas of all things. The kids in school had called him "Tex" on into high school.

She was in line briefly. Ordered. She came right back with a twelve-ounce house just like Owen's and sat facing him, having no problem putting her back to the room. Only now did Owen notice the professional laptop backpack she was wearing, which she placed on a chair with her yoga mat and Patagonia coat.

Lucy shook his hand with one hand and yanked at her tights with the other. "You might be wondering about this outfit since I did tell you I was working." She added a laugh. "Well, I was. I often dress like this when I'm on the job. Like I'm going to the gym. Helps me blend in. Me, I'll take all I can get in my line of work. Who would ever guess that a woman dressed like she's going to rowing class would actually be staking out someone, or tracking anyone?"

"Good point. Are you from here?"

"From Portland? I am. How's it treating you so far?"

"It's nice. Very walkable."

She laughed. "True. But you know why we have such small blocks? It's because the original developers back in the 1890s or whenever, Wild West entrepreneurs that they were, realized they could charge more lease for corner real estate. So they created more corners."

She talked a lot for a private detective. But then again she was probably alone a lot.

"Nothing's ever what it seems," he said.

Lucy only shook her head at that. She took a drink of coffee, then glanced outside. Her eyes landed back on him.

"How are you doing?" she said.

She had to mean *FreeChain News*. She had to know about the big announcement, plus that he was brought on from *AltaVista News*. She was also half-biting her lower lip as if stifling amusement. Was she teasing him? At least they were establishing rapport. What was he supposed to tell her? That by nearly fleeing here he'd basically ceded the newsroom to the "kids," as he termed his so-called investigative team. He was trying not to be offended by them, even though Mason Snead might've been offering them to him as golden handcuffs. *MS says mold them how you want*, Viktoria had texted him—MS, as Owen now knew, was Mason Snead. They had a point, but it still made him uneasy. Was this just a microcosm of what *FreeChain News* would be? Controlling people through their perceived freedom? The truth was, he was already rebelling a little inside. Luckily Mason Snead via Viktoria had also given him an open-ended expense account for his efforts. So here he was, out west.

He shrugged at Lucy Holden. "If you mean *FreeChain News*?

I know about as much as you. *Alta Vista News* certainly wasn't going anywhere. Meanwhile, I have a job to do."

"Uh-huh." She took a sip of coffee with both hands, warming them. She set the cup down. "You said in your email that you were looking into this Alex person, the one who did that Show Game thing?" She shook her head. "Crazy stuff. Couldn't believe it. I was on the road, for work. Los Angeles during the first one, Philadelphia the second. Everyone was talking about it."

Owen couldn't help noticing how she said "looking into Alex," as if he should drop the Dwayne Specklin angle. He needed to keep going with his original investigation. He had to trust they would lead to the same place. Plus, his mission, as handed to him by Mason Snead, started here. On his West Coast tour over the last couple days, he had met some victims of Dwayne Specklin's in person, in San Diego, Los Angeles, San Jose, hoping one of them could lead him to Alex. All men. It made sense that Alex was a male, considering what Dwayne Specklin had done to boys. And meeting man-to-man was always better, Owen knew, because you might spot nuances or even tells that could be concealed over the phone. But so many of the victims were devastated, either on drugs or self-destructive or even suicidal, and possibly unreliable narrators. None could be Alex.

"In my line of work you have to establish connections, time-lines, watertight tunnels to the truth," he told Lucy. "You know how it is."

"I sure do."

"Which brings me to you. I haven't been getting very far, to be honest. So I'm trying someone who's not actually a victim, but who has a connection that could maybe help me. Some of the victims told me you might know some things. On account of your brother, that is."

"On account of my brother what?"

"Your brother being a victim of Dwayne Specklin's, I mean."

Her brother, Andrew Holden, had later killed himself.

"I'm very sorry," he quickly added.

Lucy Holden bowed her head a moment, then pushed back the hair falling down on one side. "Let me guess. Considering all that happened, you're thinking that I was looking into things. At the people Specklin molested, at what he did to Andrew. At least for my family's sake. It almost tore us apart, you know. My parents are divorced."

Owen knew that. "I'm separated," he blurted for no reason.

"Oh. Sorry?"

"No, it's okay," he quickly added. "What I meant was, I cannot even imagine what you all went through." He wanted to be respectful, which was why he had none of his gear out. "If anything else, I really just need to hear from someone stable and on the level who isn't with the authorities."

Lucy Holden spurted a laugh. Something about the way she did made Owen sit up straight. She glared at the ceiling, and her eyes landed back on him. Her voice turned deeper, more gravelly than it already was.

"Come on," she said, grinning with one side of her mouth. "You can't be happy about this *FreeChain News* thing, can you? An old-school news guy like you?"

"This isn't about me, Ms. Holden."

"Call me Lucy. Screw it. Of course it's about you. You, *too*, anyway. I mean, they've got you investigating this Alex—instead of the actual abusers."

"I agreed to it. I was given a choice."

"You were also given the title of Lead Investigative Reporter."

"That was my old title. It's now Head Investigative Reporter."

"Ah. I see." Lucy leaned forward, and the table legs pressed against Owen's knees. "But before, though, you were investigating Dwayne Specklin, weren't you? And Alex took that from you."

She was good. But then again, she was a private detective, and there was her brother to honor—

"I think about my brother every day," she continued, "and about what the Dwayne Specklins of this world do to us all. So of course I knew what you were investigating. Victims do talk among themselves, you know. Sometimes it's the only way not to self-destruct."

"Of course. You're right. I guess I like the challenge, considering."

"And have you thought of the consequences of that? Say you find this Alex renegade, or whatever or whoever they are. Then what happens to the other truth?"

"I'm a reporter, Lucy. I'm not a Supreme Court judge."

"Have you seen what this guy's saying?" Lucy said. "This Mason Snead? He's actually been rooting for Alex in public, all while he's sending you out to uncover him."

It was true. Mason Snead had been posting on FreeChain and giving quotes that he couldn't help admiring the Show Game. *It cuts right through all the bullshit*, he'd said just this morning.

"That's just his way," Owen said. "It's good news business. He's stoking it. Spot news is sports, you know that. Plus, he's one of those full disclosure people."

"He's one of those tech economy assholes. Bullshit libertarians by another name. Peer-to-peer news? Truth sharing? Come on? He's the ultimate hypocrite. The guy doesn't just want it both ways, he wants it every way. Because he's going to monetize the whole fucking thing for himself. Meanwhile it's all chaos all the time for the rest of us. And you? You don't even sound to me like someone who wants to find this Alex person." She paused, held up hands. "Pardon my going off here. I'm really just trying to figure this out."

"It's okay." Owen added a smile. "I am too." He dropped the smile. "Look. You make good points, all around. And if you don't want to discuss any leads that you might have? Then I'll understand."

"No, let's discuss." Lucy sat up straight like Owen had just moments ago. She shot him a smile that was more genuine than he'd expected. "Seriously. Shoot."

Owen took a moment to jog his brain. He told her whom he'd already met. They discussed some of the victims, and Lucy confirmed that none of them could be Alex.

"Are you still looking into things?" Owen then asked outright.

Lucy's eyes flashed, an even deeper green. "Not after what that Alex did with his Show Game. I mean, why would I? We have about as much closure as we're ever going to get."

"Sure. True. Just curious."

Lucy did give him a few more leads that he didn't have, including a couple victims that had long disappeared. But she knew of them. "One's in Utah, the other in Vermont." She paused, abruptly, as if catching her breath.

"What is it?" Owen said.

Lucy looked around the room, like she was stalling, Owen thought. "There is another one. But . . ." Her eyes landed back on him, and they were sparkling as much as sad. "I really shouldn't even tell you. In case he is Alex. I should just be rooting him on."

"That's up to you. I'm not a cop."

"No. No, you're not." She sighed. She took a deep breath. "His name is Martin. Martin Podest."

"He live around here?"

"Sort of. In the Northwest. He lives near Tacoma. That's up in Washington State, close to Seattle."

Owen knew where Tacoma was, roughly. It was near Molly's world now. He nodded along, letting Lucy tell it.

"The thing is," she continued, "no one even knows Martin was a victim. But maybe now he's taking his revenge? And . . ."

"And what?"

She lowered her head. "And, maybe, it's because he's perpetrating the same crimes."

"Same crimes?"

Lucy spoke lower. "I think he has certain inclinations. For young men. Boys, really. But he's got it under control."

"How do you know?"

"I've seen certain records. Maybe ones I wasn't supposed to."

"Okay. Say no more." Owen thought a moment. "So, this Martin, he hates himself for it—and in turn he hated Dwayne Specklin for it. So he—"

"Whoa, easy. I'm not saying it's him. Not at all."

"No, I get it. You're right. I'm getting ahead of myself. There's also the possibility that he knows someone who is involved."

Owen got his notepad out. Adrenaline kicked in and he felt lighter, sharper.

"Martin's a Scout leader, among other things," Lucy told him. She gave him the contact details from her phone. She watched him write.

"It is an interesting angle," he said.

"The guy lives alone, never did marry, travels a lot for the Scouts. Who knows?"

"Have you talked to him since the Conrad Holmes Show Game?" Owen said.

"No."

"So not since the first Show Game either? The one for the man who abused him?"

79

"Nope. No. Knock yourself out."

"Will do." Owen finished writing, asked a couple follow-up questions, and slapped his notepad shut.

"Thanks for this. This might actually lead to something."

"Sure. I guess it couldn't hurt if you told him that I was the one who sent you. He trusts me; he might trust you more that way. But it's your call."

"Thanks," Owen said. "Listen. I can't thank you enough."

"Forget it." Lucy smiled now, a wider smile that showed off great teeth that were straight but in a natural way. "Pretty fucking awesome, I have to say, that someone did what Alex did."

"I won't argue with you there," Owen said. "You know, I was thinking something that others have to be considering too. The authorities for one. That this Alex had to have had help."

"Yeah, I was thinking that as well," Lucy said, still smiling. "He must have. There's too much involved. Maybe it's an angle?"

"Maybe. I'm not going to get my hopes up. At the most, maybe this Martin Podest might know of another someone who's likely."

Owen thought about that, the next steps—hitting Tacoma on this trip if he could, and all the logistics involved got him thinking about that gooey dark chocolate cookie again. But especially about Molly. Seattle being next door to Tacoma. But how did that work? Were they obligated to see each other, to tell each other when they were near? Probably not anymore. Yet he still couldn't help feeling sad about it, and guilty not texting her.

"You know," Lucy said, "considering my obvious personal attachment to all this, I really should be sending you down the wrong path."

"That's true. But you're like me, I can tell. In the end, you just want the truth."

"Touché," she said. "Well, I guess I better get." She got up to leave. She picked up her pack and coat and yoga mat. She stared at Owen, one elbow cocked a little higher than the other. "Good luck with it," was all she said. And she turned and left, keeping that elbow cocked all the way out the door.

SATURDAY, NOVEMBER 4
OWEN

The real heart of Tacoma, Washington, was an older downtown area with bars and restaurants facing a vast working port that opened up to Puget Sound and its broad horizon. Owen thought the surrounding landscape, with its dramatically steep slopes and ridges, was far more awe-inspiring than the Tacoma core's march toward gentrification. There was still something ramshackle about the main drag that appealed to him. Nothing too fancy. Nothing perfect. It still had the grit that had earned it the nickname "Grit City." Plenty of unwashed red brick, faded "For Lease" signs, and nearly abandoned side streets, the type of area that still had an army surplus store holding out. At the bottom of the old slope waited a massive bay, with ships in port, and grain silos, pulp mills, piles and stacks. The streets reminded him of San Francisco before it cleaned up—more *Dirty Harry* than dot-com SF. This was a place that people either fled to or far away from, it seemed to Owen. He thought Tacomans should be proud of it. Then again, though, this was also the hometown of serial killer Ted Bundy after age three.

Owen was surprised that Martin Podest wanted to meet him so suddenly and so soon—and it gave him no chance to consider telling Molly he was passing through. He didn't want to sound desperate, or put her on the spot. He wasn't expecting a meeting at first. After he saw Lucy Holden, he'd tried emailing Podest. He got no reply. He then tried texting. In the text, he said he was going to call next, which often got people to respond, especially if they were under thirty. Martin was thirty. Owen also dropped Lucy Holden's name finally. Martin texted right back. He was succinct. He told Owen to sit in the window of a certain bar just off the main drag: the Yardstick Tavern.

It was now 2:10 p.m. Owen was the only person in the Yardstick apart from the bartender on his phone and a local slumped at the dinged-up bar. The floor was gnarly wood planks like from a sailing ship, with knots and gaps and petrified chewing gum spots, and the brick walls lacked mortar in too many spots. The odd, unidentifiable shipping instruments and parts hanging from the ceiling—a sextant, a porthole?—seemed to be suspended by a network of cobwebs probably dating back to before Prohibition. The place had been here before gentrification—before Grit City probably—and would be here after.

Martin Podest was late. Owen had expected that, he always did, but now he had the feeling that he was being watched in this plateglass window. A couple side streets enabled a person to peek this way from around the corner, as did a parking garage and various darkened old windows—anything from artist lofts to warehouse storage to abandoned offices. It was hard to tell. It was getting hot too. Owen was sweating. Places like the Yardstick didn't have AC and never would. He nursed a water in a plastic pint glass he'd filled from a jug set at the end of the bar.

Five minutes later, a motorcycle pulled up outside. It had a sidecar and was two-wheel drive, with winter tires and a spare tire and racks and fog lights. The beefed-up beast was dark gray and looked vintage but was one of those newer Russian imports that a certain niche rider loved. Ural was the brand. It looked like a bike for riding across the country, which reminded Owen that the main freeways were much closer to this part of Tacoma than it seemed, with I-5 just minutes away. He wondered why Martin Podest would choose this location. It seemed like an ideal spot for a quick getaway if required.

The rider pulled off his no-frills, matte-black helmet. Martin Podest? Owen wasn't sure. Martin Podest nearly didn't exist on social media or the internet apart from a few requisite LinkedIn and Boy Scout listings that didn't include a photo. Whoever it was, he didn't look at Owen. He stomped around his bike, arranging this and that, stowing his flight jacket and helmet inside the sidecar, reminding Owen of a smaller, wirier version of that actor Russell Crowe or maybe that guy who played the cop on *Stranger Things*. A few days stubble. Forceful. All elbows and nearly bowlegged. *Guarded*, Owen thought.

The man stomped toward the window and his lumbering gait smoothed out. Then he entered and Owen noticed the clear transformation as he came through the threshold. Once inside, without that survivalist bike and helmet, he looked like any alternative stay-at-home dad picking his kid up from school. He even had on a T-shirt for the band Mudhoney under his thick cardigan sweater, and scruffy cuffed Levis, skateboard sneakers. As he strolled toward Owen he pulled on, over his thinning brown hair, an army-green baseball cap bearing a monochrome Boy Scouts logo.

Owen stood.

"Martin," he said with a curt smile and held out a hand, which Owen wasn't expecting. After the pandemic, he'd expected one of its silver linings to be the death of the handshake. But it had roared right back.

"No handshake," Martin said as if reading Owen's mind. He gave Owen a fist bump instead.

"Nice to meet you," Owen said, "and thanks for coming—"

"You want a beer?" Martin said.

"Sure."

Martin held out hands as if to say, *What do you want?*

"Whatever you're having."

Martin strode up to the bar while Owen resettled into his chair. He felt many degrees cooler now, his sweat chilling the skin under his arm sockets.

Martin set two pints down. Owen's was orange, Martin's yellow.

"Got you the amber."

"You?"

"This one's got no alcohol."

Owen's chill felt greasy suddenly, and he shifted in his seat to rub it away with his shirt sleeves. "You don't drink?"

"No, I do. I just want to stay sharp for you."

"Oh. Okay."

Martin sat across from Owen with his torso straight, leaning slightly forward, his wrists resting at equal spots near the edge of the table. It wasn't so much good posture as an alert one. So far, Owen was getting the vibe of someone who had been in the military but was kicked out, or at least discharged by mutual agreement. But Martin Podest had never been in the military.

Owen thanked Martin for coming and went over why he wanted to interview him. Lucy Holden had suggested him. She thought he might know of someone who could be Alex.

"Huh," was all Martin said. He wasn't frowning, but he wasn't smiling either.

It seemed like some kind of opening. Owen got right to it. "You give me something? I don't use your name."

"What do they call that again?"

"Deep background."

"That sounds like someone could figure out who I am. Isn't there another one?"

"Off-the-record. That's the most extreme."

"That's the one," Martin said, his tone like he was explaining it to Owen.

This Martin is cocky, Owen noticed. He wasn't expecting that.

"I looked you up," Martin declared. "You made a mistake before, with your reporting. Some guy named Shane Bagley went to prison. Right? So you don't want to make a mistake, not again."

This Martin is strategic. Offense is the best defense.

"Right," was all Owen said.

Martin smiled now, but not in a creepy way. He seemed to be just appreciating the situation, like he was telling Owen the plot of a show he was bingeing. Every character has their flaw.

But Owen was not getting cold feet. His stomach and chest felt hot, and his sweat was back. "Could we get away from this window?" he said, and as soon as he said it, clouds covered the sun and stayed there.

"There you go," Martin said. "Better?"

"It is," Owen said.

He had to turn the tables back, take the offense. So he used an old reporter card.

"You know, I could use your name with or without your comment," he said. "Just drop it into the story. Adjust the context to fit."

Martin leaned back a little. His wrists lifted from the table and found his lap. He looked out the window as if watching for an airplane.

"I'm just trying to help," he said eventually.

"I understand," Owen replied, needing to make the most of Martin's vulnerability. "So, do you know of something or someone who could be involved?"

"If there were, you seem like a guy I could tell."

"I appreciate that."

Martin nodded. He spoke mechanically, nearly robotically. "And now there's the Conrad Holmes show. So many deserve it. It's not just pastors. Say, for example, a certain senator whose own child was injured in a school shooting yet has the gall to vote against every gun control bill that comes along. Then there's the big progressive intellectual who's a closet white suprema-cist, wreaking havoc and inciting followers on sneaky online forums. Also, we got the billionaire who pays no taxes yet cuts his minimum-wage employees' health care; there are plenty of those actually. Oh, you also have that major screenwriter-director-producer guy who got lucky enough to land a big sci-fi-fantasy-comic-book series that every kid loves but who's also a major pedophile."

"All true."

"I'm not done. The big-time motivational speaker who preaches female empowerment yet forbids his female employees from wearing anything but dresses and from having any salary close to the male staff and—*and*—has had multiple rape accusations brought against him over the years, all of which he'd either intimidated, hushed up, bought off, or beat through simple financial attrition by using an army of lawyers . . ."

Owen didn't interrupt. It was like Martin was telling him his next targets.

". . . the performative mask critic and anti-vaxxer—despite his own grandma dying of COVID—who only refused to wear a mask when in public view and was secretly one of the first to score the vaccine. And, and there's—"

Martin's mouth snapped shut.

Owen waited for more. He drank his beer, leaving a massive gap for Martin to dive into.

"You know what I think of all these pigs of this world?" Martin said eventually. "Politics now? So-called business? Tech, don't get me started. They're all just another pyramid scheme. All of them."

And Martin snapped shut again.

Owen was starting to more than wonder. Could Martin actually be Alex? He felt himself rising in his seat from the excitement but kept his butt planted. He'd had a slight buzz from the beer but it vanished, replaced by surge of electricity. Clarity.

Martin was right. He could not make a mistake.

A silence found them. Each sipped at their beers.

Owen sighed. "Okay, I have to ask you, sorry: Where were you during the first Show Game?"

Martin just stared, so Owen gave him the date. Martin nodded. He looked at his phone. Stalling, or helping?

"Oh right," Martin said eventually. "I was at a Scout conference. LA. I know what you're thinking. Over many days, lots of people, events. But I know people, colleagues, who can account for my attendance."

"All right, thanks."

"Just to be sure, you're not a cop?" Martin added. With a smile.

"Nope. Definitely not."

It did fit the profile, Owen thought. No kids. No girlfriend. Martin was a cop for a while, a security guard. Coached Little League. Bartender. Had a gambling problem, Lucy had told him.

Martin slapped at the table. "Let's just go there, all right?" he barked. "Dwayne Specklin abused me and I would actually kill him if I knew I could get away with it."

"Could you?" Owen said.

"You tell me. That's your job, isn't it?"

"What about Show Game number two? A guy like Conrad Holmes? He sounds a lot like all those others you just mentioned."

Martin stared out the window again, right through his motorcycle sidecar. "Okay, maybe not kill him. Make him suffer for all those who suffer."

"So . . . for the sake of going there: Where were you when the Conrad Holmes Show Game took place?"

Martin's eyes widened, and he seemed to see his bike now. "Camping. Olympic Peninsula. With the Ural."

"Is that far?"

"Not really, just across the Sound."

They both looked out at the water. "How long?" Owen said.

"Was I camping? A few days. Five."

That was more than enough time to get to Washington, DC, and back. And Martin's actual address was even closer to Sea-Tac airport than Tacoma. He wondered if a guy like Martin could get an ID good enough to get him on a plane using an alias.

"I couldn't help noticing," Owen said, "that you live in Federal Way. Why are we meeting in Tacoma?"

Martin chuckled, shaking his head. "Man, you ever been to Federal Way? Soulless. At least Tacoma has history."

"And grit."

"That's right."

Owen took a sip of the beer, for extra courage. "Were you alone? On the camping trip, I mean."

"No, I had a few Scouts with me." Martin pointed to the logo on his cap.

"How's that work?"

"It's fun. We get together regular. Pretend we're having an adventure. Boys, kids, they never get outside. It's all video games, internet, social media."

"Are these ones boys?"

Martin nodded.

"Official trip?"

"Depends how you define it. There were a couple dads there. Friends."

Owen nodded, stalling. He was going to have to shock this Martin a little, to see what he was made of. It might get ugly. "Okay if I get my notepad out?" he said.

"Go for it." Martin took a quick drink, his eyes focused on Owen, not blinking.

The Seattle-Tacoma area had plenty of military, Owen read in his notes, from multiple bases. That kind of know-how could handle the kind of operation Alex was doing. Stealth, surveillance, abduction.

Owen looked up. "Any your friends in the military? I don't just mean on the camping trip."

"A couple, yes."

"Ever go on the dark web?" Owen said. He was just fishing now.

"The what? No. Screw you."

"Sorry, I just mean, anyone who's doing this—or anything that's breaking multiple laws, not to mention major taboos? They might be using the dark web."

"I don't like what you're insinuating."

"Insinuating?"

"Yeah. Wait, what exactly did Lucy Holden tell you?"

"Nothing." Owen added a shake of his head. Lucy had only pointed him in the right direction. Martin had certain "inclinations," as she'd called them. And Owen had confirmed that Martin Podest was seeing a counselor. "I am able to find out things on my own," he added.

Martin didn't reply.

A staring contest broke out.

"Look, I know you're seeing a counselor," Owen said finally, in his softest voice. "And I commend you. I don't know the details of course. But it sounds like you're coping."

Martin nodded. Then shook his head. "No one knows about that. The Scouts, they would dump me. Are you trying to pressure me?" He stood.

"No, no. Please, sit."

Martin marched off. He went to the bar. He came back with the same beer Owen was drinking, and two shots of whiskey. He placed one in front of Owen. Owen threw his back, to steel himself for more talk. It was almost like Martin was testing him. Martin hadn't touched his shot.

"Could you, er, tell me about these friends of yours?" Owen said, the whiskey still burning in his throat.

"We go way back," Martin said. "A couple of us were in community college together. A couple others by way of various jobs. One's a cop now, another's a teacher. Another guy's Forest Service. And, yes, a few were in the army a long time. One still is, I think."

Now Owen wondered: *Could there be a whole network of them?*

"Sounds like the A-Team," he said.

"I wish, man." Martin said it like he should have been smiling, but his face had hardened.

"So you're kind of a gang. A crew."

"Sure. Wait. Do you think this Alex is one person, or are you thinking more people?"

"Good question. I hope it's more."

Martin Podest smiled at that. He drank half his shot. He said, "Man, you really don't think I was the one, do you?"

Owen shrugged. "I would be, if I were you."

"Nah. Me, I have other ways of channeling that anger."

"Oh yeah?"

"Bikes. Leading Scouts. The camping. Pickleball."

"Pickleball? That's so popular now."

"Invented right up here in Washington." Martin downed his beer. "You want another?"

Owen wanted to. Not because the beer was good. Because he wanted to see how loose Martin would get. But he also knew he had to be wary. He had to leave the interviewee wanting a little more out of it. Martin would be here, he knew where to find him. Meanwhile, he could look into what Martin was telling him.

"No, I'm good," Owen said.

"Smart," Martin said. As if reading Owen's mind again, he added, "It could be anyone. People you know, close to you even."

Was Martin deflecting, or did he know more? Or maybe just harking back to the man who had abused him? Something about the way Martin said it gave Owen a raspy little shudder inside, like tiny cold ice slivers in his stomach. He did his best not to let it show. "True. You know what? I think I'm going to leave it here for now. I've bothered you enough."

"All right."

"Could I, uh, get the names of the friends and kids who were there camping? It's just fact-checking."

"I thought this was off-the-record."

"It is. I just want to rule things out."

Martin took a deep breath. He tapped at the table. "Sure, I get it. I'll email you. My parents can vouch too." He stared at Owen. "These boys need support, you know. They need protecting."

"I understand. That's good of you."

"And, my friends, my parents? They'll tell you what you need to hear."

"Fair enough."

They finished their beers, which included the usual sports small talk. Seattle Mariners, Seahawks, Sounders, and the slew of lesser Tacoma teams in smaller sports. Martin led Owen outside to his motorcycle, which Owen praised.

"Let me help any way I can," Martin said. He added a grin. "And hey—if you find out who Alex is, and they need any help? Tell them I'm their man."

Owen smiled. "Will do, though it might be too late at that point."

"Let's hope not."

Owen stood back as Martin pulled on his jacket and helmet and stomped on his rugged Ural and roared away. A part of him wanted a ride in that sidecar. Maybe it was the rapid injection of whiskey and beer, but for a split second an even deeper part of him hoped, and wished, that Martin truly was Alex—and they were going to speed off together and nab their next Show Game contestant. He forced out the thought with a deep sigh.

Before leaving Washington State, Owen drove to Federal Way, just twenty minutes on regular roads but even faster on I-5. He had Martin's address. The house was a standard smaller and somewhat dated suburban house on a standard suburban street. It looked like the rental it was, with little to no character and only a carport instead of a garage. Martin's motorcycle was not there. On the way out, Owen drove through the city. It was not bad at all. The area and main drag had plenty of restaurants, coffee shops, and parks. Lots of families and young professionals.

Nothing like how Martin Podest described it, and certainly not lacking soul. Not even close.

MONDAY, NOVEMBER 6
OWEN

Owen, reminding himself he had to tread carefully, wanted to keep Martin Podest to himself for now. In his back pocket. What exactly were Martin's inclinations? he wondered. Was it just toward boys, or was there something of another shade, such as violence? One crime begets another. Owen only wished he could get at the counselor's notes. It wasn't going to happen. The counselor, a woman, had gone out of her way to vouch for Martin, and Owen even wondered if they were romantically involved. He had to consider everything. Anything was possible. And Owen had another wild thought—What if the counselor was in on it too? Then he reminded himself that he couldn't let his hunches spiral out of control. He could not make another mistake. No more Shane Bagleys.

One thing Owen did know was that he needed help. First thing Monday morning, back in the looming future offices of *FreeChain News*, he was finally forced to acknowledge his young but enthusiastic investigative team.

MS says mold them how you want, Viktoria had texted him.

Out in the open and near-empty newsroom, Owen stood at the head of one of the long tables—he'd simply picked one, since they didn't have an actual conference room that he knew of. There was no one to ask, no one to call on a moment's notice. Physically working here was like being on a website with no actual contact info. He'd finally remembered they had a rudimentary new intranet for the *News* and discovered under Help that the only contact was a chat function. He'd asked the chat person, an automated fake person by the name of Abernathy, if there was a conference room. Abernathy had responded: *The* News *has no conference rooms, but we do offer an open layout for improved collaboration! Feel free to use any and every space! Is there anything I can help you with today?* Owen hadn't bothered to say no or thanks.

All the kids that were his team were on phones, tablets, and laptops, doing who knew what, so Owen simply clapped his hands for all to come over. They gathered around, sharing excited glances as if Owen were about to give out awards.

"Here's what I'll need you to do: I'm looking for any connection between the Show Game, the victims slash contestants, and anyone who could be Alex. I'll let you figure out and divvy up the work between yourselves. But you're reporters now. Whatever you learn, you'll have to keep it close to your chest. Share with no one outside of the team. Give nothing away to those you contact either."

He told them about Martin Podest. Martin, again to Owen's surprise, had already emailed Owen the names of his friends and Scouts who went camping. He told the team they had to help look up these people. All were nodding along. Some entered notes into their devices, but a surprising number produced reporter notepads of actual paper. "I'll put what I have on our special Slack, Semaphor." That drew blank stares, but they would figure it out. "Signal app? Whatever we're using. Make it secure. Someone set it up."

The nods returned.

"All right, that's it." They kept staring at him. Not knowing what else to do, he stood and clapped his hands again and added, "Now get after it!"

They seemed like the magic words. They dispersed. And he wandered back to his office, thinking it couldn't hurt. And it attached no one too closely to his efforts. He didn't want anyone too near at this point. The thought occurred to him that Viktoria and MS might be using some kind of informant to keep tabs on him. Then again, they could also just monitor his email and phone if they really wanted. Mason Snead's father had basically invented the backbone to the internet after all, and Viktoria herself certainly had some sort of special powers he wasn't sure he wanted to know about, even as an investigative reporter. Her origin story must have been a doozy.

Owen leaned back in his office chair, staring at his ukulele. Then at his notes. He'd already looked up one of Martin's friends himself—the one Martin said was in the military. DeAndre Jarvis. Jarvis had served in Afghanistan among other hot spots. He'd been on social media for a brief spell after that, with the usual partying and travel, a ton of selfies blocking the view. Oval face, wore sunglasses a lot. Were they prescription? No way to tell. Then, nothing. DeAndre Jarvis faded. Owen suspected PTSD or some kind of trouble. Martin said he hadn't heard from Jarvis in a while. His email address bounced back, and his phone number was a dead end, the line transferred to some high school kid in Idaho.

Beep. His phone. He glanced at it.

What doing?

It was Molly. He wasn't going to respond at first, not now. He should've put his phone on Do Not Disturb. But something about her text encouraged him.

Show Game, he texted. *Following up, comparing/contrasting. Plastering walls.*

He chuckled. Back when they were happy, before they were married even, Owen used to paste clippings and photos on the wall like some prosecutor in a crime show. He did it so much she made him go do it out in the garage. She used to feign annoyance but it also let her rib him a little, and they used to laugh about it over date-night drinks. But then the annoyance became resentment and there were no more date nights or even nights. Just drinks alone.

I wish, he texted.

He wished he could see her now. He could still conjure up every inch of her. Her round face with soft, eternally chin-length hair and her bangs, those round glasses. Her compact body, neither thin nor chubby but with just enough curves. From a distance she could appear plain if not dowdy, from her rotating repertoire of vintage-style cardigans mostly, but the closer you got, the more she sparkled. That curl at one side of her mouth when she had your number yet again. That twinkle in her eyes so bright it was like she wasn't even wearing lenses in those glasses. Drawing him in. The way she reached out and touched him a moment, neither too firm nor fleeting, when he got something really right. By the same token, she'd let him know it when he did not. This usually involved a darkly disappointed look like he was no better than, say, the wrong package delivered to her doorstep that she was looking down on at her feet, despite the fact that she was even shorter than Owen. That chilling silence of hers followed. The latter experience had been happening far more often in the end.

At the same time it seemed like hundreds of years since he'd seen her, as if he was some ageless creature doomed to repeat every morning, day, and night without her forever. Why didn't they just talk to each other on the phone if they were going to communicate so much? They could even do a video call. Only texting? This was silly. They weren't shy teenagers. They were conversing more now than in such a long time. Then again, he didn't want to upset the fragile balance. He figured she didn't either.

Seattle had been so close to Tacoma. In the end, he hadn't told her he was there, only that he was on the West Coast, and she didn't go asking.

Owen went back to his research. By an hour later, his intrepid team of kids were already reporting back. Many of Martin Podest's friends checked out. They were all responding quickly, and happy to help. They had alibis, could vouch for Martin, and a couple had been camping with him. *Man, these kids are fast*, Owen thought. And he himself had contacted Martin's parents, who confirmed his alibi. Everyone was so fast in responding. He didn't want to believe it. Some of them could be lying. All could be. There could've been a powwow, even right there deep in the woods of the Olympic Peninsula. Still, it was something. He checked things off his list with his usual tentative doodles—the question marks and the ellipses . . .

One parent of a Scout would not respond. The parent told Owen's reporter to "lay off." That could mean anything, Owen knew. They might just hate the media. But he put an exclamation point on that one and circled it.

What do you got? Molly now texted. Then: *Sorry, can't help it. Old habits.*

Sure, she had grown weary of his slaving away to his investigations, of his staring at the garage walls. But there were also

nights where she had stood out there with him with her glass of
wine (always a lowball glass; never a wineglass) and they had
stared together.

It's okay, he texted. *I don't have much, but I do have one lead.*
He texted her a photo of his scribbled one page of summary
notes just to confirm it.

She was a fast reader and could decipher his crappy handwriting like an archaeologist could ancient cave writings. He
didn't get a reply right away, so he texted:

*I didn't know I'd be in Tacoma. I only had a few hours or I
would've checked in with you.*

He could see she was already typing: *It's okay. I was out of
town anyway . . . Teacher convention*, she added.

He wanted to ask her how that went but wanted to give her
space, so only gave it a thumbs-up. He'd already just sent her
a photo, and he couldn't remember the last time he'd done so
just because. It was probably before the bickering broke out
into open warfare, though open warfare for them wasn't mean.
It was simply each sharing their disappointment in each other.
He needed to balance his life, she'd said. Maybe they should
think about children. What? She needed to be more supportive,
he'd said. It was because she had hated her own job as a project
manager for some wannabe creative agency. Who wouldn't? *That
hurts, Owen. I could say the same. You don't care about me. Maybe
I need my own space.* Both of them had said those last words.

The summary notes she was now deciphering had Martin
Podest, a near phantom named DeAndre Jarvis, and a couple
other guys not as likely. They were just casualties.

Wow, she texted back eventually. It was irony, but she didn't
need to mark it as such in her text because he still knew her all
too well.

Plus your handwriting's gotten even worse, she added.

I know. I know. Alex could be any of them, but my money's on Martin and/or his crew. So many disgruntled young males in the world.

At least this one isn't thinking about school shootings for once, she texted back. *So that's another plus.*

And that was it. She was probably busy. It was the afternoon, so she might even be at that elementary school. He imagined unruly kids waking up from postlunch naps. At least the two of them were trying. It was good, it was progress.

He went back to racking his brain. He'd have to find this DeAndre Jarvis somehow. Maybe Jarvis had some kind of connection to Conrad Holmes. Maybe that was why—

Wait, Molly texted.

Wait what?

You keep calling this Alex a HE. What, you don't think there are women with their own reasons? I mean, fuck. Where you been?

Owen thought about that for a minute, staring at the text, which was long enough that Molly had probably spoken it into the phone, which meant she was probably alone, which meant she hadn't been busy with other things but actually had been brainstorming this with him. Staring at that wall with him. His phone lay on the opposite page of his notebook, and her words blurred with his crappy handwriting on the facing page . . . *Digitally altered voice . . . both targets lying, arrogant, power-hungry hypocrites . . . What, you don't think there are women with their own reasons—*

"Crap!" he blurted.

Holy shit! he texted back.

WEDNESDAY, NOVEMBER 8
OWEN

Owen, tapping one foot like a tiny jackhammer, sat inside his glass office in the prelaunch *FreeChain News*. He still had to consider Martin Podest his first suspect. Camping in the woods was hardly an alibi, neither was a Scout conference. People could be covering for him, easily, or he could be putting alibis in people's heads. But Molly was so very right again. Molly was always right.

Why couldn't the Show Game be coming from a woman?

Martin had said it himself: *It could be anyone. People you know, close to you even.*

Owen, lost in thoughts running away from him, stared out at their open office, at the investigation team working away on their various devices in various positions of lounging—one with her stomach on the carpeted floor, another guy with one leg hanging off an armchair arm, a couple on a sofa with their legs on ottomans, and one, a girl, with another actual notepad, which impressed Owen, but then he noticed she was sitting cross-legged. Just the sight of all those awkward positions made his back hurt. They were so comfortable at first, then suddenly were horribly not if you got too used to them. Especially when you were his age, pushing forty.

He stared at them, wondering if he could actually tell anything about them just by looking at them. Or did we just read things in, projecting, grabbing from here and there in our own experience? One guy, Lucian, a thoughtful Black kid from Queens, liked to wear one of those camouflage hunting caps. Go figure. One girl had glasses, big ones, like Florida retirees used to wear. Did that make her smart, or just trying too hard, always needing to be ahead of the curve? On the surface it didn't seem so. He'd talked to her a couple times when she asked him for advice. Her name was Gina, he thought. And she came across as nothing less than a hard worker with a solid mind. Maybe she just liked huge vintage glasses. Maybe Lucian even liked hunting. Who knew?

He had let himself assume it was a man because of the many disgruntled young males in the world. Just look at culture, society, crime. There was *Network*, and *Taxi Driver*, *Falling Down*, *Joker*, news channels treating perpetrators like victims, shooting after shooting, schools, malls, restaurants, offices. Charlottesville. But those males with chips on their shoulders didn't even have a reason. They were just pussies. Now, a woman, she might have a good reason. And she was doing it her way. She wasn't killing anyone. A male? He'd probably kill his targets right on the video. She instead was just making them suffer in a way that so many of their victims had. She wanted them to pay, sure, but also to understand. It might make the world a better place as opposed to simply even more horrifying.

Holy fuck was right. Owen's mind raced, sprinted, ready to dive off cliffs without fear. He would have to retrace his steps, would go back through the victims for any female candidates.

But it really could be any woman. He free-associated now, thinking of women he knew who had the temperament. Forceful. Pissed. Some he knew caught up with him in his sprint to the cliff. Anne Blade. Where was she now? *They might even have reasons.* Viktoria Jett. She could do it alone, or, what if it was for Snead himself, with or without his knowledge, setting up a huge journalistic coup? *They might even have good reasons.* It could even be one of these younger cub reporters he worked with, right here in front of his nose and—

He pulled back from the cliff. And he turned away from the open workspace, facing the blank wall inside his glass office. Back to reasoning. What about Lucy Holden from Portland? She was a logical choice. Her brother, Andrew, had committed suicide, after all, unable to endure the horrible weight of being abused by the all-powerful Dwayne Specklin, who just kept getting more powerful. But Lucy herself had an alibi, as she'd mentioned; plus he'd already looked into that—she'd been working on cases up and down the West Coast during the first Show Game, and she confirmed them in their initial email.

When meeting Lucy in Portland, he'd instinctively noticed a few details about her, jotting them down after the fact like he always did. *She had a slight lisp*, he'd noted. He went through the Show Game videos again, looking for anything that matched. But the Show Game voice was too digitally altered to tell. He wondered if there was a way to detect that by analyzing speech altered by a voice changer, and he had that delegated to Gina. He looked for other patterns. *Lucy had kept her elbow out, cocked almost*, Owen had also noted, but he didn't detect that on the videos, either, because the Show Game perpetrators stayed off-screen. Of course they had.

Lucy was an experienced investigator, he knew. She would know how to cover herself. She was always on the move in her work and could find a way to make the Show Game happen despite her alibis. He also recalled that she'd seemed to go out of her way to mention where she was when she'd learned about the Show Games. Los Angeles during the first one, Philadelphia during the second. California and the East Coast. Those were close enough to slip in and out of the Show Game.

He couldn't just ask her straight out. He needed more. He couldn't give it away. He came up with a pretext to email her—he was simply following up about Martin Podest. But all he got was an Out of Office notice: she was traveling for work and checking email intermittently over the next four days.

It was already late afternoon. Owen looked around at the office space and realized the last of the team had left for the day. He had to try. He took a deep breath, picked up his phone, and texted Lucy Holden.

Hey, Owen Tanaka here. Martin Podest is a tough nut. He's got an alibi. But I'm seeing red flags.

At least he'd salvaged something from the day. Time to head home. He put his phone down and gathered his notebook and ukulele. It might be a while before she texted back, if ever.

She texted right back: *On the road for work. Bumfuck. Caught me at a good time. Fire away.*

Owen grabbed his phone, his pulse racing: *He could've been planning this a long time. He might have help. Looking for your thoughts. Any names? Maybe even a woman.*

He got nothing. He waited around. Played his ukulele, until dark. Still nothing. He trudged home, taking the bus to make sure he had a connection, but still got nothing.

As soon as he stepped off his Eighth Avenue bus, his phone dinged. Molly?

It was Lucy. *Sorry, no phone network for a while.*

It's okay. Maybe just call me?

I can't. Working.

You can't, or don't want to? Owen added a smiley face. He was taking a chance, but sometimes you just had to push it.

I can't comment about an ongoing case. Sorry.

That made his heart jump. What did that mean? He texted: *?
I don't understand.*

You're a nice guy, so I'll spell it out: I'm on the case myself.

Oh. Oh shit. Could this be true? If so, why hadn't she told him? A heat moved up his neck. He took a deep breath. *Do not text in anger, Owen*, he told himself.

You should've just told me, he texted back.

Sorry about that.

I'm spending a lot of time on Martin Podest.

I'm sorry, really. I wasn't trying to trick you. I just didn't believe him. I'm guessing you don't either? I thought maybe you could get more out of him.

Owen knew he was in a tough spot. Lucy herself had told him about Martin. So didn't he owe her? But what about the woman angle? Had she thought about it? He couldn't alienate her. Needed to go slowly. *An investigative reporter like you*, he thought, *you're like the handler for a secret agent who's betraying their country. You always have to be managing their emotions, swaying them this way or that, all while keeping your emotions in check.*

Lucy wanted to know what more he had. But what did she have?

I need to confirm some things, he first texted back.

Me too; guess we're in the same boat, Lucy texted. *We're both after the same thing.*

He pushed it a little more. *Right! You started it with Podest. So let's share findings. Win-win. How about it?* Another smiley face. What did they all do before smiley faces?

I'm afraid not. Not at this stage. I hope you'll understand.

Owen didn't text her back. He left it at that. For now. Let her think on it. Let her wonder what he was thinking. Meanwhile, he needed more. He needed a way to force the issue.

ALEX

I can't say I don't love this side effect: A whole category of FreeChain and YouTube videos has popped up to comment on all that has been happening. YouTube meanwhile was threatening to ban the Show Game. As for Mason Snead's FreeChain? Not a chance. No feed before its time, baby. Plus, he certainly wasn't going to block anything that only created more ad revenue. Me, I just want the truth out. Still, I can't say it doesn't make me feel warm in my tummy like I just scarfed down some killer ramen. At the same time, many on social media are begging Alex to please, please announce the next one with a little warning so that people can be ready to watch together— apparently impromptu watch parties are ready to form as soon as the next Show Game gets announced. I might have to oblige them, these fans of mine, since they're so sympathetic to my cause. Though that has its own risks too. Chip and I have to make sure we have enough time to get well out of Dodge. And the Show Game itself has to happen fast, just like before, because the likes of Dwayne Specklin and Conrad Holmes cannot go missing long without someone noticing. It's going to be even more urgent with the third one.

Next up, Show Game Contestant number three. One more to go until my final target. Just wait till you get a load of this sick bastard.

I have my disguise—actual fat suit, baggy clothes, long hair, big dark glasses. I'm in Minneapolis, where I've met Chip. We'd reunited on the dark web. He has a different van now, this one more utilitarian, a white Ford Transit high-roof version. It's a little too new, like a rental or worse and possibly conspicuous, but it will do. He'd gone back to his van in DC and found it, from a safe distance, in the same spot. But in the end he didn't dare. What if it was some kind of trap? If those were feds coming for us on Show Game number two, then they could've put gear on it to trace us once we came back for it.

"Man, I fucking loved that van," Chip says, shaking his head.

"I know. I know, buddy." I give him a little pat on his shoulder, which only makes him shake his head again.

It's dark out. We're sitting in the back, staring out the blackened linear side window, both of us in folding chairs. All Chip has to his name in the back of this van now is a foam pad, a sleeping bag, a few toiletries, some changes of underwear and socks. I suspect he keeps a stash somewhere in this town or the next, but I don't ask. We all have our own personal escape plan. *When* to run is open to question. Is it like last time, when the authorities seemed to be speeding down the road? Or is it simply when things get too risky, when the walls close in a little too close. Me? My escape plan isn't quite one at all. It's more like a self-destruction plan. That's when I go all in and risk everything for my final target, the one I've always been aiming at. These are only practice. To make a point. Set precedent.

"What's on your mind, Alex?" Chip says. He's holding out a bag of beef jerky to me, the peppery kind.

I reach in, gnaw, and chew. I like the peppery kind. Plus I'm hungry. It's now midnight. I know nothing of Minneapolis except Mary Tyler Moore, the Replacements, skyways because it gets so dang cold, and that they have a soccer team in MLS.

We're ready to rock this. It's time for Show Game Contestant Number Three, the next-to-last target. One Gerald Hartwell. English dude, if you couldn't guess. One of those who changed his working-class London accent for a posh one that sounds like an American actor trying to do Received Pronunciation in a Hallmark movie, which makes sense if you consider that our Gerald has been in the US since his early twenties and is one of those elusive self-made men that Americans tend to worship like royalty even though the USA was founded as a big screw-you to the very concept of monarchy. Then the Queen went and knighted the guy. Now pushing sixty-five, Sir Hartwell made his name and fortune as a pharmaceutical baron and a major international financier. You could run a Show Game on him for a lot of issues: crippling economic disparity, climate change denial, unfair elections, the pandemic running amok even. That said, the man is also a major philanthropist. As such he's also, within the last couple decades, served as the founder of LifeForce, or LF. LF is a global, nongovernmental, humanitarian aid organization that helps victims of human trafficking in all its forms.

Oh, one other thing: most employees of LF have no clue, but LF also conceals a clandestine, high-level sex trafficking network worldwide. Sir Gerald Hartwell has a clue. He must've realized, in a flash of insight and arrogant ascendancy, that LifeForce was the perfect cover. The Big Lie, as Nazi propaganda minister Joseph Goebbels might have said.

Think it sounds far-fetched? Wake up. Take a good look around. Where have you been the last few years? It's been right in front of us.

Right now, Gerald Hartwell is inside a standard Radisson in downtown Minneapolis. Peggy, his by all accounts compassionate and fully unknowing wife back in Chicago, thinks he's doing a speaking engagement in Minneapolis for one of her dearest causes—the Unitarian Church, which runs in her family. He did do that, earlier. But then he slipped into this Radisson wearing a hoodie and a cap so he could spend some time with a dominatrix on the fourteenth floor. If only we could get some film of that too. We know this because we'd been tracking him on the dark web. He was the proverbial sitting duck. What were we going to do, not nab him?

Chip sits up. "Is that him?"

It looks like Hartwell, but he's shadowed by the recessed entrance (because of the cold) and the skyway looming above. Then I catch that flash of sky blue on his cap, and that logo with a loon on it. Minnesota United FC. It's why I know about the soccer team.

"Showtime," I say.

One a.m. It's less than an hour later, and we're about to start recording. We couldn't find an abandoned warehouse so we're doing it inside a super-sketchy motor hotel on the edge of town, one of those with separate little cabins for each guest. No one's noticing a thing at this dump. Gravel parking lot. Most units dark, the shades drawn. The front desk faces away from the units and closed at eight p.m. All in all, it looks like a summer camp for serial killers. Our cabin even has a handy back door and parking spot cloaked in complete darkness for fully private access, which we were all too happy to use to shuffle the hooded, duct-taped Mr. Hartwell inside.

And here the man sits, in the middle of the room. We have our disguises on, with ski face masks this time, which the bastard probably gets off on somehow considering he'd just left a domme. All is dark except for a nightstand light shining on him. We have another metal briefcase sitting on a fold-up chair, glowing red from our tactical light on the multifunction tripod.

We've got proof inside: photos of Sir Hartwell and other VIPs with naked teenage girls, plus a written statement from one of his top ringleaders.

"You're those Show Game people, aren't you?" our man says now. Chip has just torn the duct tape off, and Gerald is sneering a little, as if he possibly likes this. Jesus.

I don't answer. I'm about to tell him the rules when he interrupts again.

"Oh." He's hopping in his chair a little, his wrists taped down. "You are!" He adds a giggle. "But of course, it makes sense."

It gives me a cold shiver down my spine coming from a freak like this.

"Shut up," Chip says to fill my pause. He didn't like this guy from the start. But there's something else eating at him. He's been quieter this time, lost in thought.

"I'm quite enjoying this," Gerald says, smiling more now, getting all his big teeth out there.

"I said, shut the fuck up."

"You two plonkers don't know I have a tracking device on me, do you? Ah, no, you couldn't have done. It's in a real special place." He adds another giggle, this one higher, like he just took a helium hit along with it.

It can't be true. Chip searched him thoroughly, though it was only the strip search. He really prefers not doing even a visual cavity search, and I can't say I blame him. We just have to hope the guy won't be noticed missing until long after we film our show.

This Gerald Hartwell has to know what's coming. We wouldn't have nabbed him if we didn't have the goods. So why the smug mug? I guess we'll just have to find out, then wipe it off him. I raise the voice changer to my mouth. He doesn't even blink.

"So," I say, "here's how this works—"

"Oh, just get on with it," Gerald says, and his smirk of a smile vanishes, and he's losing his haughty act fast. So much for that. He takes a deep breath, like a bull snorting, and juts his weak chin out into the light. "Everyone knows how this works by now, don't we? Let's have your goddamned questions."

THURSDAY, NOVEMBER 9
OWEN

As Owen hunkered down early the next morning back in the empty newsroom of *FreeChain News*, he had the tangible sensation of being kept on ice—so much so that it made him actually shiver. He sat at the end of one of their long, glowing-white communal tables, and it was like a giant frozen slab cut straight out of a glacier. The other reason for his feeling was the latest Show Game. It hadn't been released yet. But everyone knew about it. This was because Alex had honored fans' pleas to give the world as much notice as the press—and had just announced the video's arrival an hour beforehand on social media, using disposable accounts with the handle of "Show Game" and deploying the hashtag #ShowGame. That put the whole world on ice. The announcement had come in at nearly the same time Owen stepped into his glass office, as if he'd himself triggered it somehow. He certainly hadn't gotten anything done waiting for it. He sat there awhile. No emails were coming in. He checked the platforms, the press. There was no other news. He emailed and texted Martin Podest, but got no response.

About forty-five minutes to go. He kept thinking about Lucy Holden. She'd told him she was working on the case too. But what did that really mean? He texted her: *You following all this? Still in Bumfuck?*

Her response came almost immediately: *They have internet in Bumfuck.*

Where is Bumfuck? he texted.

It's North Dakota. Fargo.

She then sent a second text, of her location. It was a hotel, a Residence Inn, one of those laid out more like condos, rooms with an office area for people working over longer stays. But a location cloaking app could easily hide where she was. And he didn't doubt that she, or someone fitting her description, had checked in there under her name. He'd have his team check anyway—better yet, he'd check himself. The more he knew alone, the better. At least she was replying. Martin Podest was suddenly just as much as a phantom as DeAndre Jarvis.

I trust you, he added, with winking smiley face.

Same, she texted, and that was it.

Twenty minutes to go. Owen's team had been rushing in, their faces deep in their phones until walking right up to one another on their sofas, armchairs, floor positions. Owen scanned the outside world through the windows and could see others waiting, watching in the other buildings' offices surrounding theirs. A text came in. Lucy? He picked up his phone.

Martin Podest himself: *This should get good. Enjoy the show.*

Where are you? Owen texted back, but got nothing.

Then it came, as announced. The Show Game. The video on one-hour delay. Alex's target was none other than Sir Gerald Hartwell, Big Pharma kingpin and financial godhead and more recently the philanthropist founder of LifeForce. Watching the video, Owen listened hard for any indication of who might be running the show. *Martin, is that you?* Lucy even? But the digitally altered voice was too distorted again.

The Show Game started with little drama. On the video, Gerald Hartwell had his head lowered, his normally slicked-back silver hair falling forward strand by strand. He had a slightly bewildered look, similar to the kind of men who used to let their COVID mask slip off their nose without noticing. When he talked, it was like one of those forced statements made by a political prisoner in an authoritarian regime.

He confessed right away. "I will admit to the following. LifeForce, the worldwide humanitarian NGO that I helped found, also provides cover for a secret sex trafficking network around the globe. It was the perfect front, you see."

Ding! Gerald Hartwell won fifty points for that, of course. Next came naming his partners in crime. But he refused to say who helped him directly. He just shook his head. He added "pass" as if this were an approved play in the Show Game.

Alex let Hartwell continue anyway.

"I wish to say that I am sorry," he said. "But only to my wife." He looked at the camera now, and his chin actually quivered. "Peggy, you knew none of this. You don't deserve this." Then he lowered his head, mechanically.

There came an awkward pause.

"You haven't fully shown remorse," said Alex's digital junior Darth Vader voice. "To win that fifty points, you have to say you're sorry—to the whole world. To all those you hurt, devastated, let die thinking they're worthless—"

"No. I won't do it. And you know why? Because people are suckers, the lot of them, and they always will be. They should be apologizing to me."

In the movie version of this, the character playing Gerald Hartwell would be sneering at the screen, growling something like *you can't handle the truth*. But he was just staring, all matter-of-fact, his face unmoving.

"You haven't named your fellow criminals either," the voice said. "That's another fifty points. I'll give you one more chance. Just one. You know who. The biggest fish. Do it."

A longer pause followed, in which Hartwell simply lowered his head again, this time as if some invisible hand were settling it into position, as if ready for a guillotine to come down.

Within the camera shot, the shadows running the Show Game moved. Half of the back of a person, in silhouette, wearing bulky clothing and what appeared to be a ski mask, stepped forward toward Hartwell, just out of his reach, a little woodenly, guardedly.

The figure approached the briefcase next to Hartwell. The briefcase parted open, from the figure's left hand just out of sight (surely wearing gloves). The video didn't yet show what was inside.

Hartwell wasn't watching—or could not watch. His head seemed stuck lowered. But then it started bobbing.

"Wait!" he shouted, "for fuck's sake," and his voice strained for the first time.

The briefcase fell shut. Hartwell launched right into it. He named names. Big names. CEOs, royalty, politicians, celebrities. Big fish. More than one. They were all participants, he said. Then he fell silent, staring so hard at the floor that the camera showed only the top of his thinning scalp.

Ding ding! One hundred points.

But was it the biggest fish? Owen wondered.

"Is that it?" the voice said.

Hartwell muttered something. He shook his head.

"What was that? I can't hear you. The world can't . . ."

"Hold on," Hartwell said eventually in a soft voice, raising his head, his eyes bleary. "Let me be clear. Innocents were taken advantage of. That was the very goal. Girls were impregnated. Girls were abused. It was our own personal ring, for the rich and famous. And, me, I had the goods on all of them, 'idn't I? It only enriched my fortune. An ever-expanding circle of hell . . . But I didn't run the sex trafficking. It wasn't even my idea."

"It wasn't?"

"God, no. It was only suggested, to me. Whispered. I had the perfect cover, this person suggested. And obviously there is something about me, that I would be open to that. Corruptible in that way. I wanted to do good, 'idn't I? But I was willing to do whatever to do so—"

"Don't get off track," the voice said. "You are about to name the one running it. Go on. Take your time."

Another long pause. The video just kept running.

"My real name is Jerzy Hodak," Hartwell said. "You know that? Nah, how could you?" His parents were Polish immigrants, he added, and by this point his accent had halfway retreated to its lowborn, lower-class London self. He sounded like a small-time cockney crook. It might've been tough for him to talk this way since he'd been faking it for so long. But he wanted all to know. He was glaring at the screen now. That bleariness had given way to a sharpness that could etch glass. This was no confession, yet it was nearly more shocking than his Show Game revelations. Owen heard a couple gasps out in the newsroom.

On the video, the silhouette had moved away from the briefcase, retreating from the shot. Hartwell nodded at it, as if ready to win it all.

"I now want to say, that I am sorry, especially to everyone who's been hurt."

"Wait. The name. Who suggested it to you? We don't have much time—"

"No! I'm sorry. I really am. But most of all to Peggy, my dear."

Ding ding ding!

Hartwell won, and the Show Game video ended with him staring down again.

The news tickers below meanwhile were reporting that Gerald Hartwell's last known location had been Minneapolis, and then that Hartwell had just that moment been found, still bound but alive, in a run-down motel on the outskirts of town. Owen worked out the geography, the logistics. Fargo was about three hours from Minneapolis. In theory, Lucy could've done the deed and gotten back to Fargo by morning. She could've been with Martin Podest. Better yet, it could have been Martin on his own, with DeAndre Jarvis even. At least with Lucy, he knew where she was.

Owen made a note of all this, but a mental one only. Didn't touch his pen or phone. He wasn't sure why. He just did. Maybe it was because he didn't want to get the truth wrong like he had with Shane Bagley. He certainly wasn't going to tell any of his team. He wasn't even going to tell Molly. That made him wince a little inside, like he was cheating on her; they had been studying his latest wall together, after all. But something, his old instincts, they were telling him that he had insight that no one else had, not even the authorities. And he would need every secret wild card he could get.

His phone beeped. He hoped it was Molly, or possibly Lucy Holden.

Stop what you're doing, Viktoria Jett texted him. *MS wants a meet.*

Owen's first wild thought sent him straight to that cliff again. Could Viktoria be Alex, or be in on it? Where was she right now?

Her text sent Owen three floors up. Owen exited the stairwell to find the whole floor abandoned, or at least unoccupied. It had to be because it was gutted, with almost no walls, wires hanging down, pipes and electrical exposed, a couple garbage cans, a shop vac off in a corner. The floor was dusty. The state of things made the view outstanding though. This Midtown building wasn't the tallest, but he could peer between the other buildings nearly all the way through to the green of Central Park.

Viktoria was standing by a window with her arms crossed, her chin hard.

Fine, Owen thought, so she wasn't out of town, she wasn't anywhere near Minneapolis. But that didn't mean she couldn't be directing it.

"Hi?" he said in Viktoria's direction.

"Hey there," said a male voice. It was Mason Snead. He emerged from behind a pillar of exposed girders, pipes, electrical work. "So what do you think? It'll have high-end HEPA filters throughout."

"Sounds great," Owen said.

"Pull up a chair."

"There, uh, aren't—"

"There aren't any," Viktoria barked from the window, and turned on a heel and marched over. She was wearing the same black outfit as usual, Owen realized, complete with Doc Martens. As was MS, more or less, though the predominant monochrome was blue this time instead of gray. Did they both have expansive wardrobes of only the same outfits?

Snead was looking around for chairs anyway. He shrugged. "That's all right. We'll stand." He added that telltale tug of his nose.

"This won't take long," Viktoria added.

Considering the furtiveness and withdrawn surroundings, Owen felt like he was meeting a source or even a whistleblower.

But Mason Snead owned the offices a couple floors below, not to mention the whole building (Owen had looked into it).

Owen stepped into the middle of the room, where a conference table might be.

Mason Snead stepped over. He reached for the bottom fringe of his neat, longish, severely midparted hair. Seeing his hair in this light, with a little sun shining on it, made Owen think of one of those early '70s female stars, Ali MacGraw or Streisand. Owen even thought he was going to push stray strands behind one ear. Then Snead spotted Viktoria eyeing him and he pulled his finger down. And he grinned, wide and open.

"Well, the Show Game strikes again," Mason Snead said.

Owen could feel Viktoria glaring at him again from the windows, like she was a giant black crow hovering in the air just outside. Owen looked around as if others might be there. He pointed at the floor. "So, this is . . . we're having an editorial meeting?"

"Yes! Yes, let's call it that. I'm not really into labels or titles as you know, but sure." Another tug of his nose.

"My only instruction for you, my one and only investigative reporter genius, is to follow this Show Game thing wherever it leads. In case you were hesitant. You already have a healthy budget. You also have full editorial, investigative freedom."

"That's good to hear, thank you," Owen said. "And it does fit your credo."

"Credo?" Snead's eyes lit up. "Yes! You hear that, Vik? Credo. That's good. We should've called the *News* that."

"Maybe next time," Viktoria said.

"You won't see any obstruction from me," Snead said. "All news is good news. All PR good."

With that, a cloud passed over the light coming in the

windows, and Snead's face seemed to darken, harden along with the dimming.

Owen said, "So—"

"So keep going," Snead snapped, and it almost sounded like a bark. "And there is only one thing I ask of you. I am going to need results. I am going to need them before anyone else. I am going to need a story that no one else can get. That's my brand, if you haven't figured that out. Go after this Alex. Getting results will only confirm the power of my philosophy all the more."

Snead left a pause where Owen figured he was supposed to restate said philosophy.

"Peer-to-peer, open news sharing," Owen said eventually. "Full transparency."

"Yes. That's it."

"Right. I will."

"And you? This isn't just for me. You want to get it right. You want the truth. It's what you do."

Owen nodded.

Snead stepped closer, obscuring Viktoria in the background. "Things are moving quickly," he said. "Very quickly. So let me tell you something that no one knows. That not even your fine sources can probably tell you: Gerald Hartwell, he's already in FBI custody."

How could Snead know that? Owen wondered.

"Transparency," Snead added as if knowing his thoughts.

"Right. You have your own sources." High up, certainly; of course he would. "You know," Owen continued, "I might be able to find out a lot more if you'd share those sources of yours with me."

Snead showed his teeth, but it wasn't a smile, more like he was asking Owen if he had something stuck in his incisors.

"His wife, Peggy?" Snead said. "Word is, she's becoming, uh, unhinged. Rapidly."

Owen could only imagine. He felt his heart in his throat. He swallowed it down. He shifted in place, the reporter in him returning to take over, needing to get back down to the newsroom, to make the call. All thoughts of Viktoria vanished.

He said, "Can you get me Peggy Hartwell's private number? Save time."

"No."

"We would not have that," Viktoria added with a growl.

"Is any of this known?" Owen said. "About either of them?"

"Not yet, and you can't report it. There's nothing to report it from, what with the *News* not officially up and running yet. But it does show you what I can do for you."

Owen couldn't help it. He was nodding along frantically, as if confirming his name on a winning lottery ticket. "For me," he blurted, "for me."

"Yes, you! Look at you, it's in your blood!" Snead said. "I love it."

"There's another thing we ask," Viktoria said. At some point she had found her way over, and now stood at Snead's shoulder. "You find something big? Always be sure to tell us what you find first. That means before anyone else."

ALEX

I feel like nearly all heat has left my body, but I'm not cold, despite the temperature dropping at least ten degrees overnight and not returning. Except my throat is red-hot and clogged, and my cheeks, but then those drain of heat, too, as if losing all blood.

Peggy Hartwell, why did you do it? What in the living hell?

Usually I'm pretty fired up from what we accomplish, but something about this Show Game really dragged me down. And that was before Gerald Hartwell's wife killed herself.

Peggy Hartwell didn't just do it alone—she did it for the whole world to see, this very morning, right after I woke up. Live on FreeChain, she declared that she had a statement to give, which the TV networks of course picked up.

I watched it all live . . .

Peggy Hartwell sits on a lovely white sofa, in her own home most likely, but wears a dark silk bathrobe with Asian decorations, likely purchased on one of her many trips for LifeForce. No makeup. These are the first signs. I tense up, my intestines tightening. I right away notice the poor lighting, and as she speaks the picture keeps juddering a little—she obviously set up the camera herself and it keeps getting bumped by her stomping the floor or knocking the coffee table or both. In other words, she's alone. The most alarming sign is that her cheeks glisten from fresh tears.

"I wish to make it clear that I did not know of my husband's . . . operation, front, whatever you want to call it. I find it . . . sickening. Sex trafficking? My god. These are children we are talking about . . ." She's clasping her hands together so hard in supplication or grief or both it looks like she's trying to smash something between her palms. "If my husband were here, I would make him pay myself. I might consider killing him. But he'll find a way to survive, to even make this work for him. They always do, people like him. His powerful cohorts. I have seen this from the inside. I have suspected worse things happening inside, or apart from, our organization, and I wish I would've looked into it. But we all become complicit, don't we? Every time we condone a small transgression. They all add up, and they're major crimes before you know it, but at that point there's nothing you can do. Not even me. Certainly not those children out there, girls mostly, who had their lives taken from them and now are forced to live with how they've been destroyed. In shame. Hating themselves. Wanting to kill themselves."

Peggy Hartwell stares straight into the screen, as if right at me.

"Oh god no," I'd muttered from deep in my gut.

She stares around a moment, as if anyone else were there. Consulting the shadows. Fighting back sobs, her shoulders rocking now. "Well, I guess I should thank you, Alex. Hashtag Show Game. But you know what? I'm not feeling very thankful. Because it's too late. Because, if we have to look to some reckless vigilante using FreeChain itself of all the damn things, then we've all let this go too far . . ."

"No. No."

"You want your Show Game, America? Well, here's my Show Game. You want truth? Justice. I'm going to give you both. I'm going to win it all . . ."

As I watched, as everyone watched, Peggy Hartwell raised a pistol from beside her on the sofa, shoved it inside her mouth, clamped her lips around it, and pulled the trigger. The crack-pop was deafening even on a small screen. Her body remained upright a moment, held up by the expensive thick back cushion. Then she slumped sideways, off-screen. The camera kept rolling, of course, her white sofa sprayed and smeared red.

Right now I feel a burning heat in my chest and behind my eyes, and before I know it my chin is quivering and my shoulders rocking just like hers and I'm crying.

With Gerald Hartwell sure to be in custody if not prison, that leaves their five preteen kids—all of them adopted from poorest Africa and Asia through LifeForce—without parents. Peggy Hartwell had a top leadership role in the organization.

The hot tears run down my cheeks, down my chest, onto my wrists, soaking into my bathrobe.

The whole reason I went after Sir Gerald Hartwell? I wanted him to reveal the person who suggested he lean into sex trafficking. If Hartwell did that for me, then I would not have to do it myself. Because it was too close to home.

But now? It's all on me.

An hour later, six p.m., I have my shit back together. I took a shower. I've thrown on sweats and sip a whiskey. Taking deep breaths. I'm going back over how it went down with Gerald Hartwell for the thirtieth, fortieth time. Our announcing it beforehand on social media had really grabbed people's attention: *Stay tuned for a new edition of #Show Game from Alex one hour from now*. And the show itself keeps rolling before me like a video on an auto-play loop. I remember moving toward the briefcase, slowly, guardedly, and cracking it open—and that was when Hartwell vomited out all his truth. Who knew what the guy thought was in there? Maybe he thought we had photos from his rendezvous with the domme that night, with him probably wrapped naked in plastic wrap or whatever and his dick in a cage, or maybe he was wearing diapers. Maybe he thought of his Peggy, or of his adopted children whom he might've even loved. We will probably never know anytime soon. I'm guessing that he's now in FBI custody.

Chip watched it all, too, of course, from his van or wherever he's holed up after Minneapolis. I'd nearly forgotten about him. Now a phone beeps on the coffee table, next to my airplane bottle of whiskey—it's our burner phone.

Can we talk? he's texted.

I sigh. I hate talking on phone lines, even on the burner. But I text back a *yes*. I wait for the burner to ring.

There's a knock on the door. Shit. What now? I have my motel room Do Not Disturb sign on. Then I recognize the knock—it's our special code. We came up with a knock the first time we met in person but hadn't ever used it because we'd never planned on making contact directly apart from a Show Game operation.

It's getting dark out. I look through the peephole.

It's Chip all right, in disguise—stocking cap, wraparound sunglasses, baggy dirty hick-hunter outfit with one of those camouflage hoodies. He's even wearing makeup to lighten his skin. Fuck. I slip into my running shoes and glance at my go bag, because you never know what's going down. I fling the door open, pull him inside.

"What in the fuck do you think you are doing?" I say.

Chip doesn't answer. His shoulders are drooping. He just shakes his head. Not good.

"Where's your van?" I say. "Tell me you didn't drive it here?"

"I didn't. It's safe. We're safe. I spent all day making sure I, we, haven't been followed."

"You followed me here?"

"Not right away. After that fucking suicide I did."

Chip slumps on the sofa where I was sitting and stares at the little whiskey bottle. His sunglasses hang off on his nose and he absently snatches them and stuffs them in a pocket. I grab another bottle from the minibar and hand it to him and he sucks half of it down in one gulp. He was never much of a drinker, as far as I know. Now he's got this stare, right through me, boring through the wall opposite. Uh-oh. Thousand-yard stare, most likely. It wasn't like I'd served in combat ops with him. But what else could it be?

"We should go to a bar," he says. "There's a tavern down the street."

"No. We are definitely not doing that. You're not leaving here till it's safe again. We need more booze, food, whatever? I'm getting it."

Chip only nods. I drop into the armchair flanking one end of the coffee table. I take a deep breath and try softening my voice. I really want to slap the dumbass for coming here but that's not going to help anyone. "You can talk to me," I say.

Chip keeps staring so long I think he's never going to look up. Then his head perks up like a bird's.

"You were crying too," he says. "I can tell."

"I was. Of course I was."

Now it's me Chip's staring right through. I try keeping eye contact, but it's tough.

"That woman," he says, "that Peggy Hartwell, she did it just like we do it."

"For everyone to see," I mutter.

"She's wrecked it. She's wrecked the Show Game."

I take another deep breath. "No, she hasn't. She hasn't at all," I say, but inside I'm agreeing with him and have been even since I broke down crying.

"This was going to be the last one, you said. And now it's something else," Chip says.

I don't say anything.

So, we fix it, I want to tell him.

But I let him work it out inside his head. He raises the empty whiskey bottle to his mouth, robotically, like a mechanical Turk in a carnival.

"Torture," he says eventually, staring at nothing, his expression so vacant now it's like he's watching a planet in the next solar system over. "I did it all. All for the team. All for the CIA extraction team bestowed on me by my abilities and luck. Waterboarding, sure. Beatings, sure. Blood, sure. Sleep deprivation. You name it. Talk about mental fucking abuse. Grown men pleading with you like schizophrenic babies. I did not like what I was becoming then and I'm not sure I do even now." His mouth snaps shut.

He goes back to his solar system. I give it a second. "There's also the fact," I say eventually, "that you're undoing what you were becoming."

"We can't know that until it's too late."

"I think we can, if we only—"

"No! Don't you get it? This was never supposed to get violent. In any way."

"I know. You're right." I'm nodding along, and now I'm wishing I hadn't given him the last minibar bottle of whiskey because I'm starting to get goose bumps, the creepy-crawly kind. I can see where this is going.

"It wasn't our fault," I say in my softer voice, and even reach out and touch the arm of the sofa.

"You don't fucking believe that," he says. "It's a direct repercussion."

"Chip, listen . . ."

He gets cold feet now? I'm screwed. I can't do this on my own.

He holds up one arm, lets it drop again. "Best-laid plans and all that. Just like combat."

"I know, I know—"

"No, you don't know," he says, not angrily, but in a mono-tone I've never heard before, like he's repeating back a password.

"It's not just us. This. Mrs. Hartwell. Have you seen the comments, the posts?"

I know what he's talking about. Online and even pundits on traditional TV, some were growing impatient. They were calling for the Show Game to become harsher. If Alex and company were going to do this, they should go for the same blood that the perpetrators had no problem sucking. They should get violent on these fuckers, medieval even. String them up by their toenails. Their prize for winning the game should be an ignoble death. Others were saying the opposite and becoming just as vehement about it—the rich and powerful had rights, too, no matter their crimes, and should be afforded fair and judicial treatment. Some of them were even claiming that the rich and powerful deserved preferential treatment, just because of who they were, because of their titles, and some even demanded immunity for them. It was shocking to hear, but such were the times. It was like a giant rock had been overturned and all the worms and scorpions came crawling out.

"I have seen the comments," I say. "But then there are the others." Some were saying that violent means were shortsighted—that none of those bastards on the Show Game would ever admit to any of it if they knew their fate. The briefcase was genius. It made them think. Otherwise it would just turn into one long torture session broadcast live. "People get it."

"People . . ." Chip begins, but that's it. He closes his eyes. I'm not sure I've ever seen a guy so still. I actually watch his stomach and chest to make sure he's breathing. I wonder if it's some kind of relaxation technique.

I can't disturb such repose. It's so quiet, I can faintly hear the rush of the nearby highway.

Chip's eyes pop open. It makes me start.

"I should've been there for Wilson," he says. "Instead? I left. Then I'm practically doing deeds like Holmes did to my own brother." He shakes his head. It keeps shaking, slowly.

I shake my head at him shaking his head.

"So what's the next move?" Chip says, picking up right where we left it.

Chip's not out, not yet. I take a huge deep breath, but inside, and my feet feel like they're floating right above the floor. But I'm not sure if it makes me fired up or nauseated.

"Well, we've come this far," I say, all jaded-like.

He nods. Go on.

"There's only one way to fix it," I say.

"One last target." Chip sits up. "We need to go big. Do what no one's expecting. Do the one target you were afraid of."

"What? No. I—"

"Don't bullshit me. I know you have one. I can see it on your face."

Chip's speaking in that monotone voice again and I know exactly what it's saying.

I bow forward, elbows on my knees.

I've never revealed my final target to him. It's too big. It's too personal. I lower my head, staring between my knees at the sharp and jagged geometric patterns of the carpet.

Now Chip's got his elbows on his knees, leaning toward me, our faces just a couple feet from each other's. I can smell his outfit. It has an earthen reek to it, and a little sourness, more country drifter than hick hunter, but not too bad. At least there's no cigarettes in it.

"You know what?" I say. "Screw it."

I lay it all on him, and why. I don't have to say the target's name. The context is enough.

Chip's now sitting bolt upright, his back rooted to the rear cushion. His eyes have widened. His hands clawed.

"Holy shit," he says.

MONDAY, NOVEMBER 13
OWEN

Owen sat on a park bench in Portland, surveilling the building across the street. The modern and imposing federal courthouse had seen many an international news cycle's worth of defensive perimeter fencing, pockmarks, and graffiti from the protests that had taken place here during the pandemic, many every night for weeks on end. He eyed the courthouse's broad front entrance from his spot in the center of Chapman Square among the thick old oak trees, close to a granite pillar commemorating Spanish-American War–era glory, complete with an advancing infantryman statue at the top. This ground zero for the protests had supposedly ruined downtown, according to most reports at the time, all the businesses fleeing or battered or boarded up. Yet office workers, shoppers, and tourists filled the sidewalks, some even popping over to the Square to see where the big fiery nighttime face-offs had all gone down. Owen figured he blended in pretty well in his usual road outfit of outdoors-ready materials, lots of pocket, zippers, water resistance. Molly used to joke that he was a wannabe model for REI. But it fit his line of work. You had to be ready to go at any time. Should he wear a face mask for secrecy, or would that only call more attention to himself? In the end he kept it hung around his neck just in case.

Last Thursday in New York City, he had just been getting back to the open office for *FreeChain News* after meeting with Mason Snead and Viktoria when the suicide of Peggy Hartwell had filled the screens. He had smelled a bitter, sour smell—someone on his investigative team had vomited watching. Another, a quite young guy, had left. They never saw him again; word was, his own mother had committed suicide. Owen had ignored them all. He'd holed up in his office and would've closed the door if the open layout had allowed a door. But it was clear from his hunched demeanor, manning his desk, that he wasn't to be disturbed. First Mason Snead tells him that he knows Peggy Hartwell is liable to harm herself before anyone else does. How? Did he have a camera in her house? Could he see the near future? Mason Snead wasn't revealing his means. Owen could only assume he knew Peggy Hartwell from experience and was a good judge of human character. So what did that mean about how Snead was judging him and his actions?

One thing he knew from years on the beat: there's always someone watching.

The very thought made Owen wince inside, and sharply, someone slowly dragging a thin metal cable through his abdomen and out through his stomach. And now MS and Viktoria wanted results, and they wanted to know first. There were rewards, in future. Mason Snead had sources he could pass on to him. Neither of these disclosures fit Mason Snead's operating philosophy, that of peer-to-peer, open news sharing with full transparency. But then again, neither did Owen's or his team's own role. His was like a special team of career warriors in a volunteer army. So he had fought. In his office Owen had revisited all his angles and tried all his sources in government, law enforcement, media, but he still got nowhere.

Owen was still suspecting everyone, still running for cliffs with his thoughts. Just to keep sane, he'd tried contacting Anne Blade because he had no real idea where she was. She hadn't replied. A couple Instagram photos showed her in Mexico, Sayulita, but it was only her feet on the beach or ceviche and cervezas. Anyone could've posted those. And wasn't she originally from Minneapolis? Or was it Milwaukee? Back to Viktoria Jett. He still couldn't pinpoint where she lived. Was it close to an airport? NYC alone had three major options, not to mention Mason Sneed's private jets.

His questions had also kept coming back to Lucy Holden. Lucy had thrown him for a loop with that text of hers about working on the case too. What could that mean? It was so broad. Even if she wasn't involved, she was the only one who might know more than he. Whatever it was, he needed to confirm her role before moving on. In the meantime he had confirmed her alibi: a Lucy Holden had checked into the Residence Inn in Fargo, North Dakota, on November 8. So she might just be telling him the truth about pursuing the Show Game perpetrator like he was doing. That could explain why she had been relatively near the Show Games when they happened. But maybe she was being used somehow, unwittingly? In any case, he hadn't told Mason Sneed or Viktoria about Lucy yet, despite their instructions to tell them about anything big he had. He felt locked into Lucy for some reason, like they were a team. He wasn't sure why. He felt a clear respect for her, pursuing the truth just like he was. Besides, he didn't want to wreck any of her progress by involving others. If that made him more beholden to Lucy Holden than Mason Sneed? So be it.

He'd known he needed to make a bold move. By the end of the day after Peggy Hartwell, he'd booked a flight for Portland early the next morning.

With the time difference it was now late afternoon in Portland, the sky cloudy and neither cold nor hot, surprisingly mild for November and still no rain. Owen eyed the federal courthouse entrance with his sunglasses on, arms spread out along the back of the bench, just another casual dude. He wondered if he should be looking for a woman in a yoga outfit, or Pilates, whatever it was. It had involved a rolled-up mat. No, she wouldn't be wearing a workout outfit. A courthouse meant a professional appearance.

His phone beeped. It was Molly: *Getting anywhere?*

Not yet. But closer. Maybe? he texted back. He included the emoji of the guy holding up his hands.

And something about that made him realize that here he was again, so relatively close to Seattle. He again wondered if he should tell her.

I'm on the road, he added. If she asked, he would tell her.

Ah. Good luck, was all she texted back.

He watched the overworked-looking lawyers coming and going at the federal courthouse. A woman exited wearing a modest gray skirt suit, hair down. It looked like Lucy. She started one way, then pivoted another, and headed north, then west at the corner. Owen shot up, slung on his backpack, fast-walked through the rectangular path after her.

He almost forgot. *Thanks*, he texted to Molly in full stride as he moved on.

The woman was heading toward Portland City Hall, another scale model of the big city thing. These blocks were so small, he was able to catch up by the next light. He stood behind her along with a couple others. It had to be her. He could tell by her lopsided mullet haircut, the severe bangs, that freckled olive skin, and the way she walked—purposeful, but not angry. For some reason her courtroom attire made her look younger than her workout outfit ruse, like a grad student dressed as a lawyer for Halloween. There was something else he noticed that he now recalled from when they met before. She was holding her right arm up to her chest as if, at first glance, she was holding something, but on a closer look, it was more like she was about to defend herself with her elbow. He wondered if she was doing this because others were waiting at the light. Maybe it was a defensive maneuver left over from the darkest days of social distancing. She'd done it in that coffee shop, too, once she was near others in line, then again when leaving him. He wondered if she was even cognizant of it. In any case, he didn't want to surprise her around others. Now they waited for the MAX light rail train to pass. The elbow had cocked a little higher, as if able to put a dent in a moving train.

The train passed. The light changed.

She whipped around to face him, the others moving on.

"You're following me?" she said. That elbow still up.

"Hi. No. I—"

"I saw you when I came out. I don't know what else you call this, what you're doing."

Of course she'd seen him. She was an investigator, after all, with a keen eye for anything she'd seen before. But he could've also cloaked himself better. He'd been stretched out on that bench and right across the street, as if they'd arranged to meet. Maybe a part of him had wanted her to see him, to see what she would do? She might've even been watching from a window.

Owen held up his palms. "What can I say? If I was truly following you, we wouldn't be talking."

More people passed, approached. They were blocking the corner. Owen shuffled out of the way, along the inside edge of the sidewalk, and Lucy did the same. A good sign. She wasn't necessarily looking to make a scene. Her elbow lowered, an even better sign.

She smiled. "How are you so sure I wouldn't know?"

"If you put it like that?" He smiled back, shrugged. "Anyway, I came to see you."

"Yeah? How did you know I'd be here?"

"You were scheduled to testify for a court case—something corporate law about technology theft—in your official capacity as a private investigator and sometimes expert witness. It's all public record."

"That's true."

"I have more questions for you. It will only take a second."

"You couldn't have texted, emailed?"

"I was passing through, doing more research. Then heading up to Tacoma to follow up on Martin Podest."

He was lying. He really just wanted to gauge her reactions in person. But he did have the reasons ready. He would say he was here for Scout records concerning her brother and others and was prepared to head back to Tacoma if need be. Keep her on the defensive.

Yet she didn't ask. All she said was, "I don't have time. I got another thing at City Hall."

"By the way, do you know what's up with Martin? He's not responding."

"I don't. He does that sometimes. They all do."

"Please? It'll just take a second."

She sighed. "All right, um, the Hilton's easy. Block away. I use it all the time."

The vast and multileveled lobby of the Hilton had a café that was like a copy of a Starbucks but with locally sourced micro-brews, kombuchas, drinking vinegars.

"Not sure what I can tell you," Lucy said as they waited in line. "I told you. I can't disclose."

"I'm going to ask anyway. You're all I've got."

She sighed. "Well, in that case, we might as well get a beer."

They did have a CBD squeeze IPA that sounded okay, whatever that was. "I thought you had a thing," he said.

"I thought you weren't following me."

"Good point."

He got the squeeze IPA, she a porter to his surprise. They took a table in a back corner.

"Horrible about Peggy Hartwell," he said. He wanted to see how that went over.

She shook her head, slowly, her eyes lowered. "Yes."

Anyone might've reacted that way.

"I wonder how Alex feels about it? It must be tough to take. This wasn't supposed to go down like that."

"No."

Her eyes seemed a little glossier, possibly wetter. She took a drink of beer.

Again, anyone would shed a tear at the thought. Then again, Lucy might be thinking of her client, who could even be the Show Game rebel in the flesh. There was still the chance she was directly involved. He had to keep her on the defensive.

"I think that, whoever it is, must've had help," Owen said. "They would have to."

"You said that before."

"Did I?" Owen took a drink, let things settle. Lucy checked something on her smartwatch.

Owen said, "My wife, she thinks it might be a woman."

"Who?"

"The Show Game person or persons."

Lucy tapped her watch without flinching. She looked up, her green eyes locked on him. "Oh? She sounds like a smart lady. How long you been married?"

"We're separated. I told you that before."

"Ah. Right. Well, this life, it'll take its toll. The pandemic never made it easier, I suppose."

"True."

They both drank to that.

"Though it wasn't any better in the Before Time," Owen said.

"Hey, that's what I call it too!"

They toasted to that.

"You'd be good at what I do," Lucy told Owen.

"Likewise," he told her.

She looked around as if others were listening. "Look. What if I gave you something? Would that make you happier?"

"What if you did?"

"Go ahead, ask me."

"There's only one problem: How can I trust you?"

"Says the reporter," she said.

"Ouch. All right . . ." Owen launched right into it, no need for his notebook. "Do you know if Dwayne Specklin, Conrad Holmes, or Gerald Hartwell have said anything to the authorities about a possible identity?"

"I don't know that. Do you?"

He held up a hand. "That's why I'm asking you."

She smiled, her pint glass raised. "Well, I bet your boss, Mason Snead, could find out. He's so goddamn high and mighty."

Now she was testing him. He might as well be forthright enough. "We don't have a lot of contact," Owen said. "He believes in what people used to call self-starters. Wants to see what I can do."

"Ah, yes, the old reward." Lucy's voice had turned more gravelly again. "'You do this for me? I will really make it worth your while.' Only problem is, once you give him something? Who's to say he has any incentive to give you something in return, even when he's promised it."

Owen shrugged. "Honor?"

Lucy laughed out loud, her head tilting back, her porter nearly sloshing out of the glass.

Owen felt a little rush of blood to his head. He didn't appreciate her laughing at him. But maybe she knew that. And he'd been doing this long enough to know he needed to rein in any anger. He added a bitter little chuckle. "So," he said, "maybe we cancel things out. You tell me what it isn't?"

"Good. Okay, I'll play. Here's the thing: It doesn't involve my brother, certainly not anymore. Certainly not that asswipe Conrad Holmes. Never in a million years Peggy Hartwell. She was that rare example of being as good of a person as she appears. It was her idea to adopt those kids, you know." Lucy looked away at the thought, and her eyes took on a gloss again.

"That leaves Gerald Hartwell himself. That leaves his connections. The names he named."

Lucy only stared back, the gloss evaporating from her green eyes again, hard, penetrating. *Figure it out*, they were saying. He needed another move.

"Before?" Owen said. "I believe I'd suggested that we share findings. Correct?"

"Something like that."

"Well, now . . . Are you ready?"

"Ready."

"I propose that we join forces. Completely."

Her reaction was smooth. She thought about this a few seconds, her eyes finding the ceiling, swirling her beer for good measure. "I'm not sure I follow," she was saying. "You're thinking it's a way for me to get around my confidentiality commitment somehow? Huh . . ."

Owen noticed how that elbow of hers went up again, instinctively, unknowingly. In his mind he saw her doing it before, on the street corner, and in that coffee place when they first met, and then, like a film rolling backward, his mind's eye traveled all the way back to that last Show Game video—to when "Alex" had approached the metal briefcase, keeping Gerald Hartwell at a safe distance.

"You're thinking you would be my partner," Lucy was saying now. "So you would be privy to what I know. What I do? But that leaves your end. It's an interesting thought. There are issues with moonlighting, plus legal ones involving confidentiality, partiality. If that's what you mean. I think I'd need to check compliance on my end . . ."

It was that elbow. Her elbow up. How could he have missed it! He could see it clearly now. It was in that video, just a silhouette of it, but it had clearly been there as the figure approached guardedly. Even she had a tic. Practically a tell. She was too good to be caught saying something only Alex could know, plus there was the obvious use of a digitally altered voice to cover her slight lisp, not to mention that she was a female.

Owen felt himself rising in his seat from the excitement but forced himself to sit still. He had been getting a slight buzz from the beer but now it was sucked away, replaced by an ice-cold dousing of soberness. He tried to warn himself. This was still too small. This was just intuition. He needed to take another look at that video, as soon as he could. Man, he so hated strong hunches. He hated them because they required jumping off that cliff. A leap of faith. Investigative reporters liked steel and concrete, not thin air or smoke, and certainly not smoke up their asses. And then there was the clear fear that he never wanted to be so wrong again. But this time? It was practically hitting him over the head—

"Is something the matter?" Lucy was saying now. "You look a little pale."

Owen realized he was sitting up straight, his shoulders arching back, and his eyes so wide that he could feel the air on them. He shook his head to scare off his shock.

"I'm fine," he said.

"You don't look fine, dude."

He thought about pulling out his phone right here and watching the latest Show Game together, to pause it right on that cocked elbow.

"So I have a question," she added. Still acting all casual.

He nodded.

She said, "Have you told them about me at *FreeChain News*? Your boss or whoever?"

"No. When it comes to editorial? I pretty much am the boss."

He was fibbing, of course. But they were so close now. It was practically like she wanted him to know it was her.

So he decided to go for it.

He straightened his shoulders. He shifted his beer to the side. In a split second he went over what he was going to say, but what he did say was not what he'd rehearsed.

He leaned forward, lowering his voice. "I'm not going to tell anyone," he told her.

She pulled back, lowering her beer. "You said that already. Wait. Tell what?"

"That I think you could be the one doing it. That it's you. The Show Game."

ALEX / LUCY

I laugh so hard I nearly do a spit take, grabbing at the table edge, and then it goes down the wrong tube, and I'm coughing. Everyone's staring at me in this fake-local Hilton Hotel café. My face is beet red.

The truth is, I'm stalling.

I clear my throat, take a deep breath, chuckle some more, and then I grin at Owen Tanaka.

The poor bastard. I don't want to burn him like he's probably been burned before. He seems like a nice guy, the kind who'd offer you his hand sanitizer not because he thinks you're filthy but because he wants us all to survive. Driven, sure, like all reporters of his type are, but he's not in it for the book deal or the pundit gig, it seems to me. He's definitely an inquisitive dork, both geeky and witty, as if Columbo were a reporter instead and far, far neater and organized. Part Japanese-American, he'd told me, which explained his vaguely Asian features. Dark mop of hair but kept in control, the kind of hair that doesn't ever seem to grow or get cut. That hair tries to but can't hide a birthmark on his right temple shaped like a puzzle piece. It does hide big ears, I'd noticed (don't think I didn't, Owen!), which make his face (smaller than mine) seem even smaller, but it also make his piercing dark-brown eyes seem even bigger. Tanner than you'd think for a reporter, with lots of leathery skin and creases like a farmer—like Columbo as a National Park Service guide. No matter what this guy did in life, he was stuck being a tidy Columbo of color. But there is also something sad about him, the way he lowers his eyes. It isn't just that he is separated. There's something he needs to prove; something that he never can, it seems to me. One of those people who made a huge mistake that they never felt they could live down no matter how hard they worked, no matter how big their successes. I'm telling myself this is a good thing. I'd like to tell him there is always a way to pay it back.

What does he really know? He knows me as Lucy Holden, thirty-seven, private detective. Established. My clients are mostly law firms, but sometimes it's a company or even an individual. Occasionally pro bono. Like many middle-class kids from Portland, I went to U of O. But then a path developed. I was in that start-up right out of college, in New York City, then a sorry stretch at Columbia Law School that I did not finish. But it was enough for me to get in the door doing private investigations back in Portland, first with a firm, then on my own. Mom and Dad are divorced, my dad still a realtor but now with another young girlfriend who used to be his assistant, big surprise. We're not close, as you can imagine. We do text sometimes, but little does he know I'm only using him as an alibi. It's distant with my mom, too, but getting better. She now lives on the Oregon Coast and is half retired. We even talk on the phone sometimes. I visited her once.

As you can also imagine, my brother Andrew's death changed everything.

Of course I avenged my brother. Andrew was so outgoing and fun when we were kids. I remember he helped me learn how to ride my bicycle when the other kids were trying to push everyone off their bikes. Suddenly, around age eleven, he went dark. He stayed in his room. He abandoned all his friends. Kids were joking about others getting molested, but I couldn't have imagined it would be him. He killed himself his first year out of high school, hung himself from a tree, outside the main building of a certain junior college that promised another new start. He did it before dawn, as the earliest faculty and students walked up. He didn't even know who he was yet. Dwayne Specklin was still lurking in Portland back then.

When you're growing up, you think your family life is normal because that's all you know; only later do you realize it was far from that truth. For us, it was the other way around. My brother's death made us all realize how normal and practically perfect our family had been. It was like all our personalities had been replaced after his death and there was no returning them. Apart from that? I have a high school friend who's a rich soccer mom in West Linn who I do still like but also use for alibis. Mostly, my only real connection is to cats. I don't have any, sadly. My vigilante life does not allow for it. But I do volunteer at the shelter. Ah, when I say "shelter," you are probably thinking it's a homeless shelter. Tsk-tsk. Humans don't deserve as good a treatment as cats. Though I am mostly into feral cats.

What, you didn't think I could be a woman? And why not? You don't think we have our reasons? Open your eyes, pal.

I threw Owen off with that Martin Podest-from-Tacoma ruse. Did it again with Fargo. I'd texted him I was in North Dakota, which was true—I was there for my actual job, conducting standard interviews and meeting with a certain law firm. Then I went to a crappy car lot where I paid cash with a little extra, no questions, for a Ford Mustang with too many miles but still plenty of engine to get me to Minneapolis in a hurry, just under three hours on a Wednesday evening, Highway 94 all the way. After Show Game number three, I was back in my Fargo Residence Inn in time to put my dirty dishes outside my door before the morning rounds started, which helped my alibi even more. And in time to text Owen my location. Sorry, Owen.

Owen is now smiling at me from across the table. I'm grinning back at him and stalling. He's smiling at the people staring.

He leans back as if enjoying himself. Oh, he's good at this, I'll give him that.

"You could see why I would think that, though," he says.

Here we go. I sit up tall, put on my big girl pants, and slap on a straight face. "You know what? Okay. Let's assume I do the Show Game. First of all, I wasn't even at those places."

Owen shrugs. "There are ways around that. You would know how, if anyone."

Think, Luce, think. I take a sip of beer. I had thought of everything, but not of this, not exactly. For some reason I'd rather be facing questioning from law enforcement. Maybe it's the respect I have for this Owen. Like I'm beholden—

My watch buzzes me. Thank god. I have a nail appointment in a half hour.

I tap it away on my watch and say, "My City Hall thing is definitely on." And take a big drink like I've got to get going.

Still stalling.

"Of course," he says.

I have to look interested. I have to say something, anything to throw him off a little. "I told you," I say, "I have a confidentiality issue."

"Which could also be a convenient excuse," he says.

He's so calm and relaxed, but I can see that the birthmark on his right temple is a darker red than before. And he's quit gesturing, remaining still. In his outdoor tech gear, he's looking less to me now like some dorky National Park guide than a mercenary for an oil company in the Middle East on a mission.

"One sec," I say. I get out my iPad to take up time. Owen doesn't ask me what I'm doing. He just watches.

Now I'm thinking, *What if Owen knows more about Conrad Holmes in custody than I know?* Holmes might have told them who Chip really is, Reggie Dinkins, currently on the lam as a deserter, seeking revenge for his brother. He's definitely not Martin Podest's friend DeAndre Jarvis. Sorry again, Owen.

Owen could've been trying to snare me with his question just now about whether Holmes or the others had said anything to the authorities about a possible identity. But I have other outs. I could send him after Viktoria Jett, for one, since she's so sketchy. But how many times can I send him chasing? I know what it means to cry wolf—

A cold jolt runs through my body. I realize something else. What I can do.

"Are you taping this?" I say. "You better not be taping this."

Owen holds up his hands. "This isn't for attribution."

Nice try, Owen. "Not even 'on background.'"

I'm showing him I know what I'm doing *and* what he does.

He nods as if impressed. "Okay, let's go with 'deep background.'"

"Nope. This is completely off-the-record. Or nothing."

"Sure, sounds good," he says, all casual like I just suggested something off the menu. God, he's good. He's got all day. He probably would order another round in this shiny and too-bright hotel trap.

I take a good look around, but furtively, an eye over my right shoulder, and then my left, even though the only people in here are a tourist family of four having an argument and a probably crazy drifter who somehow made it in past security. Owen takes the looks around with me. *We're just a conspiracy of one*, his gesture's saying to me, *just the two of us.*

"It's usually about follow the money, am I right?" I say.

He nods, shrugs. *Go on*, he's saying.

"This one, it's about following the lie—the biggest lie."

"Gerald Hartwell, he was telling a pretty big lie."

"No. The one so big that even the one telling it believes it's true."

Owen takes a deep breath and thinks on it. "That's good. But there's not a lot of detail there. To follow. A trail needs at least a trailhead."

What now? Fuck.

I lean forward again, and I lower my voice. "It's right under your nose."

Owen actually looks down. "I don't see anything."

It's time. I go there.

"It's Mason Snead," I say, and repeat it, elongating the syllables. "*May-son Sneeead.*"

Owen releases the slightest gasp, like a hiccup.

What the hell am I doing? This is too close for comfort. I could be giving up the whole shebang, but what can I do? Owen was going to find out something, and it's better Snead than me. And it's too late anyway. Though a part of me needed to tell someone so bad. Maybe it's guilt. About Peggy Hartwell. Or maybe it's a plea for help. I'm not sure I want to know the answer to that. I imagine my brother. Andrew. What would he think of this? Me.

"Wait. You're after him, or he's instigated this whole plan?" Owen says.

Suddenly I have to pee, and the AC is too cold in here like in every damn American hotel, and it's all I can do not to shiver. I take a deep breath instead. I stare at Owen Tanaka, this guy from Mason Snead's own *FreeChain News*. His eyes are green like mine, but darker. I keep staring. He's got a resting mean face, his little jaw set hard like some small but predatory rainforest animal who makes the most of his tiny jungle kingdom, and I wonder if that's the way he normally looks. If this is the real him. I keep holding the stare. He's doing it back, no problem.

"Both," I say finally. "And that's all I can tell you."

OWEN

He had learned many things in dealing with sources, and even with the targets themselves. You had to go slow. You had to let off the gas right when you wanted to burst through that barrier in the road going a hundred. It was the only way to get the truth out of them. Questioning had to be incremental. Getting them to open up had to be from them wanting to do it. Thinking it was their idea, even. He guessed this was why he liked imagining he was doing espionage. Though it was more like he was the spy's handler than the spy. He was Smiley, not Leamas.

In her way, Lucy Holden had thrown monkey wrenches in his work. First it was Martin Podest. But Podest was nothing in comparison. Mason Snead was big, probably bigger than the president even, with tech leaders surpassing politicians in their importance and standing.

He'd asked Lucy if she was after Mason Snead or if he was the instigator. After staring at him with big green serious eyes for what seemed like a full minute, she'd said, *Both. And that's all I can tell you.* Like she was Deep Throat herself.

He had to admit she'd thrown him for a loop with Mason Snead. He hoped he hadn't let it show. He'd let slip that little gasp more out of regret than shock, more wincing than recoiling, knowing that he would still have to continue his slow and steady turtle's marathon. He knew this was all he would get out of her, for now. For formality's sake, he had implored her to go on record as an anonymous source to provide more details, but she had pulled back. No way, no how.

"I do my job, you do yours," she had said.

She was good, Owen knew.

And so he had left it. He let her go do her thing at City Hall, even though he knew it was likely a ruse, and hadn't even bothered to follow her. This fit his MO. He was pretending not to be sure at all now whether she was the one doing the Show Game. Pretending not to notice how she'd been stalling and looking pale.

Owen walked back to his own hotel, not too far away, a newer boutique inn he'd gotten a deal on. It rested on a fault line between the fresh and apparently endlessly thriving Pearl District and ever-degenerating Old Town. Spiffy in one direction, all squalor in the other. Two sides of the same town.

The first thing he did up in his room was watch that last video of the Show Game, again and again. Nope, he had not been wrong. That elbow was sticking out. Same angle, same persistence, everything. Despite the comfort of the rest of the well-appointed room, he was sitting in the hard little modern chair at an austere metal desktop so small it was attached to the bare concrete wall he faced. He might've been in a prison cell, or a monk even, but he liked it that way. It helped him focus.

Molly texted him: *Finding anything? I'm telling you, it's a woman behind it.*

He didn't text her back right away.

You're on to something, aren't you? she eventually texted back, then, *I bet you are.* Then, finally: *Keep going. And keep not telling anyone. The longer you don't reveal her, the longer it will all be worth it.*

Unable to leave a text unanswered, unlike so many other people, and especially one from Molly, he texted back a cryptic *OK.*

He liked that she was texting him so much, but he wondered whether it was just for all this truth he was after and not him as a person. Maybe he could be both to her, after all, he told himself.

Owen got back to work, reading up on the latest develop ments, sending and replying to emails, checking in with his sources, rereading notes. He typed out all that had happened with Lucy.

Who suddenly texted him too.

Hi Owen, it's Lucy. I'm going to come out and say it, because you're going to find out anyway. I knew Mason Snead. It was years ago.

Owen: *Why didn't you tell me earlier?*

A couple minutes passed.

I guess I was trying to keep myself out of your story. Out of what you need to find out.

He waited his own couple minutes. *Thanks for telling me.*

He turned to a window, staring out at the clean facades, balconies, and rooftops of new buildings, and a single well-preserved church spire, the horizon all construction cranes and looming green hills. He had a corner room. He looked out the other window and eyed Old Town with its crumbling brick structures that were sure to be earthquake hazards, and the lazy angry junkie graffiti, and boarded-up windows. It was afternoon. Soon it would be twilight then dark and if he looked in either direction, all he'd be able to see were silhouettes and have little inkling for how divided his surroundings were.

The more he knew, the less he knew.

Owen had to admit that Lucy's line about the biggest lie had stayed with him, and kind of creeped him out. And now, according to Lucy, he should be looking into Mason Snead himself?

His phone beeped. It was from Viktoria Jett, which of course meant MS, too, like they were reading his texts, if not his thoughts, and this gave him a little shiver as if the AC had just kicked in above his head.

You're West Coast? Viktoria texted. *What do you got?*

Owen gave it a few minutes. He thought it over. He penciled out a few responses, some spare, some overly long and counteractive. He considered just not texting back.

Nothing stellar. Tying up loose ends. Will report on my return.

So there it was. His first transgression. No, it was not, in truth—he hadn't even told them about Lucy Holden in the first place. He was rebelling, little by little. But it wasn't just that, he realized. He wanted Lucy to be the Show Game. He was rooting for her and probably had been all along.

He knew another thing too. He wasn't going anywhere, not yet, not until he knew more. After he watched the video for the seventh time, he called the front desk and booked his hotel room for five more days and extended his rental car.

ALEX / LUCY

I'd never said this was going to be easy, especially since it's never been done before. The pressure's mounting. I'm holing up in my nondescript Portland bungalow. I can feel safe here. It's surrounded by trees, at the end of a neglected street with oily gravel sidewalks and chain-link fences and the houses set back in lots far bigger than the small old homes, most properties just as overgrown as mine, the neighbors all keeping to themselves. One's a biker dude, another's probably an ex-con trying to stay out for good, another a poor single mom of three who's probably scared of the biker and the ex-con. There's a run-down trailer park the next street over, and low-income housing in the other direction filled with frightened-looking new immigrants. Welcome to America, folks! This is all standard for the Cully neighborhood, which is far more like farther out East County than the rest of the gentrified Portland surrounding it. Cully is a holdout. Gentrification is catching on here finally but it's going to take a while. Me, I picked it for the anonymity and how close it is to Portland International Airport as well as to the central city. I need to get downtown? I just take Sandy Boulevard in by car or bus like most born-and-raised Portlanders like me. Sandy is still the way. Most new arrivals let themselves get stuck on the I-84, and they can have it. I know this town like the back of my hand, not to mention the suburbs, seeing how I grew up in Inner Southeast, so I can slip out any time I like.

I have to keep this going. Events are moving faster, just like I figured they would. Things are getting trickier. Lots of smart people are asking around. I have to assume it's everyone from private eyes to more investigative reporters to the feds, for sure. One thing I've learned over the years, especially from my line of work: there's always someone watching. Owen Tanaka is watching.

And then there's Owen Tanaka's new boss: Mason Snead. It's strange, no, upsetting, what Snead has been up to. Snead likes to comment in public on what Alex has been doing with the Show Game. He pretends to approve of the concept, because he says that society should be "open" in a libertarian way. He even claims he's rooting for Alex. But it seems to me, knowing Snead, that the guy is actually mocking it deep down, practically condemning it in his smug way. That, or something even worse. It's the way he talks about it, like a rich guy bloviating about one of his prize horses running in the Kentucky Derby. Like he really does own everything in the end and it's all just a game for his amusement and we're his suckers. Oh man, if Owen Tanaka even had a clue about Mason Snead. Hopefully he'll figure it out before it's too late.

It's Monday evening now. After I left Owen Tanaka earlier, I'd headed straight for City Hall, strode up to records on the third floor, said hi to a friend I knew, then exited out the entrance on the other side of the block, checking windows and corners the whole way through. Of course Owen hadn't followed me. He didn't need to.

He has what he needs for now. He was good. He might not even believe I'm the Show Game. His accusation might've just been a way to force my hand, to see how I'd react, see what I had in me.

I'm now doing laundry for items I'd need just in case I had to hit the road on a moment's notice, if not go underground depending on how the powers that be decide to handle me should they find out.

At least I didn't sell out Chip. You owe me one, buddy. Then again, I hadn't even warned him about Owen Tanaka so that Chip could keep his guard up. Some buddy I was.

When I offered him the tip about Mason Snead, Owen Tanaka hit me up with that incisive reply about whether I was after Snead or if Snead had set all this in motion. And I can't stop wondering, worrying exactly what he meant by that. If he suspected more.

Both, I'd told him finally. *And that's all I can tell you.*

What was I, his Woodward whistleblower? Then again, he was an investigative journalist, so it was like red meat to him. Still, it seemed like I'd kept him at bay, at least for now.

But it had also seemed too easy.

So I made another tough call. I had to feed Owen more, because he was going to learn it anyway. I'd texted him that I'd known Mason Snead. It was many years ago. Let him figure out the rest. I was originally going to tell him on the spot but was scared my tells and tics might give me away somehow. One thing

I know for sure from being a private investigator: people never know what someone is noticing about them that they do not see at all. Some giveaways are instinctive, like the blink of an eye.

The dryer dings. Done. Time to get folding. After that, I'm heading down to the shelter for my cat fix, in the event I need to leave those babies for a while.

I'm preparing. I'm reacting at the same time. None of this is going to help me in the end, and I know that. Because I'm going for fucking broke. But I have to keep stalling for time. And I really do feel like Owen deserves something. But no one deserves to endure knowing what Mason Snead did to me and so many others—not just yet anyway.

I still remember it like it was today, feeling it right now like I have to hug myself from the freezing cold. Over fifteen years ago, before the launch of #AllGood, before FreeChain even, I worked for Mason Snead on his start-up called UnVest. Snead had created UnVest as an open, peer-to-peer platform, initially for victims of religious abuse. This was before apps, so we had forums, email newsletters, donation campaigns, lobbying efforts, investigations. It was growing and fast, for those abused, sure, but also for anyone involved—for friends and loved ones, pissed-off parents, but also for militant atheists and outsiders, and even, more and more, the abusers themselves, mostly those reformed, but even some anonymously who couldn't cease but wanted help. Everyone was welcome.

Mason had a way of providing an inclusive arena and was skilled in avoiding politicizing matters. We were branching out, too, beyond religion to Scouting organizations and cults and sham medicine and even (ironically) certain businesses such as big finance, adhering to that old start-up axiom about gaining as much presence as possible and working out the details later.

I was all in for the obvious reason—my brother, Andrew. I worked on a new investigations team for victims of Scout leader abuse. We did whatever it took, like WikiLeaks later before they, too, were shown to be what they were. We were vigilantes, but playing by the rules. Exposure was part of the equation, but comforting the abused came first.

There were red flags. Each of the teams seemed to work independently, and guardedly, each with their own physical offices even, and each answered only to Mason Snead. It was like terrorist cells, we joked, but with full transparency. Later I would learn that this was how dictators operated. Divide and rule. The führer principle.

We were all young. I was only twenty-two when I started, fresh out of the University of Oregon with a degree in political science and newly arrived in New York City to change the whole goddamn world, maybe even the solar system, all for my little brother. I was sharing a four-hundred-square-foot apartment in Alphabet City with a girl whose name and job I can't even recall now because she worked nights and slept over with a string of boyfriends.

Mason was even younger, at all of nineteen. He seemed to embody every bright future that ever was, JFK and Steve Jobs and Bill Clinton and JFK Jr. all rolled into one. Some knew who his father was, Myron Snead having basically created the foundation for the internet, but we all knew that Mason had skipped grades and, passing on the Ivy League, graduated from Stanford at sixteen before allegedly passing on a Rhodes Scholarship for philosophy at Oxford. He wanted at the real world. UnVest was his second start-up. His first tracked big-time corporate fraud, but it was bought out by a corporation and made to quietly die, which sort of proved his point about transparency.

UnVest was also a mildly surprising success coming so soon after the dot-com bubble had burst. Venture capital had dried up, yet we seemed to have lots of funding. Even at the time I didn't really see how any of it made any money. Free lunches just magically appeared. Kegs on Friday. Wild after-hours raves at secret locations.

We worked together, partied together. But only within our teams. Mason wanted it that way. He never combined us, not even for an open-layout office or companywide announcements or team building like all the start-ups did.

Soon you started to want his attention, to hope he would visit your team. Mason always had good ideas, and sometimes berated team members for bad ideas, but he always made you work harder. You were changing the world. There was definitely a charisma there. We became close. He visited our team for after-work drinks and always sat next to me. I can see him now in a booth in one of our favorite East Village spots, and, oddly, he looked the same age then as he does now. I was not in love, but I was definitely in awe. I never knew anyone like this in Oregon, not even in Portland.

One night late, as I was walking home, a black town car pulled up. It was Mason. In the back seat. He asked me to get in with him. He wasn't smiling. He was serious. That oddly perfect skin was creasing for the first time in the dim shadowed light, and I wondered if he was going to fire me. Maybe something was wrong with the company?

The last thing I remember, he was tugging at his nose.

I don't remember anything after that.

The next thing I knew, I woke up in a lavish but oddly sparse apartment, like one of those corporate ones used for short-term business. My head was killing me, and not like a hangover. More like I'd been inhaling gas fumes. Toxic. That or my head was in the speakers all night listening to a punk show. Was this Mason's place? Had we had too many drinks together and I'd passed out? I shouted around but no one was there. There was no phone. No TV even. I turned my crappy flip phone on—no messages, nothing. Then I realized how much my vagina hurt, as if raw, and my anus. And my insides. I could barely walk. It was somewhere near Central Park, I could tell by looking out the window, the tenth floor maybe. I just wanted out of there. I found my way out, passing through the building alone. It all was austere inside, all marble with no carpet, not even art anywhere. *Like a mausoleum*, I couldn't help thinking. It was even that cold.

I called in sick for half a day and then made it a whole day. I didn't know what to do. Confront him? Go to the police? Talk to HR? Right. There was no HR, not in a start-up, at least not by that name. Then I thought, maybe it hadn't even been him? And would he fire me? I still wanted that damn job so much. I was so naive, so stupid, so young.

Mason wasn't at work the next day, or at least not to my knowledge. I spotted him briefly the day after that from afar, but he was with another team and we had a huge deadline and there was no way to get to him.

Two nights later, I was walking home. The town car pulled up. It was Mason again. He smiled this time, but it was an overly concerned if not unknowingly smug smile, like you'd give to a homeless person when you don't have any change but do tell them best of luck.

I got in the car. I did. To this day, I do not know why. Maybe I just wanted answers. He kept his distance. He said it was being reported to him that something was wrong with me at work.

"Didn't you like the other night?" he then said.

My hand clawed at the door handle, but still did not open it. "What? What happened? What the hell did you do to me?"

He placed a flat hand to his chest, like one of those concerned aristocrats in some old movie. Oh my. "You don't remember?"

"What happened!"

"We had such a lovely time. Drinks at Insert Bar. That early cabaret show."

I'd never heard of either bar or club. He kept that straight and concerned face on me.

"And then you went home," he said. "I wanted to take you but you said you wanted to walk."

He added that telltale tug on his nose.

I remember all the air leaving my chest. My head felt as it had been drained of all fluid, of brain even. It took me like a minute to speak.

"I have a very good memory," was all I could say.

And that was the last thing I remember.

It happened again. Incredibly, horribly, the sickest joke there ever was. I woke up in a similar and equally grim apartment, in the same building, five minutes after midnight.

I sprinted out this time, bleeding raw, fuck it. That building foyer was all marble, too—and so cold—with a marble counter even, but it was void of devices and had no concierge or doorman outside either. It could have been a grand vestibule in ancient Rome. Yet I felt eyes on me, all over me, so much so that I had to hug and rub myself to make them go away. I noted the address on the way out.

I was crushed. I didn't go to work. I curled up in my apartment in a ball and told my roommate I was sick.

I was starting to believe it myself, what he was telling me. Doing to me. And if I went back to work, and let the criminal become normal, bit by bit, then I would believe it forever.

I quit UnVest two days later. They were going to fire me, anyway, because I'd been taken off my team for a "lack of commitment." My self-performance review just happened to be due then, too, which I had ignored.

I took it upon myself to retrace my steps. Gathering all my strength, along with a shot of whiskey from the nearest open bar, I found the apartment building the next morning. It had a doorman now. It had an awning when I would have sworn there was not one before. I could also see the silhouette of a concierge inside, behind the marble counter. Why hadn't I taken a picture of that? The doorman was tall and big-boned, with a soft face that might have once been boyish. I cleared my throat. I strode up. I put on a taut smile.

"Hi. I know someone in the building, but I can't remember his unit number."

"All right. What's the name?"

"Mason. Snead."

Doorman checked a notepad-size directory in his pocket. "Sorry, ma'am. No one under that name."

What was I doing? But it was all I had. *Think.*

"Oh . . ." I made myself look truly dejected. I even looked at the ground, and then rose my head up with my eyes as big as I could make them. I took a step closer. My more promiscuous friends used to tell me that if you got your face close enough to a guy, that was all it took.

"Look, sir. I don't know how to say this, but this person, he didn't treat me very well. I'm thinking of taking legal action. But I need to identify him. This building."

"Do you have a picture?"

"Yes!" I fumbled for my flip phone and showed him a grainy photo of Mason Snead.

Doorman stared at it. He stared at me. His thick jaw seemed to grow in size, or maybe it was my head spinning from what he said next.

"I don't recognize this person," he said, flatly, like reciting a phone number.

"But . . ."

"Ma'am, I'm sorry, but—"

"Don't call me ma'am."

He blinked, once, but that was it.

Shit, what was I doing? I put the smile back on, tilted my head.

But now his brow loomed larger, too, as if being puffed up, pumping. "Look, lady," he said, "I've worked this building for ten years. I know everyone here. Who comes here. Leaves. I have never seen that man in my life."

"You don't know who Mason Snead is?"

"No. I'm afraid I do not."

"Son of Myron Snead? No? Look, I'm just trying to confirm that, that . . . Oh, forget it."

A kindly looking and dapper elderly couple passed, and the doorman tipped an imaginary hat to them.

He waited for the door to shut behind them completely. He turned to me. "Come to think of it? I've never seen you either."

Blood emptied from my face, head, and plummeted down through my gut like diarrhea, pooling around my feet, red-hot. I had to steady myself. I took a step back.

"You're not always here. There was no one here a few nights ago."

The hint of a smile raised one corner of his broad mouth, a long and oddly bright red slit wider than my whole face. "Lady, I work nights. Right now I'm filling in for Jones, who's late on account of a family issue."

"Well, you weren't working the night of the fourteenth." I wagged a finger at him like he was a bad boy, flashing smiles at him, trying to keep my wits. But it only made me look crazier.

His big eyebrows raised, like two toy mice pulled by strings. "As a matter of fact, I was."

He was flipping to another page in his little directory, which looked like a book of matches in his huge paw.

"No, no," I muttered.

"What time?" he said.

But I was already backing up. Still muttering. "I was on the, uh, tenth floor, had to be," I was saying, but then I looked up, and the building had five stories max. Though the building next door was taller. A few nearby buildings were taller. One next door was. Had I been transported secretly from another? But from where? My head was spinning around at all the buildings, and I nearly stumbled. I kept backing up. "No, this can't be . . ."

"I even have video to prove it," he said, his head turning to me on a swivel, his feet still planted. He added a full smile now, no teeth, and it was like a finger smearing a line of red.

My face was hot, rigid, holding back tears. I backed up all the way to the street corner before I burst into tears, shaking, and had to prop myself against the wall.

The doorman might as well have been testifying in a courtroom. That was the point, I now saw. That was how powerful Mason Snead could be. They probably even had cameras on me right then, my body language making me look like a madwoman.

I pulled myself together again. I checked the bar and club Mason said we went to, and a bartender and server at each said that they'd seen me there, the last around midnight. The problem was, I had woken up a little before midnight in that apartment. This wasn't right. I couldn't believe what I was hearing. Both kept a straight face, just like Mason, like placating that homeless person they were never going to help. I literally backed out of that cabaret club.

My phone showed no activity for either night, like it had been turned off for the duration both times. There was only one call out, to a number I didn't know, the night I was raped a second time. The day after I quit, I got a voicemail on my phone, the number private. It was Mason's voice. He said, "We should go back to that club we went to that second night. You know, the private club. I'm a member. You liked it so much. You told me. I have your message about that still, and I'll keep it, too, I like it so much." And he played it, right there on that voicemail.

It was me, my voice. It was saying, "Oh, Mason. We had such a lovely time. We should go back to that club we went to that second night. You know, the private club. I liked it so much. We stayed until two! Can we do it again real soon? Can we? . . ."

And I went on, gushing. It was me but not me, like a bimbo version of myself, mentioning those clubs I was supposedly at but couldn't have been given the time I was in those apartments and raped. Was it me via some kind of early AI? An impersonator? Was it just me drugged? And I mentioned the private club of the second night. Of course the name wasn't said. And that he was a member was the only thing my voice message didn't corroborate. So it didn't exist, not publicly, but who knew? I imagined some imposing brownstone on the Upper East Side with just a bronze plaque somewhere and a vague society name. Come to think of it, that fit the description of that apartment building exactly.

Within a couple months, my stomach started spinning. I was throwing up. I was pregnant. I wandered the city like a zombie, not eating, sleeping. Was it even Mason who did it? Or someone else? Maybe he had a whole posse. I felt like Mia Farrow in fucking *Rosemary's Baby*.

I ended up having an abortion. I probably could have found out who the father was from my blood and fetal DNA, but by that point I didn't want to know. Then I did. I stayed in NYC a couple years, out of defiance more than anything, and I tried investigating on my own. I consulted lawyers, good ones, big ones. No one would touch me. I eventually entered Columbia Law School but dropped out, then limped back to Portland a different person a year after that. Not quite devastated, just warped forever. I didn't know who I was. I actually considered changing my name. I wished I were an alcoholic, or drug addict, because at least I could've numbed the pain. I tried. Vomiting and no sleep weren't helping matters. The dudes I met were even crazier than me.

And then it happened, finally: A year into that scene, Snead was arrested on sexual abuse charges. He even went to jail. It saved me. It was like seeing a rainbow for the first time. My mind cleared. I lost the losers. I waited for those lawyers to call me back. None did. I called others, I called reporters. All counseled patience, again.

Jail for Snead lasted a week. The charges were dropped, his accuser made to look unstable, and she disappeared from the face of this earth. It could have been me. It was like being buried alive. It shook me to my core. But this time my marrow was boiling, my mind stayed clear. I knew why, how. Mason Snead got off because of his money and connections, on a technicality. And this time it didn't nearly kill me.

I had tried to get past it. I did. But it kept coming back stronger. In my face. Forcing me to deal. Could what happened to my brother really have happened to me? It was the same. It was an abuse of power. Sex was only the tool. The real Mason Snead isn't some wunderkind. He doesn't want to make a dent in the universe. He wants to transcend even the most powerful, keep young girls captive, rape them, and leave them like a garbage bag for pickup on the sidewalk. He doesn't want to go to the moon or even own an island. Nothing like that figured into it. His was a secret but ancient ambition. I actually wouldn't be surprised if he wanted to create a colony in the middle of the earth, he's that mad. They're all fucking mad.

My brother's fate was horrible, but that was only the spark. This was my volcano. I was going to smother those mother-fuckers with hot lava, as many as I could, my trail of scorching, cleansing molten rock consuming as many as I could until I buried Mason Snead.

I had thought about ways to do it. What if I just got close, then threw him in front of a fast car?

Then I had realized: I was simply going to do to them, and then to him, what he did to me. Destroy. Warp them forever.

MONDAY–SATURDAY, NOVEMBER 13–18
OWEN

He turned his Portland hotel room into his office. Holed up. He sometimes used his favorite of the seven surrounding coffee shops to get away from his tiny desk. Plus housekeeping needed to come in. But he didn't go out too much and didn't cross West Burnside into the compact downtown area because he didn't want to run into Lucy Holden by accident. Anything was possible. She would wonder why he was still here. She would figure out that he might still be on to her. Before he made his next move involving her, his plan was to get more on Mason Snead. This was his show now.

Owen used the investigative reporter's trusted resources for getting at the truth: consulting the online databases; public and private records; checking sources and rechecking interviews; analyzing, comparing, and visualizing data—spreadsheets, PDF extraction tools, mapping software. And when those didn't work, he started emailing, texting, and even calling trusty contacts, old friends, all using his personal accounts. He couldn't use his team back in NYC for this since that inevitably meant using the team's supposedly secure new chat tool. To cover himself, he occasionally did use his *FreeChain News* accounts and their new chat. Most of the team, he saw, appeared to be using it as just their own personal Twitter, that or TikTok, but one was on the ball: Gina. She had checked with experts and reported back to him that "analysis of human speech altered by a voice changer could not detect the person's true voice." It was possible, however, to reverse-engineer vocals if the perpetrator's voice was known. But the Show Game voice was not known. All the more reason for Owen to confirm it.

He finally got hold of Anne Blade, his former editor. This was on his third day in his hotel room. She had indeed been in Mexico, helping to care for her ill father. They talked on the phone in his room at four a.m. PST, before her new job back east began for the day.

"I was hoping you'd get in touch," she said. Owen could hear the subway station behind her, yet she still spoke in hushed tones. "You want something on Snead? Good. Fuck that guy."

Anne Blade had a good tip for him. He pursued it immediately, not even bothering to get out of bed, just grabbing his tablet and laptop and notepads off the floor and plopping them onto the sheets. Before he knew it, it was ten a.m. and he hadn't eaten yet.

He got a text from Molly: *It is a she, isn't it? Mum's the word!*

If she only knew. He tried stalling, but finally texted back: *Hold on to your hat.* Plus a grimace face emoji.

That afternoon (it took Owen a second to recall which day), after a quick shower, a few stretches, and making sure the Do Not Disturb sign was on the door, he started calling in a few favors, screw it. This led him to a couple fellow investigative reporters, including some in the business world that Owen didn't know. It helped his cause that he told them he wasn't building a story but simply discreetly assessing his current employer. This was absolutely off-the-record. That opened more minor floodgates.

He kept going. Took quick walks for food and fresh air. Worked into the night. The following afternoon, his fourth day—Friday again already, he summarized his findings in a little report that he would normally refer to for building a story, for working into the narrative . . .

It had been rumored that Mason Snead was not Myron Snead's biological son, something Owen had been able to confirm. Mason Snead was adopted, but his parentage was unclear. He had been in a couple foster homes early on, but their locations were equally unclear. No one knew whether he'd even taken a DNA test. The boy was too smart for his own good, according to a former au pair who demanded never to be named (reporter suspected she'd been paid off to keep quiet on top of the usual NDA). Au pair said that Myron Snead and his third wife, Clarice, didn't know how to handle young Mason. The au pair said it was awkward, like when a parent senses they're raising a serial killer. From a young age, Mason was ambitious, driven, had a chip on his shoulder. He never backed down. A business reporter had been preparing a book on him but was threatened with so much legal action he gave it up. But business reporter was happy to talk to Owen off-the-record, on a different phone Owen had to call. Reporter filled in some details. Mason had excelled in everything, even sports, despite the somewhat frail look he had now. He was gifted at soccer but gave it up because he realized that a body would give out in its thirties; he only wanted to cultivate that which would last a lifetime if not longer. His mind was constantly demanding more training, more experiences. He skipped high school for college, then traveled the world with a backpack instead of accepting his Rhodes Scholarship. He cozied up to his first investor on the heels of that.

"Here's where it gets weird," business reporter had said. "Brace yourself."

Mason Snead's start-ups never actually got very far. They bled money. Yet they looked profitable, and the hype always enhanced the impression. He already had money, so he didn't need start-ups to survive. He only needed his endeavors to get enough attention that he could use them for his own ends.

"What ends?" Owen had asked.

"That's where you got me. That was where I hit a dead end every time." Reporter left a pause.

"But?"

"But, if you ask me . . ." Reporter lowered his voice. "I think he was blackmailing people."

"People?"

"The rich and powerful. His own investors."

"Wait. Blackmailing them into . . . investing in him?"

"There's a chicken or egg question here. But you didn't hear it from me."

Owen then talked to an investigative reporter specializing in church issues. Mason Snead's odd business behavior had evolved with UnVest, then #AllGood. These orgs allowed him to reach more influential people that he could lure in and fleece. Certain priests were not uncovered. Instead they were only blackmailed, and continuously.

"Continuously," Owen said. "What does that mean?"

"I hit brick walls there, but I take it to mean that it was ongoing and might even still be."

Meanwhile, #AllGood attracted the powerful and wealthy as a high-profile way to give to charity and win on taxes.

Owen had always sensed something was off. But he hadn't wanted to know. He had told himself certain things were not true. He kept working into the evening of his last day, Saturday.

He thought about adding a couple more days on his room, but that was going to start looking suspect to Viktoria Jett, which meant to Mason Snead himself. By now he was having his team look deep into poor Martin Podest as a ruse, since Tacoma was so close to Portland.

Mason Snead's organizations were practically fronts, Owen now knew. Mason Snead was a glorified straw man and front man—for himself alone.

Some people had attempted to take him and his companies to court, Owen had learned from his legal and law enforcement contacts. So how come none of this had ever been made public before, or taken to trial? Snead, Owen recalled, had also been charged and jailed briefly for sexual assault some years ago but got off on a technicality, this after his accuser appeared dubious at best. Again, how? The answer gave Owen shivers. Snead was too big, and the people involved too powerful to let any of it to be known. The best sources Owen was likely to find were whispers.

Owen took another look at Lucy. She had texted him that she'd known Mason Snead years ago, sure. But Owen did more research—and found out that she had worked at none other than UnVest.

He was by now rewearing his dirty laundry. He'd washed underwear and socks in the sink like an international correspondent in rough country. He was getting desperate. Before he left, he needed something on Lucy herself.

He needed female insight, a woman's angle. He even thought about enlisting Molly. She'd studied journalism in college. She certainly knew how the game worked. But it would take too long to explain. The thought of them working together calmed him down, though, like a hot bath in that nice tub he'd never even used in this hotel. It was the closest he'd gotten to justifying a video call.

It was now six p.m. again. Owen had resorted to texting Lucy herself that afternoon, offering her tidbits of what he was finding, hoping that she would confirm. She hadn't texted him back. She wouldn't talk before, but maybe now after he'd done his due diligence? He had then emailed her, too, twice, and got her Out of Office both times. All it said was that she was working on a case and would get back at the earliest opportunity.

He called back Anne Blade. She didn't answer. He was about to leave a message when another call came through. He pushed accept.

"It's me. What?"

It was Anne Blade. She, too, had another phone.

"You said 'fuck that guy,' right?" Owen said.

"I did, and I meant it. You found some things. What d'ya got?"

Owen gave her all he'd learned. He didn't tell her where he was, and she did not ask.

"It's some kind of racket," he said to sum up.

She didn't dispute it, not any of it. "Tell me you're on a safe phone," she said after a long pause.

"I am."

She said nothing.

"It's a burner app," he added. "Hushed."

"Okay. All right."

"Did you know any of this?" Owen said. "Is that what you're saying, Anne? By not saying. Or you know of something else?"

"Uh-huh," she said after the longest pause yet. Her voice sounded smaller, now, and fainter, like she had backed away from the receiver.

"Fuck that guy," Owen said. "Remember?"

"There were allegations," smaller Anne said, eventually.

Owen didn't answer. *Don't force her. Give it time.*

"There were allegations," she repeated after another while,

her voice growing strong again, "that he had done stuff to some women. Young women."

Allegations, plural—not one accuser, but more. "All right . . ."

Another long pause. Owen actually had to check his phone to make sure they were still connected.

"Remember, Anne, this is all completely off-the-record," he said into the silence after another few beats.

"Snead, he's worse than the Show Game's targets," Anne sputtered, her voice now hard and staccato. "There were stories. Girls. Employees. Scary shit. Waking up not knowing where they were." Her mouth snapped shut with a gasp.

"That's why," Owen blurted.

"That's why, what?"

"When you got laid off, when I saw you in your office, you had this look on your face. Ghost."

She didn't reply.

Owen cleared his throat. "Take your time."

"It was relief, that look," she said finally. "No way I was working with that bastard anyway."

Owen was sitting on the edge of the bed and cradling the phone like it was a porcelain artifact thousands of years old. His chest was tightening. He took a deep breath, but it didn't help much. "Were you one of those girls, Anne?"

The small voice was back. "It was a long time ago," Anne said after a while. "I saw a couple lawyers, Owen. The law even. But no one would touch it. So I put it behind me." She added a sick giggle. "Until you come along. You fucker."

Owen gave her the same sick giggle. "I had to, Anne. It's what we do."

"I know."

"When was it?"

171

"A long time ago."

"I have that already," Owen said.

She sighed on her end, but nothing followed.

"We'll play a guessing game. All right?"

"All right. Okay."

"Did you meet him somewhere? Bar or a party, friends, acquaintances?"

"No."

"Work situation."

"Yes."

"You worked for him?"

"What did I just tell you? It wasn't like he was working for anyone."

"Was it #AllGood?"

"No."

Owen's pulse raced. He stood, strode over to the window, but it was all a blur. He was too focused to see. "Was it . . . UnVest?"

A pause where she might have nodded. "Yes."

"Can you tell me more?"

"I worked there. On one of their teams. Thought it would be more rewarding than journalism. What an idiot."

"I could find that all out on my own." He needed more, in other words.

"Right."

"Look," Owen said, "if you can't tell me, if it's too hard, I understand. Think it over. Call me back when you're ready."

"No."

"No?"

"No, it's okay. All I can tell you is someone threatened me. In a parking garage. Threatened my family, my parents back in Milwaukee. It's a big reason they retired in Mexico. I mean, who does that to people?"

"Fucking bastards," Owen muttered. The words came out before he even thought them. He was lowering back to the bed.

Another thought shot through his skull, like hot wasabi. He popped back up, his heart thumping.

"Anne, I have another question."

She sniffed, surely from sobs. "Okay."

"You're doing great."

"I know."

"Do you know the name Lucy Holden? She worked for UnVest, too, back then."

Anne didn't take too long or not long enough. "It's hard to say," she said, "we worked in isolated teams, completely siloed. There was this one woman, though, she was going around discreetly asking questions. But she didn't get very far. I gave her nothing. I regret that too."

Owen described Lucy, pacing the room, stabbing at air. "That sound like her? Her hair would've been different."

"Sounds like her," Anne said. "God, we were all so naive."

"That's no excuse. Ever."

"No, of course not. Listen. If this Lucy Holden is a source? You have to warn her to watch her back. She might be getting into trouble."

"Oh, I think Mason Snead is the one in trouble."

"Good. But you didn't hear it from me. My dad, he has Parkinson's."

"I'm sorry. Okay. All off-the-record. Thank you, Anne."

"Thank you. For making me talk. Now go out there and hunt it down. Him. Because if you don't? I just think I might someday. And beat you to it."

Spoken like a true editor. "Will do," Owen said, with all the respect in his heart.

Once he was off the phone, he went to the window again. It was dark now. He could see every detail of every raindrop on the windowpane, but all else was obscured. No inkling.

He touched the window and wanted it to be chilling cold. It wasn't. He then felt an odd compulsion to open the window, but it was sealed of course. That transformed into an urgent need to finally write to Shane Bagley in prison, to tell him what he was doing. He took a deep breath. He closed his eyes. Something told him, inside that darkness, that Shane Bagley would not yet approve. Not yet. That damning quote now echoed in his head: *Nice try—dumbshit.*

He opened his eyes and peered at the dark city in silhouette, in the direction of Lucy's home far across the Willamette River. He'd already retrieved her address from databases on that first day he'd extended his stay. That was the easy part. But of course she would've known that. He tried texting her again and got nothing. Her email still had the Out of Office. He phoned her. Voicemail. He didn't leave a message. It was already seven p.m. now.

He was pulling on his clothes and mapping his route to her house not far from the airport. Forty-five minutes by bus and train, but no more than thirty minutes in his rental car.

"It is you, isn't it, Lucy?" he said, to the rain now rolling down the window like tears. Her tears. All their tears.

Five minutes later he was exiting the hotel into that rain, bouncing on the soles of his feet he was so worked up.

ALEX / LUCY

It's evening now. It's been raining, I see from the streaks on the windows. I'm thinking about my next move. It's all I think about.

I went to the cat shelter today to get my mind off it, if only for a minute. Sometimes I go down there outside of volunteering, just to watch happy, normal people get their kittens and cats for the first time. It helped, but it didn't last. My mind refocused on the mission as soon as I was back inside my car.

I'm on the sofa with the lights down low. Keeps me calm. I can't read for fun anymore, and I certainly can't start streaming a new series. The Show Game consumes all. But I need to check in with Chip again. He was right, I know it. With so much coming down, we need to hurry. Smash and grab, he said. *We act incrementally, we're only increasing the chances of compromising the mission. We need to go big. Do what no one's expecting.* But I still don't think his whole heart is in this. I need to cut to the chase for the operation's sake as well, because I don't know how long I'll be able to keep Chip, especially considering that thousand-yard stare I'd witnessed. He hadn't exactly looked over the moon when I'd told him we're going after Mason Snead next. So I'd told him why we were doing it—Snead had raped me and other girls, and who knew who else was in on it. And he did all this while polishing his tech-philanthropist veneer, all the better to exploit the whole damn world. Chip had nodded, okay, and that steel returned to his eyes. That bought me some time. When I last checked in with him, he said he was fine. He was back on the East Coast, already casing the target. He had the van. This was all good news, but he could be anywhere, really. And his head could be miles away.

I remind myself, there in the half dark, with my feet up on the ottoman, that I've come such a long way. I'd rebuilt myself after limping back to Portland so many years ago, all while keeping my eyes on the prize. First, I had investigated. Found out what little I could as I built my career as a private detective. This was the perfect front, and by design from the start.

Over time, I discovered that Mason Snead had done the same to others, many far more vulnerable. I started looking into individual cases. The woman were getting younger, just girls more and more underage, unprotected ones either new to the country as asylum seekers or refugees, then it was girls abroad. Snead had even been collaborating with ICE, it was said. A few had tried to sue him, prosecute him, but they always got nowhere. I assumed some were bought off, and I knew others were threatened. Mason Snead wasn't pulling every string, of course. This wasn't some TV thriller. He only had to exist for others to do his deeds for him, for others to be so goddamn willing and able. He was seducing, compromising, owning more and more of the rich and powerful with his sick narcissistic crack. UnVest, #AllGood, it was all bullshit. Mason Snead believed in nothing. If he believed anything at all, it was that power for power's sake and dominance were the ultimate realization of his bullshit libertarian principles.

Meanwhile, I had done all I could to cover myself. Pretty damn well, I have to say. The line from my brother's abuser to Mason Snead is not clear. An investigator would, first of all, have to know who I was. If anyone was looking, they would have to understand the big picture. It's the flip side of the Big Lie. The Big Truth. That Mason Snead and his horrible deeds are the ultimate result of unchecked power.

This makes me think of Owen Tanaka. I toast him with an imaginary whiskey. Bravo, Ken Burns reporter guy in your functional outdoorsy gear. Owen gets it. Don't you, Owen? The dude just doesn't know it yet. I only hope he figures it out before it's too late for him. That he can act on it. If he doesn't, he'll regret it till his dying day.

I hear a jet overhead, a faint rush, taking off from the airport, but things are otherwise quiet here on my secluded street. I can see out the living room window. The only other two houses I can see in the dimming light are just silhouettes among the oak and fir trees that have been here long before me and will remain long after. But will they outlast the evil machinations of the Mason Sneads of this world? Sometimes I still can't believe people like him actually exist. They and their realm would be too preposterous in a movie. I snort at the thought, and I again wish I had a whiskey in my hand. But I need to stay sharp. I have a couple go bags packed, waiting in the threshold to the kitchen in case, and I glance over at them there near the back door just to make sure.

I start. *What was that?* A shadow moved, at the window over the sink. A branch? But it's not windy.

My heart's racing. I'm sitting bolt upright, digging into the leather chair arms. Paralyzed for a moment.

I take a deep breath and slip into my running shoes, my eyes darting from the kitchen window over to the living room window and back. There are no cars out front. Maybe it was a neighbor in their backyard? But any yards are too far for shadows to reach, even under the strangest light, and they're blocked by too many trees and bushes.

I'm at the light switch now. I slowly push the dimmer off all the way. An animal? We sometimes get raccoons. But what kind of racoon stands tall enough for its shadow to reach my kitchen window?

I'm in the kitchen now, crouching in the dark, regulating my breathing, not letting my racing heart get the best of my lungs. I watch not only the window but the cabinet doors, and stove, and walls around me for any reflections or shadow not clearly from the window. Creeping through the room, half my height, all those squats coming in handy now. Considering my next move. I have a pistol in one go bag next to me, unregistered. My registered detective Glock is in my den, locked up. I hate that I immediately think of going to the gun, but we're all conditioned that way, as would be any intruder, so I have to think it too. I need something. I'm at the drawers now. Listening. Nothing new. So I pull open the drawer and withdraw my handy utility knife, cost me a lot at Kitchen Kaboodle but worth it when I do cook. It'll prove itself now.

I tense up. One of the stationary shadows on my cabinets shifted, just slightly. I go over my whole backyard in my mind. I still don't know what it could be. It's no tree or shrub that I can recall.

I creep over to the kitchen back door, lower than the door window. Rise to the lower right corner. I got a cute little curtain from Target but it doesn't quite cover the glass and I can peek out . . .

I start again, pull back down. "Jesus," I blurt, "fuck."

I'd accidentally banged my elbow on the door, but nothing happens.

I peek again. Hold my stance.

It's a silhouette, all right, of a person. Wearing a hood. Standing at my back door, casual stance, arms at their sides but ready, with shoulders back, like someone making a delivery. But what delivery person is going to find their way around the back through all my shrubs and fences?

It's not Chip. I know his silhouette. Maybe it's a homeless person? That's certainly feasible. They've been exiting the central city for so many years now when not forced out, just like all the once fairly stable lower-middle-class folks displaced by gentrification.

I sigh, pondering a new next move. Maybe I'm not here? I just keep quiet. I peek again. The silhouette has all evening, apparently. It just stands there. I lower my knife, down and away from me. I peek again. I can't make out the person at all. They're just contours filled with black. Do I turn on my back-door light?

It says something. I can't make it out.

"What?" I say in a normal voice.

"Lucy Holden? Open up, please."

It's a female voice, high in tone but with an edge to it, like a rusty saw.

I pull the curtain aside a little, both eyes peering out, scanning the silhouette. Her hands are empty, hanging loosely.

"Who the hell are you?" I say.

"Open up, please. Let me in."

"What's wrong with the front door?"

No reply.

I look out again.

Silhouette Lady shrugs.

I'm smart enough not to turn on the light. Something tells me Silhouette Lady doesn't want that either.

I crack the door open, propping one shoulder against it just in case, and look out.

"Hi," Silhouette Lady says. With my eyes adjusting, I can see that she's wearing a hood because it's been raining out. The hood is that of a standard, likely high-end rain jacket.

"What do you want?" I say.

"To talk to you."

"I don't know you."

"But I know you," she says.

The woman's voice is still high but firm and civil, reminding me of a public service announcement.

"Who are you?" I add.

"It's starting to rain again," she says.

"I'm armed," I say.

"I know."

How does she know that?

"You'd be careless not to be," she adds, "what with me hovering at your door like some ghost. Come on." She puts her hands up.

I nod and place the knife on my little dining table, within reach. I pull the door open, slowly, keeping my shoulder to it.

She steps in sideways, still hands up. She stands in the middle of the room for me. Cooperative.

I nod, thanks.

She shrugs, don't mention it.

She pulls her hood off to reveal sandy-whitish hair, a full head of it. She's in her early fifties, I'm guessing, and is moderately attractive though her face is a little drawn. Something about her reminds me of a male Latino character actor whose name I can't recall, which is weird, but with a woman's full curves from the neck down. Her warm brown eyes are helping matters. She has olive skin like me.

She doesn't say anything, just lets me take her in. I stand back a step, the knife behind me. Sure enough, she's wearing a North Face jacket. It's not even black, more like navy.

"Let's get to it, shall we?" she says, adding a smile.

"Cut to the chase?"

She nods.

"Who are you?" I say.

She shakes that head.

"You want a little light, some water maybe?" I don't know why I say this. Maybe I'm a little embarrassed now with us gleaming here from the dim full-moon window light.

"That's kind of you, but no."

Something about the way she said this confirms that there's no point in asking her name again either.

"Look. I know what you're doing," she says.

That makes me try anyway. "Who are you?" I repeat, adding a little edge to my voice just to test her out. "What's your name?"

"You can cut the act. We're two adults here, right? Plus we're women."

Good point, Silhouette Lady.

"Right," I say.

"I know what you're doing, and I am not going to tell anyone. Okay? Let's establish that first."

I nod. I shake my head as if to say, *Lady, I got no idea what's going on here*. But I don't say yes, and I don't say no either.

"Are you from a client of mine? Is that it?" I ask her.

She adds a smile. It's disarming, but only just enough. "You know it's not."

"So how did you find me?" I say. Trying that out, but giving nothing away.

"Nope."

"Nope? As in, you can't tell me that either?"

"Yep."

"Why?"

"Because I have things to tell you," she says. "It will help you."

"Uh, help me how? I don't get it."

Silhouette Lady pauses here. She bites her lower lip and nods at a thought. She's making a decision here. She's going to give me something. "Because you know my daughter, or at least who she is. Her name was Hayley."

"Who? Wait, *was*?"

"That's right. You might know her now as Viktoria Jett."

OWEN

By 7:55 p.m., and full darkness, Owen had made it to Lucy Holden's street. The rain was light, but nothing his Gore-Tex rain jacket couldn't handle. He parked his rental car at the end of the street, then strolled his way in, hood on, head down, hands in his pockets. Just a dude walking along in the evening.

The street was dark, the houses mostly bungalows and more spread apart than in most neighborhoods in this part of the city, with plenty of trees and bushes surrounding each. He smelled the faint odor of smoke, maybe someone's backyard smoker. No one noticed him. Not one car had come or gone.

He wasn't spying. He was going to confront Lucy once and for all. He'd been trying to come with an angle that was ethical, at least journalistically. According to Mason Snead's no-rules libertarian logic, a reporter could likely report on a murderer while he was planning it. That wasn't what he wanted. Deep down, knowing what he now knew about Mason Snead being a dangerous high-end fraud, Owen wanted to give Lucy a chance to explain herself. He might be able to get away with an off-the-record-type tale, or even as "not attributed," as long as he didn't know what she was planning exactly. That could make him an accomplice—or so he'd guessed driving over in the rental. He wasn't sure. This was all moving so fast, and he had to get at her while he could. And, he had to admit to himself, he really wanted to hear her story for himself. Not to feed the news beast or Viktoria Jett and Mason Snead or for any sort of accolades.

What exactly had made her come this far? To sacrifice everything? He knew one thing—he'd never taken such a personal interest in a story, not even close.

He passed Lucy's place once on foot, not breaking stride,

side-eyeing the house, on down to the end of the street, a rare city cul-de-sac. Paused. Stood under the cover of a tree. After a couple minutes, he passed back by Lucy's.

Then he walked up the little path to the front steps.

ALEX / LUCY

My face burns, my eyeballs too. It's like Silhouette Lady just slapped me right in my own kitchen.

"He hurt you, didn't he?" she said.

Meaning Mason Snead, of course. First she tells me Viktoria Jett's her daughter, and now this.

I don't answer at first.

Then I say back to her, "Did he hurt your daughter?"

Silhouette Lady sits up straight, as if hearing a threatening noise in the distance. She probably was expecting my reply.

"Did he hurt your Hayley?" I add, throwing my investigator self right back at her, whatever she might be. Something about her makes me think of a judge, but that isn't quite right.

Now she doesn't answer at first. And then she nods at the hard and reflecting veneer tabletop.

"I'll tell you what I can," she says. "Whatever horrors that you're imagining? About the evil of Mason Snead and his ilk? They're only the tip of the iceberg. It's organized, international, right here at home in front of us. Truly untouchable. Dangerous."

I think for a moment, staring at the floor in the dark, and it might as well be a murky cave filling with black water. "Sex trafficking?" I say finally.

She doesn't nod, but she doesn't shake her head either.

"But that show already ran," I say. "It was Gerald Hartwell, the founder of LifeForce. LF, Hartwell, he says it's a humanitarian aid org helping victims of human trafficking but it also runs its own high-end sex trafficking network worldwide and—"

"I saw the show. Of course I saw it."

"And he admitted to it."

"Did he?" Silhouette Lady shoots back, the first time I hear her raise her voice. "Did he truly? I'm talking all the way."

I don't think she wants me to know too much. Could someone try to harm me for what I know? I think of that big doorman and my return visit.

"You tell me," I mutter finally.

"It's far worse than you fear. Think of the worst, then double it. The truth is the opposite. *All* victims are not the object to be helped, but to be exploited." She holds up a flat hand and moves it along an imaginary flat plane. "All along the line."

"Gerald Hartwell was only part of it," I say, swallowing hard like from the worst acid reflux. "Powerful as he was. Is."

"That's right."

"And me? What about what happened to me?"

"It was getting started before that," Silhouette Lady says. "It's been progressing and growing ever since. I hate to say it like this, but you? Girls at his companies? You were just a sideshow. Why? Because he can. They can."

They? That gives me a shiver. I actually have to hug myself.

I quickly find my way back to steely composed Lucy, relying on reason. I ask Silhouette Lady basic questions: Who is she? Who told her about me? Why now? She doesn't answer. I don't want to say too much before I know the full score. But the assumption is like a zeppelin inside the room. It was the only thing we could be talking about. Mason Snead was All.

This is about her daughter, Hayley aka Viktoria Jett, sure, but it all stems from Mason Snead.

"So what do you want me to do?" I ask her.

"Just watch your step," Silhouette Lady says.

"Watch it how?"

"For starters, do not use an FBI disguise, or any fed for that matter. It will only get you into worse trouble if you're caught."

"I'm going to need more than that."

"I will try and let you know if you're making a wrong move, but that will sometimes mean revealing what you're doing. To me. Can you do that?"

OWEN

He stood at the front door of Lucy Holden's house. It was dark inside, though the living room lights appeared to be on the lowest dimmer setting.

He knocked on the front door.

ALEX / LUCY

Knock knock knock!

Silhouette Lady ducks down even faster than I do. She glares at me in the dark, I glare back.

"Someone trailing you?" I hiss at her; I'm pissed.

"No, not possible," she says, and the calm way she shakes her head tells me it's true. "I took every precaution."

We're crouching a foot from each other. "I'll see who it is, maybe just a neighbor, delivery—"

"No. Anyone ever come to your door?"

"Nope. Never."

"Don't take the chance. Those your go bags?"

I'm already thinking it, my pulse calming, my mind seeing next steps. "Yes," I say.

"Good girl."

OWEN

He waited. Then rang the doorbell. Waited. He listened, but the light patter of rain prevented him from hearing anything inside.

He backed away, watching the house, the main living room window, the rest all dark. Back up the street. At the corner, under the cover of a big oak, he thought about texting her. But he didn't want to freak her out or, worse, give her a chance to avoid him.

He emailed her from his phone instead: *Hey. I'm back in Portland, got a couple questions. Leaving tomorrow. Is tonight bad for you?*

He spotted a dive bar up the main cross street—he could hole up there if he had to. He checked his email and saw he'd immediately gotten her Out of Office email again.

Then Owen felt the most overwhelming urge, deep inside him, and it scared him, like when you're holding a sharp kitchen knife and wonder what it would be like to harm yourself or, worse yet, someone you love. And yet the urge felt so warm, and comforting, the truest truth in the world.

ALEX / LUCY

Brrring brrring bring!

The doorbell now.

I tense up and feel it from Silhouette Lady too. We're both perched on our toes.

She helps me pull my coat on, I grab the go bags.

I push the back door open, the two of us crouching, crab walking.

"We'll have to split up," she whispers in my ear, "for safety's sake—"

I hold her by both hands. "You need to come with me, I need to know more."

She nods. "I'll follow you."

OWEN

After the email, Owen walked back to front door, which had a peephole. He kept himself as visible as possible. He still didn't want to freak her out.

He knocked again, this time hard. Heard a dog bark in the distance.

"Lucy? Hi. It's me, Owen Tanaka!" He was doing his best to remain upbeat.

He stepped to the side, peering around, then kept going over to the main window. Stepping into sodden bark dust, no match for his also Gore-Tex hiking shoes. He took another peek around the street—the last thing he needed was a neighbor with a pit bull or worse coming after him. What if Oregon was an open carry state, and what were the defense of property rules? Was it Multnomah County or state—

When he glanced back again at the dim living room, he thought he saw something move inside, someone rushing through. He ducked down. Sidestepped over to a corner of the window. Peeked in. His pulse racing, his chest thumping, not caring if a neighbor could see him.

He spotted a kitchen, back through the living room, barely illuminated by a sink window. Another shadow. Was it two? One unmoving. Another darted and bent down and he was bobbing up and down trying to see better but now the shadows were gone.

ALEX / LUCY

We use my planned route out the backyard, rushing through specific bushes and out via a neighbor's yard beyond. I lead and Silhouette Lady follows, watching our backs. We hear a dog bark but that's it.

Once we're out, I turn to her.

She's gone.

The woman shook me off, and deftly, too, like she knows these bushes better than me.

By the time I reach one street over, to continue my escape plan, I keep looking back. But it's like she was never there.

OWEN

He rushed to the side of the house. It had a high fence. He jumped up, but he couldn't pull himself over, so he planted his foot at the base of the two lowest branches of the closest tree; the branch snapped and the dog barked again.

"Crap."

He sprinted around to the other side of the house, found another fence there but this one was shorter, flimsy, bending his way when he grabbed it. And slippery it was so old.

It had a gate. Locked, though. He pulled himself up and grabbed the latch on the other side, flipped it up, dropped down, pushed the gate open, kept going.

The path led right around to a kitchen door, the rear exit. He stopped in his tracks, wondering about local laws again. What if someone had already called the cops? His breath steamed into the light rain. All he heard was that damn dog woofing, and some of the surrounding bushes and branches swaying in the wind that was picking up, flinging drops of rain.

He took a deep breath. He walked up to the door. Knocked, politely.

Nothing. He waited. Getting his lungs back.

"Lucy, it's me. It's just Owen Tanaka. You can open up if you're there . . ."

Nothing. He peeked in the kitchen back door window. The kitchen was small and spare, the dining table in the middle completely cleared. He spotted the open threshold to the living room. The floor equally spotless. Didn't exactly look lived in. He sighed at the thought. But he'd definitely seen shadows.

He took a deep breath. He waited for the dog to quiet, at least. He tried the doorknob.

It turned. He took another deep breath. He pushed the door open.

Listened.

"Lucy? It's just me . . ."

A shiver shot up his spine, making him gasp a little. He paused, midstep.

What if it wasn't Lucy he'd seen?

He listened again, got complete silence.

He stepped backward, feeling for the kitchen back door, and the first thing he found was the door lock. For some reason, for Lucy's own good surely, he turned the lock so that the door would shut behind him. He kept backing up and out and pulled the door shut. He tried it, to make sure. It wouldn't open now. Good, good. And something about that gave him hope, that he'd at least salvaged something from this.

SUNDAY–WEDNESDAY, NOVEMBER 19–22
ALEX / LUCY

I'm out, gone. Vamoose. Gone to the mattresses. It's two days later. I'm on a Greyhound bus now, afternoon, nothing but flat brown land and gray sky. It's a four-day odyssey east, Greyhound and Amtrak and bus again, alternating IDs every time, paid in cash. This was always the plan. I'm just doing it sooner, and it's not unexpected considering all that's going down so fast.

The final nail was when someone showed up at my front door unannounced—not soon after Silhouette Lady, waiting patiently at my back door, had found me. I was pissed at her for a second for leading someone here but she'd taken every precaution. Shame, though, because we'd just started having a nice little revealing chat that made me want to smash a window and curl up in a ball crying at the same time.

As I'd moved on down the street, I had that creeping feeling you get when you go on vacation and think you forgot something. Did I leave a burner on? Did I lock the back door? So much was going on, I really can't remember. And I will never know the truth of that, either, because I'm never going back there, and that was burning me up more than probably anything, the fact that I'll never be able to check that burner and possibly lock that door one last time. The tiniest things are the hugest tragedies.

For about two seconds. I'm already over it. It's not my door anymore, not my stove, not my house. Not even my city now. To be honest? I'm glad.

And then came the second tragedy. After Silhouette Lady vanished on me, I'd checked my email one last time before I gave up my normal phone for good, and I saw that none other than Owen Tanaka had emailed me right before someone showed at my house: He was in Portland, had a few questions. Leaving tomorrow. Wanted to meet up that very night?

Oh, Owen, you with your careful ways. Don't you know that they are extinct? He could've been the one who showed up at my house, but now I will never know. I sigh at the thought. That Owen would've made a fine investigative partner.

It's currently a cold and slate-gray November morning here somewhere in Utah or possibly Colorado and I'm curled up in a back seat of the bus all to myself, dressed like a near-homeless ex-junkie in my cheap hoodie and unwashed jeans and stocking cap and eyes red from tears. For the next stretch I'll have the foreigner-seeing-America-on-the-cheap look, all it takes is a few minor tweaks, all of which are in the go bags, including the hair dye. Some guy a couple seats up keeps farting meanwhile, though, and if he doesn't stop I might just have to break character and become the ex-con husband beater.

I think about Silhouette Lady again, for the millionth time. Man, she was good. Something about the way she spoke, so precisely, and moved, so efficiently for her build, it was like Chip. That made me wonder if she had military or cop experience or, gasp, might even be a fed. By that logic, her saying *I'll follow you* might just mean more than through the backyards. It might mean she'll continue to surveil me, even like this.

Two days later. I've passed through some truly gloomy Midwest weather, all black sky and sheets of sleet, then sharp bright sun, then dirty snow on the side of the road already, and I don't even want to think of what that portends. A long Amtrak, a cramped but cheap Chinatown bus, and now here I am: New York City baby.

It's Wednesday. Thanksgiving is looming tomorrow, with people coming and going in ways they don't normally, and I'm not sure if that helps or hurts. Screw it. I hit the ground running right off the bus and I'm on the street in my privileged NY grad student outfit, which truth be told isn't that different from what I sometimes wear on the job. I'm even carrying a yoga mat. At least I didn't get snowed in or out.

It's afternoon, not much colder than Portland, crisp blue sky. I really like my chunky new dark sunglasses. My name's Josie if anyone's asking. I keep thinking someone's going to ask because I have another creeping feeling that I'm being tailed. Silhouette Lady left that feeling with me—thanks a ton.

I zigzag plenty of blocks and check lots of window reflections just to make sure. I keep telling myself I'm only paranoid. That we're safe. Chip and I are on full burner phones and encrypted email and darknet and disguises now—the whole deal, for the one final job.

The problem is, I'm operating off-plan right now. The plan is supposed to be surveilling Mason Snead and his movements. But there's something I have to do. It's dragging me along, by industrial winch practically, a steel cable looped around my chest that keeps tightening.

I'm on the Upper East Side. I'm a block away now and my lungs are so tight they feel like they want to collapse. I'm regulating my breathing but it still sounds like wheezing. I turn the corner, slowly, walk the opposite sidewalk, side-eying across the street under my sunglasses. Trying to walk normal but inside it feels like I'm sprinting, then trudging along, sprinting again, slowing to keep myself in check. And there it is.

The brownstone from years before. Oh, I've researched it over the years. Don't get me wrong. There was once some kind of private club there, and as such it was all but vacant from any directories online or even in physical records. Some vague holding company owned it. But then it was vacated and sat dormant. It was sold ten years ago. It's been renovated. It now has a taut new, forest-green awning, a normal concierge, no doorman, and regular tenants. I watch a couple come and go. Man, if they only knew.

I realize I'm standing in the middle of the sidewalk and blocking everything like a tourist or a crazy person. A lady in a mink goes round me with her little dogs. "Sorry, go around," I mutter in a hopeless New York voice like I meant to be there, like I'm checking across the street to see if I left my apartment light on or something.

Now my chest wants to burst, like it's full of air. I let out a big sigh. And, to my surprise, I smile, a big grin that stays on my face all the way to the next corner.

I needed that, I realize. Just needed to see it. I'd never visited it in the flesh so long after the fact. It had always been blurred on Street View, not surprising since any user can submit a request to have a home, a car, or even themselves obscured. And then I had stopped looking. I just didn't want to know. If the building were still dormant, I would've pitched to Chip that we use it for our next Show Game, so poetic that would be in its justice. But we have a different plan for the next show.

Minutes later, I'm sitting in a coffee shop having a turmeric tea just blocks away, still owning my past like a motherfucker. I'm not grinning now, but I'm sitting at the window and looking out in full view, just people-watching with glee like a tourist. If I see that big oaf of a creepy doorman, maybe I'll just spill my hot tea on him for the jolly fuck of it. Thinking of him and Mason Snead now makes me think of his creepy-as-hell right-hand woman, Viktoria Jett, which makes me think of Silhouette Lady again.

And my hint of a smile drops like a concrete block in the Hudson River, and I slump in my chair. I still can't believe what Silhouette Lady had told me. This is all even worse than I thought. They will get away with it, forever. That sick bastard or one of his cronies will probably even run for president someday and privatize everything like some asshole from an Ayn Rand novel. No regulations! Abuse away! Silhouette Lady's look was not helping her credibility, though, with her rumpled clothes and her shortish hair frizzing. If I only had a photo of her, I could do an image search and learn who she is.

Silhouette Lady also really threw me a loop by naming Viktoria Jett as her daughter. Though I wasn't surprised that Viktoria Jett was not the real name of Mason Snead's number one. I wouldn't have been surprised to hear that he suggested such a preposterous name himself, and she of course had obliged, because why not? She was already all in, already completely sold on his bullshit and had made it her own. Even though she is a woman. It won't be easy finding out Viktoria Jett's full name as there will certainly be no original records if I know my Mason Snead. But I will find out in time.

I turn away from the window, my jaw grinding away like I have a bitter taste in my mouth. I should've spent more time looking into Viktoria Jett. She had come after, so I hadn't. No time. And there is now so much to do. I have to get everything right. I take a deep breath with my head down. My few moments together with Silhouette Lady in my dark house are so vivid now, it's like I'm sitting right at my kitchen table instead of here in this café. Even the light outside suddenly seems to darken. Then it's like someone poured my hot tea onto my own face. My face burns, the backs of my eyeballs red-hot, too, and I face the realization all over again. I remember every word that Silhouette Lady had said.

He hurt you, didn't he? she'd said. Meaning Mason Snead, of course.

She had proceeded to tell me what she could. *Whatever horrors that you're imagining? About the evil of Mason Snead and his ilk? They're only the tip of the iceberg.*

Far worse than you fear, she'd told me.

. . . think of the worst, then double it. The truth is the opposite. All victims are not the object to be helped, but to be exploited.

Silhouette Lady and I were really getting somewhere. Then someone knocked on my kitchen back door. Owen, was that you? And Silhouette Lady and I hit the floor of my kitchen. And we scrambled, went our own ways.

But I have the cruel gist of it now: it all stemmed from Mason Snead.

I thought I was taking down a gargantuan monster when I exposed Gerald Hartwell, but I was only scratching at the surface, like tearing a piece of bark off a giant, hundred-year-old tree. And what did I get for it? An innocent woman dead, his wife. And the rest of the world thinking a great injustice has been righted. Hell, Mason Snead probably even applauded. And in fact he had: I remember how he had praised it all so much on FreeChain.

I'd already realized I'd have to go after Snead myself, that I can't run from it. And now Silhouette Lady is giving me even more reason. I cannot, not ever, back out.

This realization of it all had been getting up on top of me during that odyssey across the country, practically smothering me like that unending granite sky covered American's vast exposed plains, a leaden gravity blanket over a sleeping infant and it's nothing like a hug.

The memory of that now makes me push my tea away here in this café. I go over everything again, comparing, recombining, starting with Chip coming to see me with such remorse and ending with Silhouette Lady telling me that she will follow me.

Her warning about wearing a fed disguise sticks in my craw. Was she talking about the possibility of it, as in general, or had she known that I had used an FBI disguise before?

Only a few people could have known that. And they were all my victims.

Except for one.

I feel a tugging inside my gut, but sharpish, like a hook.

Chip!

I rush out the door.

I find Chip's Ford Transit van after he gives me the location by encrypted message. It's down near Battery Park, on a back street, but we both know he can't stay there long with its proximity to One World Trade Center and other landmarks. Too conspicuous. But Chip had sighted Mason Snead taking meetings in tall glass buildings full of money that had doubled in value after the pandemic from all the wheeling and dealing and predatory manipulation.

This isn't a planned meet. I don't tell Chip why I'm coming. He just unlocks the door when I'm in close range and I step in.

He's in the back, slouched in one of his two fold-up lawn chairs with green-and-white webbing like something out of 1975, but they're brand-new, a real find. I take the other chair. It's stuffy in here and a little sour-stale from his few items of dirty laundry, I'm guessing. I sigh at that. It's dark inside, too, despite the up-front windows, because Chip now has a shower curtain behind the front seats as a partition, all pineapples and flowers. He's got a high-end cooler, too, and his foam pad covering this floor that he sleeps on resembles sand in this light.

"All you need is a palm tree and you're good to go," I joke, trying to break the ice. I had calmed down on the way over. Stopped along the esplanade and stared across the Hudson for a few minutes, letting the late-afternoon New Jersey horizon blur. Maybe none of this is what I'm afraid it is. Maybe there's a great explanation. But I'm going to have to broach the subject.

He looks at me from his chair like I've just spoken Magyar. He only shrugs.

The rest of his gear is stowed away shipshape, I see, always ready to go any second. He's got a go bag, too, a new high-end tactical job. I'd normally ask him how many compartments and pouches it has, but I'm in no more mood than he is.

"How's it going?" I say.

"I saw Snead and that Viktoria Jett enter and exit one bank building. Now they're in that financial center across the street."

I look across to street level, one of those smaller bagel chains catering to the white-collar grunt workers. Then I look straight up from it, and keep going. The glass must reach fifty stories. I'm assuming that Snead and Viktoria are up there somewhere at the highest point, where the sun's glare in my eyes starts to blind me and blur the glass.

"We have a problem," I say.

Chip sits up, nodding, and pulls his hands from the pockets of his fleece. He raises his chin and resets it in a harder position.

I'm going to get right to the point. It's what he always advises. Plus I need to do it while I'm still calm. I don't exactly care for all the surly attitude Chip is bouncing off the inside of this van.

"You're two-timing," I say.

He stares at me a moment. He shakes his head, not denying it, more like I'm speaking Magyar again.

"A woman came to see me. At my own house."

Now his eyes widen. About time. "I . . . don't understand."

"She wouldn't tell me her name. Who she works for. She wouldn't tell me how she knows. But she knows. She was good, no slouch. Discreet contact, all via the back door."

Chip's face is still a mask, but the chin is losing shape and those eyes are widening even more. "I'm not sure where you're going with this."

"You're not, not at all? She says her daughter is Viktoria Jett."

Chip sighs, then shifts in his chair, which creaks. That's it. The final tell. I was expecting something more dramatic, to be honest.

We sit in near dark silence a while. We're both staring at the foam padding.

"My guess is she's a cop or similar," I say eventually. "She had fed written all over her."

We hear a siren far in the distance, police, and listen to it fade. Leave it to NYC to hammer it home.

"Hayley Gonzalez," Chip says after a while.

I stare at him now but he still can't look at me. "Who?"

"That's Viktoria Jett's real name. I'll spare you the research."

"Thanks."

"Her mom, that's Berta Gonzalez. She's FBI."

I can feel the heat in my fists and face, but it's draining fast. I'm cold in seconds. "Fuck, Chip."

"She's semiretired," he adds.

"That's reassuring. How? Why?"

"Always have backup," he says.

"She come to you, or vice versa?"

Chip only side-eyes me but then I realize he's still doing his job—watching the exits through the dark window that he'd darkened even more with window tinting.

"I was getting worried . . . as to whether Conrad Holmes would spill the beans about me to the feds," he says after a couple seconds. "So. I knew Berta from way back. She was a special teams liaison, FBI-CIA. I made discreet contact."

I sigh before I can stop it. "You did it in DC, I'm guessing? When you tried going back for your van."

Now *he* sighs. "She was reluctant at first. She knew I was a . . . had gone AWOL. But I also knew that Viktoria was her daughter. Long estranged. Not many know about that."

"Well, this sure is plenty to take in . . . So *did* he? Holmes, I mean."

"What, spill the beans? No. That's the irony. He hadn't told them I was part of the Show Game—at least, that was what Berta confirmed for me. She did say Holmes had requested that they, the authorities I mean, go lenient on us, whoever 'we' are. Quite contrite, our Conrad."

"Yeah, right."

"No, get this: He's fully repented, apparently. He even told them how he really lost his arm. He wants to pay the price."

"I'll still believe it when I see it. Why haven't you told me?"

"Haven't exactly seen you, have I? Plus I didn't want to dump anything incriminating into our communications, not even over the dark web. You never know."

"Huh," I say, shaking my head, genuinely amazed.

"Go ahead," Chip says. "Let yourself believe it: he wouldn't have come clean if we hadn't done what we did. To him."

I can't tell if I'm proud or sad at how pathetic we humans are. How have we even, somehow, gotten this far? You'd think the earth would simply stop spinning in protest. I shake my head again. That thought only confirms that it's sadness I'm feeling. Maybe it's because this, my sensible little confrontation, is now suddenly sounding like a major breakup.

"So I guess you're off the hook," I mutter.

"Luce, she's doing us a favor," Chips says finally.

"Don't call me that."

"Sorry, Jane," he says, as in *Jane Doe*, my brand-new Show Game name. I've killed off Alex. No more ambiguity. This final episode will reveal that its creator is a woman, which has been the plan all along. At least that's still on track.

"How long?" I ask him. "Have you been tipping her off all along?"

"No. It's not like that. We've only made brief, nonrevealing contact. She cares first and foremost about her daughter. She wants to save her somehow. Appeal to her. But she'll arrest her first if she has to."

"So, this Berta, she does approve of what we're doing?"

"Yes. Yes, she does."

Suddenly I'm waving my hands around, my chair creaking and wobbling. "Well, I got news for you all. That just makes her an accomplice! FBI or no—"

"Calm down," Chip says.

"You calm down. I'm the one who has to deal with this from here on out."

"True—"

"I'm the one who's going to have to keep this alive, juggling it all; then there's that reporter, Tanaka. Good dude, but unfortunately he also happens to work for Mason Snead—"

"Wait." Chip sits up, his voice raising too. "Who? What?"

"Owen Tanaka. Don't worry. He's just a reporter; okay, maybe he is an investigative reporter. He got hired for Snead's new *FreeChain News* thing."

"Snead hired him, you mean. You never told me about that. Jesus."

"Don't worry." I sputter a bitter laugh at the very thought. "Poor guy, this Owen. I think he's got more of an interest than he even knows. And you know what? I don't think he's let anyone at *FreeChain News* know a thing, let alone Viktoria Jett or Mason Snead and . . ." I freeze up. Grab the chair arms. My head rotates slowly toward Chip, as if on a swivel. "Wait, what did you say?"

"Nothing. When?"

"I said I'm gonna have to deal with this from here on out, and you, you said: *True.*"

Chip nods. He takes a peek outside, ever diligent. Then his eyes return to me and he doesn't take them off me. Unblinking.

"I'm going to complete our surveillance," he says, "so that you can take it from here. But I'm done. I'm done, Lucy."

"Oh." My head lowers. The inside of the van spins a moment, and I have to hold on to the chair arms. I take deep breaths. This wasn't how it was going to go down at all. I was going to set him straight. We were going to patch up this Berta Gonzalez thing. We might even have had to trick her, send her on a wild goose chase. We wouldn't have needed much. We were so close now.

"Come on," he says softly, "you can't tell me you were not suspecting it."

"We were so close," I mutter.

"And we still are. You are." To my surprise, he puts a hand on mine, and it's soft, and it's warm. "She's my gift to you," he says.

"Who is?"

"Berta. It's an upgrade. I was unhappy anyways."

"No shit." I yank my hand away. I cross my arms on my chest like some pissed-off sorority girl and I hate myself for it already.

"Don't be like that, come on . . ."

I take another deep breath. I loosen my arms. He watches and waits until I've let it sink in.

"What does that mean, she's your gift to me?" I say.

"Like I said: always have backup. I wasn't going to leave you without help."

"Help? How's she going to help?"

"I don't know exactly," Chip says. "You'll have to feel her out."

"Great. That's just great. Why, though? You still haven't told me why."

Chip waits to watch a town car pull up and unload a couple men in suits slapping each other on their backs. "Gross," I mutter.

He fixes his eyes back on me. "Did you know I had a wife?" he says.

"No. I didn't know that."

"We're divorced. Good thing, too, because with all this going on? She'd just assume I was having an affair. Anyways, I've made contact."

That's another risk he's taken, but I don't scold him for it. Who am I to talk, anyway? I've been stringing this Owen Tanaka along in secret like he's in line to be the next Chip.

Chip's eyes are full of gravitas, but there's also a twinkle in them. "Did you know that I have a daughter of my own? She's eight now—"

I rise up, out of my chair, and stand over Chip, pointing in his face. "Exactly! You have a daughter. That's exactly why you should stick with me."

"That may be true, but—"

"See!" I lower my pointing finger, take a step back, give him some room. "Maybe we can talk this out, go get a beer in disguise to celebrate. Okay, so you have a source or whatever she is and she happens to be FBI, and her daughter is Viktoria Jett. So what. We'll make it work. More the fucking merrier—"

"I'm not finished speaking," he adds now. Chip's eyes are filling with actual wetness, something I've never seen before, and his voice is squeaking a little. "I mean, what if my daughter doesn't have a dad?"

"Oh," I mutter for the second time. I find my way back to my chair. I have no response, which is nearly as maddening as the rest of it. I always have a response. I flop up one arm for a second, but that's about it.

"Berta will find you," Chip says after a while, his voice soft. "I'll help her find you if need be. Is that all right?"

"Sure," I say absently, like I'm talking in my sleep, "sure, man."

"You have to trust it."

"Sure."

"Anyway, I do have some good news," he adds. "Viktoria is usually the only security Snead has nearby. Physically anyway. That's all I'm seeing. Sometimes he doesn't even use her."

"That's because he's cocky. Thinks he's fucking invincible. Well, fuck him."

I'm practically snarling it.

Chip only nods, then waits for me to come back around. It takes a minute or five, but we get there. The dim light helps. Soon we're staring at each other, nodding, a little smile on each of our faces in recognition of all we've accomplished together.

"That was one wild ride," he says.

"Yes, it sure was. I'll never reveal your identity, if it comes to that. Ever."

"Thank you. Me neither."

"Thank you, for everything."

This should be the happy part, the bittersweet goodbye, but then his smile vanishes and his face darkens.

"We are what we're becoming," he says. "Me, I was getting scared of who I'm becoming. And you should be too."

WEDNESDAY, NOVEMBER 22
OWEN

Owen had returned to New York City the previous Sunday, the day after pulling Lucy Holden's back door shut again. It was now Wednesday evening. Thanksgiving Eve. He was holed up in his office at *FreeChain News*. He still hadn't told anyone that Lucy Holden had to be running the Show Game. He should have been reporting it to Mason Snead, or at least to Viktoria Jett. It wasn't just about getting fired. This alone could be seen as criminal conspiracy, it might be argued.

Other updates from his team only confirmed it. Martin Podest had only been on another road trip with his beefed-up Ural, this time up in the woods of BC, and the last of the Scouts' parents had finally checked in to say all was well and Martin did indeed have an alibi for the other Show Game. Even DeAndre Jarvis checked out, in more ways than one. He'd been in a mental health facility this whole time and likely wasn't coming back out. Yet another casualty of senseless wars. No wonder Martin was so angry.

Lucy becoming the mastermind behind the Show Game certainly fit. It was getting back at those, men mainly, who abused power and money and corruption for their own perverse ends. She had turned vigilante after seeing her younger brother abused and then, later, certain female colleagues working for Snead. This was confirmed by Anne Blade. He, meanwhile, had also learned that Snead's own organizations were practically fronts, that Mason Snead was the front man for himself. The latter meant following the money, but Owen still didn't have anything more on Snead that matched what he'd learned from his research and working his sources from that hotel in Portland. He was becoming desperate.

Most every staffer had left for the day now as well, on account of the holiday. Owen was holed up for a reason. He was waiting. He waved goodbye from his office to the staffers leaving.

And still he waited, eyeing the deserted open office layout, looking more like an office furniture showroom than an actual office. He picked up his ukulele. He strummed it, but mechanically, just random strings like some carnival automaton on the fritz. Biding his time.

On Monday, his first morning back, he had learned from his excited investigative team that Snead now had an office right there in *FreeChain News*. It was probably just for show, Owen figured. Snead had only been in the office once, as far as the team knew—to do an advance interview about the new organization. But then Lucian, the thoughtful Black kid from Queens who liked to wear that camo hunting cap, told Owen about something weird—not on chat but in person, whispering. Snead, Lucian told him, had stayed in that new office of his one evening, all alone and presumably working, until after the last of the team had left around nine p.m.

And then something even weirder happened.

Earlier this very evening, Gina had come to see Owen in his office. Gina, the go-getter with the big-framed, Florida-retiree glasses. She'd done a great job confirming details about Martin Podest and others, as well as researching voice changers like the one used for the Show Game. Owen had been working away at his desk. He didn't even notice her come in. He simply looked up and there she was on his sofa, staring at the floor.

"Hi, Gina. Hey, thanks again for looking into that altered voice stuff for me."

She opened her mouth to speak, but nothing came out.

Owen sat up. "Are you all right? Wait. How long have you been here?"

She tried shrugging, but that only made her chin quiver.

Owen looked out around the open newsroom. Most everyone else looked like they'd left for the day. Maybe she'd been waiting for that.

"It's okay," he said in a lower voice. "Take your time."

She nodded. She stood, eventually. She turned to leave, her arms hanging at her sides.

"Wait."

She turned to him, slowly, as if on a swivel.

The look in her eyes made Owen wince. They stared right through him. It scared him so bad he blurted, "Look, now you're freaking me out."

She shook her head.

He lowered his voice. "Come over here. Jesus."

She floated over to him, like on rails. That gave him a shiver. She arrived at his desk. He waited for her words to land. Her chin quivered some more and she gulped back tears.

"Take it easy," he told her. "Just take your time."

She nodded, pulled herself together. "I can't tell you, not exactly," she said finally. "I thought I could, but . . ."

"You're distraught. That's okay. Why don't you go on home. Tell me if you feel like it."

She had nodded again, but it came out with a grimace, like all her teeth had been replaced. Her eyes even wider now. She'd turned to leave.

"Wait." Owen had stood. He couldn't help himself. "You'll have to throw me a bone, something. I'm sorry, it's what I do."

Gina had stood in the doorway. Her arm had raised, mechanically, as if by a wire. It was pointing toward Mason Snead's imitation new office. "His . . . computer," was all she'd said, and then had wandered off, through the newsroom, out the door.

Owen now got another shiver just recalling it. Now he wondered if maybe Mason Snead was using that office to do some work off the radar? Something that might lead Owen to a money trail never before known. This was how desperate he was becoming. And this was how stupid. Because now, at the end of his two days back, and with everyone else gone home, Owen decided to resort to entering that office. It was crazy, he knew. There might be a camera somewhere. But he couldn't spot any camera. And Viktoria Jett had herself told them on the team chat that the building didn't have any—they wanted their employees to feel protected from the constant surveillance of the rest of the world. Which might hold all the more reason for Mason Snead to do his straw man work in there. Unlike the few glass-walled offices here, Snead's did have a door.

Still, they were practically asking Owen to try it.

He texted Molly, just a simple text, not telling her what he had in mind: *Should I do it?*

Her text, within five minutes: *You know the answer to that.*

And so he tried the door. It opened. And he went in.

The office had frosted glass chest-high and was as spare as could be, as he could tell from out on the floor when advancing toward it. It was simply a standard office chair, a desk, and an iMac like those distributed throughout the open floor for anyone to use. It was also spotless. Owen saw no beverage marks or spills or even dust atop the desk, no smudges on the black screen gone to sleep. Owen ran a finger along the top of the square clock on the wall and came up with no dust even there. It was like Mason Snead had wiped the room down before he left.

Owen peeked out onto the floor. Still no one. Gina had been the last to leave. It was now 8:17 p.m. The cleaning people wouldn't be coming for at least a couple hours, if they were even coming at all before the holiday. Though if someone spotted him or questioned him, such as security (did they have any here? he wasn't sure), he would simply stall by saying he didn't know whose office it was and he was checking it out for a possible switch of offices. He pulled open the two drawers in the desk. Nothing. Completely empty, and just as spotless, never been used. He clicked the mouse.

The desktop flashed on. To Owen's surprise, Snead didn't even have his own user account. There was one account, called simply "User." It wasn't protected by password, and the desktop setup looked default. He opened Mail. It had never been used. Same for the other apps. He opened Photos.

"What the? . . ."

He took a step back, wheezing. His heart thumping.

He checked the floor. Still no one. He blinked at the screen, refocused.

He saw photo after photo of girls, little girls. Anywhere from ages twelve to eighteen, he guessed. Most were naked or close to it. The positions were mostly compromising, showing their most private parts exposed. Some were smiling, but most had a dull look on their faces as if they were exhausted or worse. A few showed fear. Some wore COVID masks. Many photos showed them being assaulted by men in various ways, sick ways, unimaginable ways. The men were often older, much older, well older than Owen even, and some could be his grandfather. Most were naked, too, though the ones clothed always had more on than the girls. The men had gray hair, sagging skin, and faces full of joy, or lust, or hate. There were often two or more to a girl.

Owen couldn't stop staring. Refocusing. There were a little over three thousand photos in the Photo Library, from well before the pandemic and right on through, as confirmed by the girls in masks. All Owen's muscles had tensed up. A heat had surged through his body that recombined in various places as anger, deep sadness, resolve—in his chest, his throat, his head, his fists. Many of the men's faces were blurred out, but never the girls'. Some of the men's faces weren't, though, and Owen made himself scan them even though he was gritting his teeth so hard he thought one of his molars might crack. He recognized a couple of the men. Powerful men. Famous men.

And then his gut was swelling and pinching tight at the same time, an implosion of hot metal right in his stomach. He wheezed, his head spinning, that fire rising up his throat.

Owen shut the door to Mason Snead's new office slowly, silently, a sickening nausea swelling in his abdomen. He continued on through the open offices with his head down, trying to stop the spinning, the bitter acidic taste rising up his throat like the worst heartburn imaginable.

He rushed into the restrooms in case he had to vomit. He pushed a stall door open. He flung the toilet lid up and knelt down to it, his mouth hanging open.

But nothing happened. He only gasped, and gasped, and his insides calmed down.

He stood up, eventually. Leaned against the wall.

He started, from another jolt—he'd left the photos open on screen!

He rushed back through the offices and entered the room with his head down and one arm up like a fireman entering a smoke-filled room and he closed the photos and for good measure wiped his fingerprints off the mouse and keyboard and desk and door handle with the hem of his shirt. Like he was the fucking sociopath reprobate himself. This made him want to vomit all over again.

Owen walked out. He wandered south, street after street after street as if distance itself were a disinfectant for his infection, the surrounding darkness shrinking all contagions. He ended up in the Old Town Bar, the same one where Anne Blade had gone after she was fired. Eighteenth Street close to Union Square wasn't exactly on the way home, but he didn't do so out of any tribute. It was the first place his hot, blurring, teary eyes wandering through the night could focus on. But such was the irony of life. The bar was half full and all dark wood inside and it might have been 1890. He sat at the end of the long bar, in the semi-darkness, and drank a double shot of neat well whiskey and a pint of cheap beer like one of those worn-down old journalists he'd never wanted to become. The only thing missing was the menthol cigarette. He chuckled at that, but then his eyes lowered back to the bartop again.

He thought about that so-called office of Mason Snead's again, about the meaning of that. For the fiftieth fucking time. He kept coming to the same conclusion:

Mason Snead thought he was so powerful no one could touch him, even if they did see his photos. It was almost like a test. Come and get it. What are you going to do about me? Nothing.

Why did he do it? *Because he can.*

Owen took a pull off his whiskey and it burned again and the fire down his throat gave him the sick thought that Snead having an office like that might even have been Viktoria Jett's idea.

By the second whiskey, his brain had calmed down, and slowed, and a sadness slowly washed over him like an oil slick weighing down tropical blue seawater. He felt like the bird trapped in it. He was a reporter, sure, but where to even start with this? He wanted to tell someone, anyone, but who? He couldn't tell Molly. It would only sadden her more than anger her. Stories remotely like this were part of what had dragged down their marriage.

Like all sad and slightly drunk people in every bar practically the world over, he checked his phone, for a text or email, maybe an AP Breaking News notification mercilessly announcing the end of the planet on account of a giant meteor about to strike any moment. Something, please. No such luck. He noticed the latest Out of Office reply from Lucy Holden after he'd tried her again early today. He was trying her every day on this or that pretext, and today he'd finally just emailed her that he had stopped by her place in Portland last Saturday. Still nothing came back but her automated reply.

He kept arriving at the same thought, and it made him nod with bitter recognition.

What's more important now, exposing Lucy Holden or Mason Snead?

"Fuck," he muttered under his breath. The bar was nearly empty now, the bartender far at the other end chatting with a local. It was so dark back where he was, Owen could swear someone had turned off some of the lights. He liked it that way. He sipped. Submerged in a black fog.

He felt something. Someone. A person had sat next to him, despite ninety-nine percent of the long bar being open. He shrugged at that. "Hey," he said.

"Evening."

It was a woman.

* * *

She had brought her own drink over, two actually—exactly what he was having.

Huh. Owen shifted his eyeballs around, searching the dim light for any reflections he could spot, trying to sneak a look at her. He had no angle, so he finally just dropped a shoulder and looked at her like drunk people do.

She had shorter hair, salt and peppery, nice eyes. She was staring back at him with them. She was probably midfifties, with a certain presence to her, and he told himself she looked smart as well.

Owen held up his whiskey. "Good choice," he said, late in coming like drunk people do.

Then she did the funniest thing. She took her eyes off him and turned to the long room, watching it, even though even few patrons were here.

"Thanks, Owen," she said. "It is Owen, right? Owen Tanaka?"

Owen didn't do a spit take or fall off his stool, but close. He gave a little gasp that unfortunately leaked a little saliva that he had to wipe away with his thumb. It also made him sit upright again on his stool.

The woman waited a moment for him to compose himself. She spoke in a low but firm voice.

"You know Lucy Holden? From Portland, Oregon. Private investigator."

It was now like someone had turned up all the lights, closing time. Owen might have even squinted from it. He didn't reply. He glared at the woman. He felt instantly sober, or at least halfway there.

"Don't make a big deal about it, please. I simply asked you a question."

Owen stared at his whiskey and beer a moment and mentally pushed them away.

"Yes, I'm Owen Tanaka. Who are you?"

As he asked the question Owen finally found the woman's profile in the bar mirror. It showed the other side of her face.

"What happened to your face?" he blurted before she could answer.

Her right eye was swollen and red, soon to blossom with all the colors of a bruise.

"Never mind that," she said.

Owen, still not quite sober, sputtered a laugh. "Which part? Who you are, what happened to you?"

She turned to him, her face hard. It obviously didn't hurt, or at least she wasn't letting it show. She took a large draw on the whiskey and then the beer as if to prove it.

"Not here," she said.

She pushed a beer coaster over to him. It had an address written on it, around the edge.

Owen nodded at it.

"Meet me here, as soon as you can. Can you get there? Good. But don't rush it. I'll go first. Give me about ten minutes. Make sure no one's following you. Do you know how to do that? Double good. And don't drink any more of that."

"Okay."

With that, she downed the rest of her whiskey and beer. Owen wasn't going to object—she surely needed it more than him after what had happened to her.

She patted the bar twice, stood, took a deep breath that sounded more like a sigh, and left the bar. Owen noticed right away that she was limping, and he hoped that she didn't have more of those bruises on the rest of her. The bartender waved good night but didn't look up from his local. Owen watched her steady herself along the bar as she went, in a way that looked like a drunk to someone not in the know. Owen could see she was stiff, sore.

"Okay," he repeated and pushed away his beer and whiskey. He committed the address to memory, tore up the edge of the beer coaster to destroy the address, and checked the time.

It wasn't just dark now. It was cold out, too, shockingly so, a sudden plunge that made Owen's heart race, and he wished he'd brought the quilted Thinsulate liner jacket that zipped into his raincoat. The address was a nondescript apartment in the East Village, a fifteen-minute walk from the bar, Owen passing happy or at least hopeful NYU students from all ranks of life. Owen rang the bell and was buzzed in without a conversation. A rare walk-up, third floor. Climbing the stairs made his alcohol-soaked head throb and his lungs strain like he'd climbed twenty floors. But he proceeded like an automaton, not halting, not questioning. Apartment 3B. The door was open. He stepped inside. It was furnished plainly but with cheap new trendy pieces, like an Airbnb or maybe a for-sale unit being staged. It then occurred to him that this might be a safe house. He realized he was even farther from his home. What if he never made it home again? What if he couldn't text Molly? That made his heart race, and the booze made it worse.

He stood in the middle of the main room, on hardwood floors, all the walls white, and the only discernible smell was possibly fresh paint. The only other rooms were a small kitchen and bathroom. The one window was well blocked by a darkening shade. There was no bed, though the sturdy blocky sofa was likely a hide-a-bed.

"Hello?" he said finally.

"Anyone follow you?" he heard from the kitchen. It was the woman.

"No. Nope. I've worked with sources before."

The woman entered the room holding an ice pack. "I'm not a source," she said.

"Okay."

"Water," she said, nodding toward the kitchen.

"I'm okay."

"It wasn't a question. Glasses above the sink."

"Oh. All right."

Owen proceeded into the cramped kitchen space and poured himself water from the fridge, suddenly feeling sheepish if not a little cowed. He had met with plenty of sources in private before who were wrecks physically and mentally, and he couldn't help thinking that now the tables were turned. He took a deep breath, regained a little steel, and strode back out into the main room.

"I'm not a source either," he declared.

"Sit," was all she said. She was sitting on the sofa, holding the ice pack to her face.

A simple wood and faux leather armchair stood at an angle to the sofa, a cheap little oval coffee table between them. As Owen sat in the armchair, she wrapped the ice pack into place using a scarf. This made her look like Elephant Man and Owen even more uncomfortable.

"Who did this to you?" Owen asked her.

She only shrugged. "First things first."

"But you're all right? Can I get you anything?"

"I'm fine."

"So am I," Owen quipped.

They shared a chuckle at that, quite the icebreaker.

Then the woman's face opened up, and the smile faded. "I thought you might know how to contact Lucy."

She went on, "I made first contact with her a few days ago." She told Owen how she'd gone to Lucy's house in Portland,

STEVE ANDERSON

just recently. "We got rudely interrupted, had to break it off. I'd always had access to her movements, more or less. Now I've lost that, too, at least for now. So I'm coming to you."

Owen didn't respond. He had set his glass on the coffee table. He was holding out for more, though he didn't like the taut yet creeping feeling in his gut. The woman stared at Owen a moment, firmly but with a concern in her eyes like he was a little boy she was going to tell a grandparent had died. One end of her scarf hung down the side of her lopsided ice pack head.

"I'm going to tell you," she continued, "because a reporter like you would find out anyway, my name is Berta Gonzalez. I'm with the FBI—or was. Semiretired. My daughter is Viktoria Jett."

Owen's eyes widened so much he could feel the dry air on them.

Berta said, "It's a lot, I know. Her real name, or at least birth name, is Hayley. Gonzalez. Just listen. Bear with me. I'm going to tell you what I told Lucy, even more of it, actually, because she and I didn't end up getting much quality time the other night."

"Oh. All right." Owen took a quick drink of water.

"Your new boss is Mason Snead," Berta said. "What do you know about him?"

Owen told her what he'd summarized in the little report he'd written up. She nodded to confirm his findings, but it was a slow, grave, brooding nod.

"Mason Snead and his conspirators, they're far worse than you might think. Way worse. It's not just that he's a fraud, or that he and they launder money, and it's not about the money trail. That's just the means. It's not even that they blackmail whoever's susceptible—priests, politicians, the rich and powerful. Seduce the most powerful. Your Sir Hartwells of the world. He, they, exploit the opportunity double. Snead is actually funding and

218

perpetrating more of it. And he's using his organizations and nonprofits as covers to do even more. Set them up for blackmail, for example, by hooking them up with young girls and boys. That or whatever the weakness may be."

A series of questions were already scrolling in Owen's head. He wished he had his notepad. Mason Snead had powerful friends, which meant he had sadistic thugs at his disposal. Any one of them could've sent Berta that message to her body. Owen, with a shudder, then realized that it could have even been Viktoria Jett herself giving the orders.

"Why did they do that to you?" Owen said.

"Someone must suspect that I know more than I do. I have been looking into, uh, things, for a while now. Well before the Show Game. Snead, he has people everywhere. Could even be from inside the bureau."

"Did they say anything?"

Berta shrugged. "It was like the movie version. There I was in a parking structure, all alone. Some big guy appears out of nowhere, beats the crap out of me, and when I'm on the ground he says in my ear, 'Stay in your lane, Gonzalez.'"

"What exactly do you know? How does Lucy fit in?"

"Lucy had worked for UnVest, years ago. You might know that by now. The team she worked on at UnVest, it was really meant to corrupt priests further, and to make them pay up of course. Now #AllGood would take this into every realm. You name it. World hunger, developing countries' health care, gun control. UnVest made WikiLeaks's betrayal look like a gouging lemonade stand. Whatever the cause was, Snead would appropriate it, exploit it, defile it."

"What about LifeForce? The org run by Gerald Hartwell?"

"Oh, that," Berta said. "That was basically just a subsidiary, huge as it was—is. I mean the sex trafficking one."

"But Hartwell didn't name the one big name: Mason Snead."

"Yeah, and why do you think Hartwell didn't?"

Owen held up a finger. "To protect him. He threw others under the bus to protect Mason Snead."

"Correct! You get an A."

Berta continued, "Gerald Hartwell was diverting as best as he could. Tough spot, though. He was avoiding worse repercussions. Mason Snead, you see, could and can sic his powerful partners on him."

"Going with the lesser evil, as it were."

"Yep."

"So Conrad Holmes was warning us in a general sense, while Hartwell was hinting in a specific sense, in his way," Owen said.

"Double yep. It's a funnel to the truth. Lucy, she was on to something. Is still. But she has no idea just how big. Mason Snead was and is Al Capone posing as the fucking pope of the tech economy, new media, sharing economy, social media, whatever you want to call it. All the same old snake oil."

Berta batted at her hanging scarf like it was a snake hanging down.

Owen held up his own hand. It was like he had a question, but he didn't. This was simply too much. This was the logical evolution of a cynicism and nihilism that had infected developed societies since the beginning of the Enlightenment and classical Liberalism had festered into a full-grown virus. Talk about a major pandemic.

"Do you want me to stop?" Berta said.

"Yes. No."

"I know what you're thinking: you want to ask a question but no question can begin to make sense of it. Right? They might as well be cannibals, Owen. #AllGood cannibalized itself. It says it's a nonprofit corps but that's just part of the big lie. It might as well be a crooked church. The money gets funneled into all types of corrupt operations. More money comes in from corrupt operations. Similarly, they have laundering partners abroad, from many countries. This didn't just evolve. Someone got greedy or more degenerate or whatever. It was planned from the start. Cloaked the whole time."

"But Mason Snead wasn't just born fully formed," Owen said.

"No. Though there is a progression from rapist to black-mailer to, today, full-on sex trafficker for the rich and powerful. Need I point out the final, ultimate expression of this? Mason Snead was part of a deadly wheel of degradation that turns and turns, degrading more and more with each revolution."

Owen picked up the water, then put it down. He wished it was that whiskey he'd left behind; he had such a horrible taste in his mouth that needed dousing. Normally he would've been inclined to question all this, to have to confirm. But he had also just seen what was on Mason Snead's computer.

He told Berta what he'd seen, what had driven him to that bar.

Berta only shook her head. "He thinks no one can touch him. Hell, he probably wanted someone to find it. They look? Then they're implicated too. Incriminated. That's what they do to people. Pull them in so that they feel trapped. If they have any scruples at all, that is." Berta pushed the ice pack back into place, staring at Owen. "Tell me you didn't leave any traces?"

"I wiped it all down. There's no cameras in there, either, as far as I know."

"Good. Okay."

"That Snead," Owen said, "he might as well be the priest that fucked Lucy's little brother."

"Owen, it's worse than that—"

"Why aren't you investigating?" he blurted, cutting her off. "The bureau, I mean? Whoever? You meeting like this, this doesn't exactly say funded operation."

"No. Why do you think, Owen? We've tried, believe me."

"They're too powerful, you mean."

"That's right."

He had more questions and she kept answering before he could get them out, interrupting right when his mouth opened like she was receiving a readout of his mind in an earpiece.

"Why now, why—"

"I told you. I lost access."

"How long have you—"

"Since before Lucy, or her current plans at least. I had to be discreet for all the reasons I've just mentioned."

"So it had come up—"

"In the bureau? Yes. More than once. But it kept getting squashed, buried. And they didn't know the half of it."

"Who did that—"

She flung a hand at her scarf, making it swing. "You want to know who did this to me? I don't know either. But we'll have to expect the worst. It's a warning. They know I'm Viktoria's—Hayley's—mother, so they will have to be sure that I feel the warning." She lowered her eyes. "She will."

Meaning Hayley.

As Owen listened, he felt like he was climbing those stairs again, his lungs strained. It took him a while to find his next question.

"Why me?" was all he could say.

Berta pointed at her swollen face. "I told you. No one can be trusted, not even from inside my organization. So I need someone clean."

"I'm going to need more than that, Berta."

"This thing, it's giving me a headache." Berta unwrapped her scarf, and set down the ice pack. Her swelling had lessened around her eye but now it was bright pink. "Lucy, she had a helper. I can't tell you the name. But that helper was my connection to Lucy. My access. And that helper has gone AWOL."

"Lucy won't even return an email to me, or a text."

"She will. Give it time."

"What makes you think I will?" Owen blurted, but before he'd gotten the words out he was reminded of Mason Snead's computer again. It was so out in the fucking open. On the way over, he'd even wondered if any of his investigative team were involved. Or maybe they were just all there to watch him? What if they had tracking devices on him? He felt like some sick psychology experiment in that open layout office, one that made the Stanley Milgram experiment and *The Truman Show* look like children's books. *The Matrix* was more like it.

Berta had fixed her eyes on him. "Because it's what you're becoming," she said.

Spoken like a true spy handler. Owen didn't reply at first. He only sighed. Eventually he said, "You sure you weren't in the CIA—"

"They raped her, Owen."

"Hayley?"

Berta lowered her eyes again. She nodded, slightly, but then she shook her head too. "Lucy," she said after a while. "Maybe Snead did, maybe more than one. They probably did it more than once."

"Jesus."

"Yep."

"How do you know?"

"I just know. Well, I suspected. And then I could see it in her eyes when we met. But then someone showed up at Lucy's."

223

Owen held his forehead. "The other night . . ."

"What?"

"I have to tell you: that might have been me. It was Saturday night, right?"

Berta nodded.

"I went over there," Owen told her. "To Lucy's. I was going to confront her about it, that I knew for sure she was the one doing the Show Game."

It was the first time either of them had called it by name.

"Shit," Owen added.

To his surprise, Berta only chuckled bitterly. And she read his thoughts again. She laid out her FBI card, then set out a tablet showing a few news stories about herself, and finally accessed the FBI intranet to show him that she was exactly who she said.

"I'm also not wired," she said. "Because this here? It's nothing like that."

Owen didn't have to ask why. "How long has Viktoria been with Snead?" he said.

"Years. Something completely changed with her. I could suspect what, but I really just want to reach her. We were long estranged, and I had written her off. But I couldn't help looking into this over the years. And then Lucy came along. I want Lucy to succeed. But first I need to get Hayley out of the way. If I can. There's a big *if* there."

"How? What do you really want from this?"

"I told you. Okay, yes, it's more than getting her out of the way. Hayley. I want to save her. This might be my last chance to get my daughter back." Berta paused a moment, her eyes widening, blurring, lost in thought, staring at the melting ice pack wrapped in scarf on the coffee table like it was a small dead animal. "And if I'm honest? If I don't, my husband and I will never be able to get on with our lives. I have to know she's all right. I can't quit the bureau until I know she's all right."

An image flashed before Owen's eyes, of him and Molly traveling the world happily, older together now, holding hands even. An alternate universe. If only . . .

"I understand that," he said. "So this is completely outside of the bureau, what you're doing?"

"Yes. Well, I do have access to certain resources. I am only semi-retired after all. I at least want to get to my daughter. Appeal to her. I'm not asking you to change anything you're doing. I just want to be involved. I won't interfere, not in any way that restricts you."

"You say that like I'm the one doing the Show Game. I'm just the reporter here."

"I know. Yes. That's what I meant." Berta added a strange smile, with a slight tilt of the head. "Just so we're clear. I'm just hoping to get Viktoria alone. My Hayley. The threat of the Show Game or worse might make her more responsive to that. Otherwise she won't come." Her eyes found the floorboards again. "I used to try. She wasn't even ignoring me. It was beyond that. Like she had no idea who I was. Amnesia."

Owen was now staring at the lump of ice pack and scarf on the coffee table. His eyes had blurred too. He sighed. "Okay. Let's say, for a moment, off-the-record-like, that I was to somehow help?" he said. He couldn't believe he was saying it, but he was. "What would you like me to do?"

"Keep an eye on Lucy."

"How? I don't know where she is."

"I don't, either, not yet, but you'll know when I know."

"How would you know?"

Berta didn't answer. She raised her chin.

"This has to be a give-and-take," Owen added. "You know that—you seem like a person who's dealt with reporters before."

"All right. On deep background? Fine. I told you Lucy has a helper. They were feeding me info and vice versa, when I could. We went way back. *Had* a helper, I should say. They have decided it's best to part ways."

"No he or she? *They* as in Lucy and them, or just the singular, as in they the helper—he or she?"

Berta shrugged. "I promised confidentiality. All I can tell you is that my contact has ended for now."

"What about Snead?" Owen said. "Hypothetically. Why would I handle that?"

Berta held up her hands. "Only you can answer that, Owen. Lucy, she's not just getting her vengeance—she's saving people. So many. I was wanting to tell her that. Then we got cut off."

"Right . . . If only she would've opened the door."

"Things work out like they work out. If only I wasn't in that parking garage, Owen."

They drank more water. Berta gave Owen all the time he needed. Owen asked her questions like a reporter would since remaining professional was his way of keeping his head screwed on. Berta was born and raised in California, in Oakland. She liked rare '70s and '80s new wave. She had a longtime husband who loved her, but he just wanted her to retire for good so they could relax finally, do some traveling. "He considers our Hayley lost forever," she told Owen. "She fell in with the wrong crowd, a superrich crowd, years ago, and she changed almost immediately."

Owen was nodding along, storing the details away for notes, but he couldn't actually write any of this down. None of this was working. A sick truth was creeping up on him, and it wasn't the booze wearing off. It was like a small but rabid animal with long claws climbing up his back, digging into his shoulders, grasping at his neck, his Adam's apple.

"What's the matter?" Berta said, leaning forward.

Owen only gasped, waving her away. He felt a lump in his throat. It burned. He tried not to make the connections in his mind but they were swarming his brain like a dunk in a hot bath, the waves pulsing deeper, opening pores and canals, clarifying.

He, too, was being lured in. Implicated. *FreeChain News* was just the start.

He jumped up and paced around the room. Berta stood, holding out her arms as if to steady him.

And what does that make me? Especially once I'm filing this story, and seeing more success?

He had to get out before it was too late. Before it corrupted him. The truth was just a lure, a commodity, an ideal to be itself caught and trapped and strangled, forever.

Owen's head spun, and he had to sit down again, and Berta helped him sit, on the sofa, and the wildest visions entered his head like he was on mushrooms or worse. Once upon a time in America, or even in that greater world that once looked to America to set the standard, it would've seemed improbable, maybe laughable too. A cartoon. But such were the times. They were entering a new age where not just virtue was threatened but the Truth itself.

"What if . . ."

"What if what, Owen?"

"What if Mason Snead is just using me as a tool, for rooting out any and all remaining stories about him? He will then put it all in a vault or burn it, after paying off or legally threatening everyone capable of touching him, all this via Viktoria Jett. What if Snead were only using me to uncover the Show Game before it gets to him?"

"Well, I'm sorry to tell you this, but I would not at all put it past him."

MONDAY, NOVEMBER 27
ALEX / LUCY

I'm all over Manhattan, moving from one Airbnb, hotel, Craigslist rental, hostel to the next. It's been five days since I got here. Right now it's a cloudy Monday afternoon in a laundromat west of Midtown I don't even know the name of, but it's a great place to hole up while I'm washing my disguises. There's that yoga gear, suburban jeans, power suit, party girl outfit, you name it. I'm sitting in a hard plastic chair with my feet up on my pack and charging my burner phone. Right now my outfit is homeless lady in my oversize hoodie and cheapo jeans, and I'm not washing them so as to keep in character. It makes me flinch thinking about it, how close I am to actually being homeless. Not only that—I'm anonymous. Off the grid completely. A ghost. The ID I'm using right now is a deceased woman from Wyoming. I have enough untraceable funds accessible for another week or so, so I have to make this happen.

It's just me now, an army of one.

Saying goodbye to Chip was harder than saying goodbye to my life in Portland. We had hugged, right there in his van. It was dark, but I could see the wetness in his eyes. He had offered to stay on longer, but he'd already done enough valuable surveillance. He even offered me the van, but I didn't take it. He would need it more than me. I'd wanted to remind him that he was AWOL and on the lam, so his chances with his daughter weren't much better than they were sticking with the Show Game. But he would've replied that continuing with the Show Game only made things worse. Family, children, siblings, they were like a cult, I'd wanted to half joke—they make people do the strangest things and so out of character. But by that point I was getting dark forebodings like I used to get with my brother when I was trying to keep him from falling apart, and my eyes were wet by then, too, and I pressed Chip to me for a few seconds longer until my chin had stopped quivering from love and fear and who knew what came next.

I watch my laundry go around and around, rising, dropping, helpless.

I check my phone. No messages, but I can't help checking the internet, FreeChain, social media. There is a clear movement growing online, a backlash against the Show Game. It's getting picked up by the major media. People are saying the Show Game is not the way to do this. Others defend traditional investigative journalism as the better recourse. Even Mason Snead came out against the Show Game the other day in a post. No surprise there—the man's MO is chaos if anything. *What if what the Show Game presented was fundamentally untrue?* he'd posted. *What if the whole purpose of the Show Game is to present the exact opposite of the truth? Those poor victims could have been tricked, or coerced, or drugged even? Who even knows who's behind it? Secret forces, governments even. Who knows what CGI and AI can do with video these days? Maybe the Show Game perpetrators themselves are the ones who've been defrauding and abusing America?*

And then, like clockwork, the physical protests appeared, just small groups of weirdos at first, the usual mix of unattractive males playing dress-up for one another. In their tired comic-book style, they started calling themselves the Ultimates. This brought well-meaning counterprotesters, and then the antifas-cists, and the anarchists. In Dallas, the police didn't step in soon enough. One reporter who got too close got her skull cracked and went into a coma. Others were severely injured.

Snead is building a worldview that claims the rich and powerful deserve preferential treatment, if not immunity, sheerly on account of their being rich and powerful. No matter the crime. Unlimited monarchy, basically. Fascism without the expensive military. The campaign against the Show Game seems too orchestrated, especially on FreeChain. Too human, fewer bots. This freaks me out. I had only imagined the positive attention. Or maybe I'm just getting paranoid? I need to shrug off the bad thoughts. I should not be shocked, considering what I'm up against, and certainly I am not horrified. It only makes my cause all the more urgent. The truth has to be laid out, again and again, all the way to the top. Go ahead, just try turning it all on its head—I'll just expose that too.

The dryer is done, but at the moment I have nowhere else to go. I load more money and run it again in case anything still needs to dry—and gain another hour here. The laundry inside rises up, drops from the top of the drum, tumbles over and over. Just like the truth. This makes me think of Berta Gonzalez, mother of the young woman formerly known as Hayley. Berta knew how it felt. Her own daughter has been turned upside down.

Then I feel a shiver. Or had Viktoria welcomed it? After being devastated like she surely had been, then rebuilding herself into someone else? The idea that her solution could be the opposite of mine turns my shiver into a hard, cold ball deep in my gut.

Berta Gonzalez said she would follow me, but how could she now that Chip is gone? My only hope is that Chip will let her know the plan. We didn't discuss this when we said goodbye, such was our overwhelming sadness. But now I wish I had. To that end, I took the chance of sending a message to Chip yesterday using our usual encrypted channels. I haven't heard back and do not expect to. I just need to hope. I can't think the worst. Maybe he's too spooked now. Maybe he's being followed. Threatened. Arrested. *Stop!*

Two hours later, I've left my laundry, all back in my bag, at a luggage storage shop near Penn Station. I'm now in my yoga gear, complete with mat, but with the wig and glasses and MUJI windbreaker of my privileged NY grad student outfit, which doesn't provide enough defense against the chilly gray sky. According to Chip's surveillance, Mason Snead often eats, sometimes even alone, at a certain Japanese restaurant in Hell's Kitchen. I'm heading over to confirm the regularity as a possible spot to make my move. It's getting dark. I'm getting desperate. None of the options revealed through Chip's surveillance are panning out as realistic—not for one person. The postrestaurant grab is a drastic alternative—out on the open street—but I have to start considering every option. Of course, if I were simply to shoot him? . . . problem solved.

I'm two blocks from the restaurant, on Forty-Seventh, a nice normal gentrified residential street with brownstones and stoops and actual trees. It would be a nice stroll. But remove some of the air conditioners in the windows and exposed fire escapes and it reminds me of that street on the Upper East Side where Snead and his people kept me so many years ago.

I take a deep breath. I pull my sunglasses on. I'm just another Manhattanite coming home from yoga, planning to draw a nice bath maybe, wait for my handsome civil-rights lawyer husband to get home. Once I pop out onto Ninth, I'll do a pass-by from across the street and then find a spot to surveil longer if I can. Hopefully he's got a seat near the window, so I can—

A man comes around the corner. The light is growing dim fast. He's slender, his pace measured. I touch my sunglasses to make sure they're there, adjust my posture upright, yoga gal all the way, chin up.

Shit.

It's Mason Snead.

Fuck. My heart races and my hands clench up. Worse yet, my legs feel so weak, like they want to buckle.

I can tell it's him. I'd know that waxy face anywhere. It seems to glow even in the twilight. His monochrome outfit is so simple and casual and yet spendy, he could be a dude going to the same made-up upscale yoga place as me.

We're maybe fifteen yards apart but closing fast. I keep my stride. My chest heaves because it's getting tight like I have a mask on and I wish I had a mask on to hide behind and I stick my chest out and straighten my shoulders, screw it, just a confident big city gal making my way. Looking straight ahead, behind my dark sunglasses, and I hope the light's dark enough to hide it. I glance at him.

He tugs at his nose.

I remember that. It's him. It's really him.

Five yards now. His eyes are dead and black in the twilight, but I see one corner of his thin paint stroke of a mouth curl up in a slight smile.

At me.

I don't acknowledge. I pass him, keep going. Don't look back.

The next corner is almost there. Once around the corner I'll sprint away, far down into the subway if I have to. But right now, this second? No. Don't give him that. He might see me run from him. Screw him. Give him nothing. And don't go into the subway. They might ambush you there. Just be you.

A woman marches around the corner, nearly runs right into me. I see a flash of black clothing and a pale, painted-on face with spiky hair, like she'd just traveled in time from 1981 London. Ghostly in the twilight.

Her eyes flash at me. She glares as I pass, and I feel her eyes on my back like two laser pens as I turn the corner.

That was Viktoria Jett. It had to be.

Go, Lucy, go. I keep my pace, checking whatever windows and reflections I can find, but I spot no one, nothing, not them. I keep my disguise-stride until the next cross street, West Forty-Eighth, I think, and then I turn the corner and I pull off my sunglasses and I clutch my yoga mat and I'm sprinting, not even checking for a trail now.

I slow down to a fast walk, catching my breath. I spot a grungy little gay bar with Saloon in the name, perfect. I rush in, head to the far end of the counter, the place half empty, no one paying me much attention. I'm just a big city gal here to meet her boy BFFs. I can view the street from here but no one can see me, and I order a straight vodka on the rocks. I eye the men around me. Most look pretty tough, or at least ripped.

I slurp at the vodka like it's ramen, holding it with both hands. My mind still races. What if he recognized me? Did he? He saw me. He knows my body, that bastard. And there I was wearing these stupid yoga pants. I slam down the drink, tug at the yoga pants suddenly smothering my legs, muscles, blood flow.

The drink calms me eventually, just like ramen. Then I think. *Think, Lucy!* Sipping the drink now. Of course it was coincidence. He wouldn't have remembered me, not after all those years, not with me in disguise, not after all his victims. Their victims. A bitter smile forms on my lips and I can't stop it. You know what? I'm glad he saw me. It only makes me more steeled. I can do this. I just need to tweak the plan.

I think more. I chew ice cubes. Okay, okay. I imagine the various thugs, button men, mercenaries, and simple sociopaths for hire I've met in my line of work. I could contact one. They'd join up as long as I gave them enough money and a getaway. I could even find a hit man. But what does any of that make me? No different than the likes of Mason Snead and his legion of henchmen. Once I become that? I might as well be Viktoria. This makes me think of Berta.

I order another now, this time for sadness. Then, inexplicably, halfway through that next drink, I think of Owen Tanaka. I actually consider the notion of planning this with him. Then I stop myself. I have to laugh away the thought so hard that heads finally turn.

"Hey, you okay, dear?" the nearest guy says to me with a smile.

"Yeah, I'm okay. I'm good. Just having a day is all." And I hold up my phone as if I'd just been checking it.

"Well, that's your problem right there. You work too hard. We all do."

OWEN

The morning after he met Berta Gonzalez, Owen was still stewing. He roamed the streets, which were oddly vacant, and then he remembered that it was Thanksgiving. He'd forgotten all about it. And that made him think of Molly, who texted him "Happy Thanksgiving" at that very moment. He texted her back, but neither dwelled on it because they'd rarely enjoyed a proper holiday with his job.

On Saturday, November 25, he sat down at his prisonlike desk in his apartment and finally wrote to Shane Bagley. He had wanted to write so many times, but never knew what to say. Now he wrote mechanically, as if reciting a script:

Dear Shane,

I'm sorry. You surely know that. But I'm working on making it right, at least on my end—on being a dumbass no more. I originally was going to write to you that my worst fear was repeating what I'd done to you—getting the truth wrong yet again. The next thing worse being that everyone will believe it forever. I was scared that I'd die getting it wrong.

But now I see it's more than that. I was going after the wrong truth altogether. I was going after the little guy when I should be exposing the devil incarnate. My mom once told me something I'd long forgotten: don't blame a person, blame the system they're stuck in. I have to take on the system. It's the Mason Sneads of this world that I have to take out, and I now know that a simple, well-researched exposé just isn't going to begin to cut it.

I should've been going after the mob itself, not you. But you were easier, I now see to my horror, and that is something that they are always betting on, whether it's the mob, the system, or the devil incarnate. I don't expect you to forgive me. But I simply wanted you to know that I haven't forgotten the horrible damage that I have done and I suppose I never will.

Thank you for inspiring me,
Owen Tanaka

He'd thought about deleting that line about Mason Snead, but then he purposely did not. Let them find it after the fact, the bastards. Let them use it as evidence, even, because if that was the case, then it was too late for him already.

It wasn't a letter. Sending paper by mail didn't seem urgent enough now. He was using an electronic messaging service for inmates that Shane's lawyer had told him about. Owen sent the message as soon as he was done.

That first Monday back at work, November 27, Owen was stewing even more. From his office he glared across the open so-called newsroom of *FreeChain News* at the office set aside for Mason Snead. All was the same there. Just a computer on a desktop. And Gina wasn't coming back, he knew. She'd deleted her profile from their chat account. Good for her. But he wondered why she had picked him to tell, of all people. Maybe she'd read his mind in that spooked state of hers? She knew what he always knew.

In the afternoon, his phone beeped. He had a text from Viktoria Jett: *Meet us upstairs.*

Owen glared at that, too, actually baring teeth. He didn't know what was coming over him. Events were turning him into some-thing else. Or was it already buried there, deep inside? He felt strangely energized, this despite not sleeping a wink last night, nor over Thanksgiving weekend for that matter. He'd just stared at the ceiling, eyes wide open half the time. Thinking. What if Mason Snead really was just using him as a tool? He'd be helping Snead destroy anyone capable of exposing him, all via Viktoria Jett. Imagining. What if he didn't help Snead uncover the Show Game before it reached him? Planning. What if, instead, he took it even further than that? What if . . .

This time, Owen took the elevator the three stories up to

the unoccupied floor. He had tried the elevator after taking the stairs up that first time he'd met them, and it had never opened on this floor. Now it suddenly worked? Now he wondered if Snead and Viktoria controlled the elevator itself somehow.

The door slid open. The floor still looked like no work had been attempted. No walls, wires hanging all over, pipes and electrical exposed, stray bolts and staples strewn about, that shop vac off in a corner, now inexplicably tipped over. Chaos. The chilly gray sky looming in the windows like deep ocean. Viktoria again stood by a window with her arms crossed. Owen again shuffled over on the dusty floor. As he did, he felt someone appear behind him, so he stopped and checked over his shoulder to make sure it was who he thought. Mason Snead, sure enough. When Owen had stopped, Snead had halted too. Snead rocked on his heels with his hands stuffed into his nearly invisible pockets. His thin stretched smile reminded Owen, disturbingly, of a scenario in which one man followed another to the edge of a building, intent on pushing him over.

Owen faced him, his feet planted, wanting to ball his fists. "Well, hello," he said, baring those teeth again, this time holding the fakest smile that ever was. "I figured we'd be meeting in that new office of yours downstairs."

"Oh. Yes, we could have. But you're too important for that. That's just so the team knows that I exist."

"Ah."

Viktoria had slid over as if carried by a silent zip line mounted to the ceiling. She stood at Owen's shoulder.

"You've been all over," she said. "What do you have? You haven't been reporting in."

Were they testing him? Did they know something? Suddenly all that lack of sleep hit Owen in a way that gave him no good answer. Still smiling, he looked to Snead, who gave a shrug as if to say, *she's the boss.*

Owen turned to Viktoria, his shoulders straight. He was fuming inside, all adrenaline, but he held it in, suddenly like a supporting mob guy in a Scorsese movie. He even held the smile like a wannabe made man.

"Who are you, exactly?" he said through his teeth. "I mean, I know Mr. Snead, of course, but you? I won't lie. I looked you up. You don't seem to exist."

Viktoria laughed, to Owen's surprise. A nice smile, actually, maybe the best thing about her. Yet Owen also noticed she took a half step back. "You got that right," was all she said.

They were facing each other, Snead just a spectator, eyes darting back and forth between them, tugging on the tip of his nose.

"Which part did I get right again?" Owen said. "I'm confused."

Viktoria's smile was fading. "I serve Mr. Snead and his interests. It's not important that anyone knows about me."

"You know that you have a nice smile?" Owen said, like someone else was now feeding him these creepy lines, but he couldn't help this urge to test her somehow. "And yet," he added, "you keep it hidden. Why is that?"

Viktoria swallowed her smile now. She only glared.

Owen snapped out of it. He was taking this too far. He slapped her on the shoulder, grinning now, laughing, from deep in his throat. "Hey, I'm just kidding you! Come on. Come on!" Now he was the same old male coworker every woman had ever faced in any office. Gross.

Viktoria's shoulders had drawn together, as if she were cold.

Mason Snead rocked on his heels again, and his thin lips stretched into another amused smile. "O-kay. Take it easy, everyone."

Owen adjusted his grin to a smile. "We're fine. I was just playing around." He faced both of them, holding out his hands. "You want to know what I got? I was on the West Coast about this Podest fellow. Martin Podest. I thought I had him, so I had to follow up with the locals."

"In Portland. Oregon."

"Yes. I told you. There's an investigator there, among others." He had to mention this, though without revealing Lucy Holden's name. It would look suspicious if he hadn't. "I can't confirm Podest is the one, but I'm not ruling out that he's connected somehow. He's good. Puts on the right face every time. You'd think he was reformed, or possibly the reformer himself. Crusader even. You know what? You never know."

Owen kept his eyes on Mason Snead as he said this, but Snead only tugged at his nose again. Viktoria meanwhile showed Owen a concerned face, but with all that pale base makeup and overdrawn lines, Owen couldn't help thinking of a mask for some enigmatic ancient ritual.

"Maybe you're working too hard?" Viktoria said to him. "Maybe you need a break?"

"No. I'm good."

"Then we'll need a full report, with names et cetera."

Owen gave Viktoria a little salute.

Then Snead shot Viktoria a glance that made her step away, back over to the window.

"So," Snead said. "Stellar work so far."

"Thanks."

"We didn't call you up here to interrogate you," Snead said.

"That's good to hear."

"No, I wanted to spring my own idea on you. Are you ready?"

Owen nodded.

Snead held out his hands like a TV pitchman. "Monetized whistleblowing. We start offering rewards for users' whistleblowing. It's still peer-to-peer. But they'll be competing."

Owen only nodded again.

Snead seemed taken off guard a little, maybe expecting more. "We're, uh, just iterating, you see, based on prelaunch focus grouping. Oh. Your end? You, as head investigative reporter, would benefit directly. You can pursue more stories. You will rise quickly here. Now, you wouldn't be running the whole news org, of course, not at first, but who knows; in any case you're still a big player."

"To what end?" Owen asked.

"What? Oh, to, uh, snag more bad guys? Of course."

"Of course."

Again it occurred to Owen that they were testing him, but this time it was Snead alone. Whatever he did, Owen felt the overwhelming sense, like a dire thirst, that he needed to get them to trust him, for whatever came next. So he went for it.

"That's good," he said. "But . . ."

"Go ahead. Please."

"What if we . . . dare I say it?" Owen put a sick smile on his face, sicker than any ancient mask. "What if we, say, used that information we gain to take it even further? We could even apply leverage on the powers that be that we want to expose. We blackmail them, basically—I'll just go out and say it. For them to give us even more for a story. Get them to throw someone else under the bus. But they're never quite free of that thing we have on them. That way, it's something we can always hold over them. Then they're implicated."

Mason Snead did a little air clap, like a child watching a cartoon. He even bobbed up and down.

It was like someone else had taken over Owen's body. Like

he was watching it in a wide shot from outside those windows. "Everyone's doing it," he continued. "Always have been. I don't know how much you know about journalism at this level. But it's just a big game involving access and expose. Carrots and sticks. Us? We're just 'monetizing' it, as you put it in your marketing-speak, mining the user base."

"Yes, yes. Oh yes. How does that end?" Snead asked.

"End? There's no end. Oh sure, we buy the story from not just the so-called whistleblower but also from any accusers that arise. We promise to run the story one day. But we just sit on it. Exposé after scandal after cover-up. Like money in the bank. Let chaos reign. Plus, we implicate anyone we can at the same time. Promise to make a given scandal go away eventually. There's no win-win. Only we win."

Snead tugged three, four times at his nose now, like a tic. "Did you hear that, Viktoria? I knew we picked the right guy."

Owen shrugged. His teeth-baring grin mask was back. "What can I say? It's just taking things further. You call it monetizing. I call it weaponizing."

"Bravo," said Snead.

"How do we enforce it, though?" Owen said, pushing it now.

"What?"

"What if the leverage doesn't work?"

"It's a good question . . ." Snead left his mouth open, didn't elaborate, seeming to search for the right words.

But Viktoria had come back over. "It's not just blackmail. It's threat. There, I said it. We have ways. People could get hurt. Families even. Loved ones. Does that concern you?" She glared at Owen, not blinking.

Owen just shook his head.

"Well, I think we should leave things there, at least for now," Snead said. "Thanks for your contribution, Owen. It really helps us iterate."

Owen just nodded.

"So what's next?"

"Got some leads here in town," Owen said. "There's an FBI contact, another investigator, all deep background. You can imagine how I'm a little sheepish about sharing my sources. It's the way I've worked my whole life."

"Of course," Snead said. "And now you're becoming something else. It takes a little while. I know we're only getting started. I mean, it's only been a few weeks, if that."

"We're ready when you are," Viktoria added.

"Thanks. I'll get that all for you though. Just need to wrap my head around it."

Owen said bye and turned and passed through the big open floor and he could feel their eyes on his back, like two directional antennas. Then they were two cattle prods. Then red-hot brands.

He glanced back at the last moment. They stood shoulder to shoulder, still watching him, but in that split second he noticed that Snead had one hand clamped around Viktoria's elbow, so hard and harshly that he could see the white knuckles. Both were smiling.

Owen didn't smile. He took the stairs. Screw that elevator. He tried the stairway door after shutting it behind him and of course it had locked, whereas the other floors' stairway doors didn't. He knew because he had tried them all as part of the meager workout he did when he forced himself to take a rare break. As he headed down the metal and concrete stairs, thudding along, Owen's phone wouldn't work at first. It took two floors for it to come back on.

Something about that released a panic inside him, finally. It made him weary, his leg muscles all a cold gelatin. He sat on the landing, slumping against the wall on the next first step.

Why him? Why did they trust him? Did Snead see something in him that he didn't? It made him shudder, and all the concrete and metal around him wasn't helping.

He sat up, taking deep breaths. He texted Molly: *What have I done?*

It was all he had to say. The only time he'd ever texted her anything like that was when he was causing their breakup by favoring work over whatever was left of their marriage.

Keep going, she texted back right way. *Just, please, please, watch your back.*

It was not what she'd texted back last time. Her exact words had been, *You fucked up, that's what*, and if he scrolled up enough through their texts he could even confirm it. But he didn't need to. Molly was now giving him the steel to press on. He sat up and took another deep breath and seemed to suck in all that metal and concrete around him, giving him more strength.

Weaponize this, he thought, grinding his teeth. *You can go fuck yourself with your monetizing, and your iterating.* He so hated those words.

Owen stood and pressed on, down the stairs to his floor, thinking, *if only I had been wired.* But would that even work? Who knew who they had in their pocket? Berta had alluded to such, and she was in the FBI. Then he thought about his phone. Maybe it didn't work so close to that one floor because they blocked all transmissions there somehow. Electronics even. Snead's father had basically invented the underpinnings for the internet, after all. Owen imagined himself wearing a wire and afterward hearing, in horror, only static.

He was going to fight back. If only so that he could never see what he saw on that computer screen ever again. If he ever was anything like what Snead saw in him, then he would be seeing plenty more such images in his new role.

He was going to betray Snead. All of it. He just did not know how yet.

TUESDAY, NOVEMBER 28
OWEN

Home Depot, West Twenty-Third. Monitor entrance for the next two hours.

Owen had just gotten a text from an anonymous number. It was nine a.m., the morning after meeting with Mason Snead and Viktoria. He was just leaving his apartment, about to head into the offices of *FreeChain News* to provide cover for himself, to keep himself legit in their eyes. The ambitious scheming reporter ready to sell out the future big-time.

But what was this text message?

It had to be from Berta. She didn't name Lucy as the target. Then again, why would she need to? They had never come up with a code for Lucy before Owen left that safe house or Airbnb or staged apartment or whatever it was that Berta had in the East Village—Berta had wanted it that way, for now. He wished they had. What if the text was referring to Viktoria, and not Lucy? What was he supposed to do about that? He wasn't Berta's gofer.

He took a deep breath, huddling in his apartment doorway. *Don't overthink this*, he told himself. But then a rush of heat filled his chest and head and he broke into a sweat.

STEVE ANDERSON

Or maybe it was Snead, leading him right to Lucy so that Owen could expose her? Just like they'd talked about. He couldn't know how much Snead knew. No one could.

Think, Owen, think. But what if this was coming from Viktoria herself? What if they were only fucking with him? That, or Viktoria was sending him some kind of cry for help?

Don't think, Owen, just go.

Next thing he knew, he was standing inside a temporary walkway under scaffolding across from the Home Depot on West Twenty-Third, which, with its ornate white facade and columned entrance, less resembled a massive home improvement store than some cocksure nineteenth-century bank and probably had been at one point. He was wearing sunglasses and a stocking cap, a hoodie in case he needed extra concealment. This was his usual and only look when he wanted to trail someone, which wasn't very often. The passageway helped and kept him in shadows. He wished he had one of those reflective vests to make him look more like a construction worker here; then all he needed was a pack of cigarettes to fake-smoke. Meanwhile, he told himself that Berta was looking out for him, choosing the right moment that could help him.

The people kept coming and going and none of them resembled Lucy, even in disguise. They included tourists from every continent, performers in drag, children unattended, elderly couples, more tourists, and the usual New Yorkers on a mission. Owen stuck to his spot. He didn't have a choice. There was no other good vantage point, no cafés or bars on this side of the street with windows he could watch from.

Cabs and Ubers and police cars passed both ways on Twenty-Third between him and the Home Depot, a constant flow that sometimes moved right along and sometimes backed up. Every time a large panel van or bus or truck blocked his view for more than thirty seconds, he had to choose a direction and scramble along incognito to spy on whoever might have come out.

This time it was a tourist bus. Crap. Owen did his shuffle and then returned to the chain-link fencing along the passageway. He checked his phone again. Nothing. He'd been here for forty-five minutes now. He hoped whoever he was trailing wasn't watching from all those windows inside, because he was starting to look more conspicuous than the usual weird New Yorker loitering in a passageway. He chewed on an energy bar, peanut butter and oats. He was thinking about taking the chance of loitering across the street by the entrance when a sudden thought hit him so hard that his body tensed up and his energy bar clogged his throat.

Why wasn't Berta doing this surveillance? Why wasn't she *simply doing this?*

He chewed and chewed what he had left in his mouth but it only added to the clogging.

He wanted to slap himself on the forehead. Then he felt a sick grin on his face.

Was it because she saw something in him that he hadn't—not until, that is, he was again face-to-face with Mason Snead and his henchwoman, Viktoria?

He swallowed hard, then harder, but the energy bar just sat there. He had no liquid to wash it down; he hadn't brought any liquids because he didn't want to have to pee while on surveillance. But now he needed water. A hot dog stand stood across the street by the entrance.

He waited for traffic to clear, keeping one eye on the entrance, then crossed and bought an overpriced bottle of water from the hot dog stand guy. *Oh, she was good*, he thought as he washed down his clogged swallow. Berta was a true handler. They steer you in the direction you don't even know you're heading yet. They know what you are becoming before you do.

It was now safe for him to take another bite and he did. Of course, there was also the chance that Berta had other reasons. Maybe she was simply sacrificing him because she didn't want to get caught herself. Maybe she couldn't be exposed because of some other reason. *Maybe she was just scared after getting beaten up like that*, he thought now, and his bite clogged his throat again. He chugged more water to wash it down, now off to the side of the stand, the Sabrett umbrella wanting to poke at the top of his head.

A woman passed, just exited the Home Depot. Cuffed Levis, clunky shoes, checkered button-down shirt, and heavily framed glasses. She wore a baseball cap, though with her hair tucked up inside when he would've expected a buzz cut to go with that look. At least in TV shows. But she also had a mask on, one of the many still doing so for a sense of security and who could blame them. Then he noticed something else. Her walk. He knew it. He'd seen it before. She had a resolute gait, that one elbow cocked.

This could be Lucy. She was the same size, for sure.

He must've missed her going into the store but was lucky enough to catch her coming out. He couldn't lose her now. She hadn't looked back.

He pulled on his hoodie and followed her, on to the the corner of Fifth Avenue, kitty-corner from Madison Square Park.

The light was changing but she darted off anyway, picking up speed, and a UPS truck honked at her for slowing traffic.

Shit. Owen crossed the other crosswalk, trying to keep an eye on her while watching the Fifth Avenue traffic for a break in the action, the narrow Flatiron Building looming above like a giant domino.

She was moving through the public plaza edging the park, a reclaimed street now dotted with outdoor tables populated by the lunch crowd and exhausted tourist shoppers.

Two one-way lanes of vehicles were still coming, but Owen jumped out at the slightest hole and hoped no one would honk and give him away. They didn't. He slipped past a slowing van and—

Screech. "What the fuck, man?"

A bicycle had slammed to a halt in the bike lane, just inches from him. He froze.

A blue Citi Bike, but definitely no tourist. "I'm riding here!" the guy added.

"Sorry, sorry, man," Owen said and pressed on, moving through and around tables, practically pushing tourists out of the way.

He looked in every direction. He actually turned in a circle.

She was gone.

Ah, crap. He stood there a while. Pivoting every ten seconds or so. Nothing. He held up his hands for little reason, then checked his phone for even less reason. He crossed Broadway, which cut through a corner of Madison Square Park, and entered the park. It was a rectangle with circular intersecting walkways. He strolled them all. Nothing. No one.

He had been so close.

He found a bench and slumped on it, watching the strollers and office types pass. He drank the rest of his water. Didn't matter if he had to pee now. Lot of good a stakeout back at Home Depot was going to do him at this point, even though he'd have to head back and make do, knowing all the while that he might have missed her either way. He stared at his phone a second and thought of Molly. What would she tell him to do? He stared at the anonymous text again, wondering if it were possible to respond to it, or if that would compromise him somehow, or if it would even work.

"Hey," he heard. He looked up.

VOTE, her mask read.

ALEX / LUCY

I stand over Owen Tanaka sitting on that bench in Madison Square Park. I pull down my mask. He just stares at me. He pulls off his sunglasses and his hood, revealing that mop of hair and those goofy ears always wanting to poke their way out. I think about pulling my cap off, letting my hair fall down into place, but I can't.

"You had me for a sec," he says.

"What gave it away?" I say.

"Your walk. Same one as in Portland. You walk at a steady clip, as my dad would say. One elbow up."

I sit on the bench next to him. "It's a weakness. It must've started during the pandemic. That or I do it when I think someone's following me."

Saying that makes us both take a quick glance around, in silence. The coast seems clear, but it's so hard to know. Ever since I accidentally passed Mason Snead and Viktoria, I keep getting the feeling I'm being watched. Stalked. I had lost my pursuer pretty easily in this park, but then I'd watched him from behind statues and trees and food stands and confirmed it was Owen.

"You should talk," I say.

"Oh yeah?"

"That birthmark of yours. Cover it up if you're going to

wear a disguise. Don't get me wrong—I like it. It's looks like a puzzle piece."

Owen contorts his face and shifts his stocking cap lower with one hand. "Better than Texas. That's what kids in school used to call it."

"Fuck those kids."

"Yeah. You're right."

I want to be mad at him for scaring me like this, for following me, for possibly blowing my cover. I could've just split, left him hanging. But something made me come back. Maybe it's because I have no one else on earth now.

"How long you been waiting for me to come out?" I ask Owen.

"Hour and half? At the most."

"You see anyone else doing the same?"

"I didn't, Lucy. Or do you prefer Alex?"

I pause, staring at him.

"I'm just me, from here on out."

He nods at that, slowly and firmly, as if in complete approval, and I'm not sure what to make of that.

"How did you know where I was?"

"Take one guess."

My heart says Chip, but my head says Berta. Or maybe it's the other way around.

"Viktoria Jett's mother," I say.

"Yep."

This means Chip finally told Berta where I'm operating. He had checked in on me this morning, to my surprise, all encrypted, and I had told him my latest moves because he was making it sound like he wanted back in. Now I'm pissed at him because he might've been tricking me to put Berta back on my trail. That was Chip for you—tricking you into letting him help you. But I don't know if it's really helping. This likely means that she's only known where I was since this morning, via Chip. My chest tightens from all the unknowing and I have to release a deep sigh.

"Lucy, I know it's you," Owen says. "I know what you're going to do next. Last."

Does he mean Mason Snead? I saw this coming. All I can do is chuckle now. "Hey, I was just popping into Home Depot for some duct tape and zip ties," I say. I'd left mine in Chip's van. I hold up the baggie.

Owen does that nod again.

We sit in silence for a moment, glancing around again inconspicuously. Some of the same strollers and office people pass again, but I tell myself they're only promenading the park repeatedly like people do for a little exercise.

"We can't sit here long," I say eventually.

"No."

"Fuck, Owen. You should've texted me," I say.

"I've tried that. I didn't want to freak you out."

"You're kidding, right? What do you call stalking me?"

"I'm not stalking you. I'm helping you."

This makes me sit up fast, like someone yanked me up by a cable. I face him. "Helping how?"

Owen stares at me, his features hardening, his cheekbones showing, those piercing eyes. "I know what Mason Snead is. What he does. He's a monster."

My mouth might've dropped open. I'm not sure for how long. I shake my head.

"I know what he did to you," Owen adds. "Not the details. I'm not sure I want to know those. But I know."

A few more seconds pass. He's sitting up now too.

"You should leave," I tell him. "You have what you want for your story."

"I'm not doing a story, Lucy."

"You're not?"

"No. I'm going to help you."

"You are?"

"I have no choice," he says.

"Yes, you do. I don't. I'm doing this on my own."

"No. You need help."

"I have help." I'm lying.

He stares at me as if seeing right through me, like I hadn't even replied, let alone lied.

"My whole adult life, I've pursued the truth," he says. "I've sacrificed everything for it. Never had kids. It's more or less killed my marriage." He shakes his head, those piercing eyes softening. "But the thing is . . . It's not that I can't get at the truth. It's that the truth is now in such jeopardy. And, by working for Snead, I might be the one helping to kill it off for good."

Now it's me nodding along, slowly and firmly. I know he's telling the truth. I can see it in his eyes. They have seen things that I have seen. About a minute of silence passes between us amid the rush of the city.

I say, "You know what another reporter told me once, when I wanted her—her!—to look into this? Everyone thinks that, in the big interview about their guilt, that monsters like Snead will give us some kind of deep insight into their crimes. Know what she said? 'It's a crock.' No interview will just magically reveal all truth. Never happens. So you know what I think? The Show Game might not either."

More silence. Owen, he just stares. I'm starting to wonder if the guy has some condition that doesn't let him blink.

"I was going to say the same thing to you," he says finally.

"Goddamnit, Owen."

"I know. I can't help it."

I close my eyes a second, open them. Sigh. Screw it. "All right. Can you meet me in two hours? I'll go over it all."

"Can you give me three? I need to make it look like I'm still working away at the *News*."

"Okay." I give him the address. "I'll leave first. Give me five minutes."

"Got it. Oh. One thing: I locked your back door for you, by the way."

"Back at my home?" That lifts such a weight off my chest, oddly. I sigh with relief now. "Thank you. Seriously. I'm never going back there again. But it's still good to know."

Three hours later, just after dark, Owen buzzes my rental. I found it cheap on Craigslist, that easy. It's little more than a former workshop on the last scruffy far edge of the Meatpacking District, one of the very few holdouts not transformed by the High Line and ensuing gentrification in the final days of the Before Time. Surrounding me in all their thousand-square-foot glory are concrete floors, brick walls, and chipped fiberglass washtubs down one side wall, along with the remains of shop machines pulled out ages ago. I have to make sure I don't trip over the exposed bolts and metal plates in the dark because this place has no windows. It's an old warehouse with For Lease signs on it, surely about to be sold and turned into yet another boutique hotel or home store or Starbucks Reserve Roastery any day now by all the rabid postpandemic wolves prowling for real estate prey. This space was most recently used by an artist, I can tell, because paint colors have been left everywhere, especially on those metal tubs. I can still smell the paint, which is better than the whiff of grease I sometimes get. There are two big ventilation fans, but I'm not running them. I want to be able to hear everything, anything. Still, the place does have a corner with a bed, love seat, and kitchenette fresh from IKEA, which makes such a striking contrast. The bathroom, on the other hand, is basically an enlarged closet with an industrial shower and a metal toilet, the only sinks those fiberglass tubs or the kitchenette. So be it. Could be worse. I paid some dude cash. He didn't even want to know my name.

This is my final location before the last Show Game.

I meet Owen at the nondescript side door. He holds his personal phone out to me like he's offering his wrist to the fearsome bouncer of some elite but imposing after-hours club.

We're using burners, but I'd shown him how to cloak his GPS location just in case we need to throw off Snead and Viktoria. "Did you do it?"

He nods. So I bring him inside, the short staircase down all wood, with steps so battered the edges are rounded down.

"Didn't know spots like this still existed around here," he says once we're in the place. He's smart enough to know not to talk until we're inside.

"It's been hibernating," I say.

I lead him through to the brand-new IKEA setup gleaming like a new car in a wrecking yard. He cocks his head at it and drops onto the love seat.

"It's your fault, you know?"

He just looks at me for the answer.

"You were too good. You were getting too close. You were practically forcing me to act. Sooner, that is." I add a smile.

"I can't help it, I told you," he mutters. Then he just stares into space. I know that stare. It's that look of someone leaving their old life behind. Becoming something new. Reborn. The staring can help you focus on the one or two things you never want to lose, despite your new life. I take a stab at what one might be.

"I'm sorry about your wife," I say. "What's her name?"

"Molly. We still text."

"At least you've had someone. Me, I have certain hurdles, as you can imagine. Not exactly the best Tinder date."

Owen only shrugs. I'd been trying to break the ice a little, to warm this cool calm before the big storm, but it's having the opposite effect apparently. I give him a moment.

After a while, a minute maybe, he looks up at me. "Molly, she would approve of this. You know, it's almost like she can sense it, that I'm moving on to something big. She keeps texting me to go for it."

"Maybe it's your way of winning her back?"

"Maybe."

That leaves a hole in the conversation because he has to sense that soon he's going to have to go AWOL on that part of his life too. It's the only way we'll be able to do this. It was the only way Chip did it. I eye him for a minute, sitting there, wondering if he's got what it takes. Hard to know if a guy is capable of kidnapping a major public figure and risking life in prison or worse when he's slumped on a purple-and-turquoise oversize houndstooth love seat and likely ruing his ex-wife.

I get him a water. I have a beer. I lay it all out for him, everything I've got. Chip did a fantastic job doing recon.

"I can confirm that Viktoria Jett appears to be the only security he ever has at his side. Physically at least."

Owen squints at me as if trying to believe it. "You've been doing that much surveillance all on your own?"

I'm not telling him about Chip, but he has to know I've had help. And the less each knows what the other knows, the better.

"Sometimes Snead doesn't even use her—I nearly ran into him myself that way," I say, which probably only confirms to

Owen that I had help. "Plus, the guy's cocky, you know that. Thinks he's invincible."

Owen nods. "Well, I guess we'll find out."

As for the Show Game: I'm planning on doing it right here in this space, I tell Owen. He doesn't object. I have a couple possible locations where I could grab Mason Snead. I tell him those. One is the restaurant in Hell's Kitchen near where Snead and I happened to cross paths. I shake my head at the memory. "It was him. He even did the thing."

"The thing?"

"He tugs at his nose."

Owen perks up a little. "Yes, you're right. It ruins his demeanor. Creeps me out."

"Yup." No need for me to elaborate.

I turn to Owen, facing him. I'm standing in the middle of the living area. I take a deep breath.

"I need to be honest with you. We might be exposing ourselves to the greater public somehow. Even with disguises. He might figure out who I am, if he hasn't already. No amount of voice changer is going to help there."

Owen is staring at me, wanting more. His features have hardened again, his eyes back in focus.

"So," I tell him, "I was thinking of using myself as a lure. I confront him on the street. West Forty-Eighth Street is pretty secluded. Trees, low light. We could get lucky."

By now Owen is shaking his head.

"What? What is it?"

Owen sits up. "You are not subjecting yourself to him like that," he says. "At his mercy."

"Screw it. This is the final episode."

"No," he says. "If something goes wrong, before we do the Show Game? Who knows what he could make you out to be.

257

He could destroy you all over again. Say you were coming on to him even."

My eyes widen at that. One eyebrow even goes up. I really don't know what to say.

Owen stands and paces the living area with confidence. "You're omitting the obvious," he tells me. "The best way to snag him? It's for *me* to lure him."

"You?"

"He trusts me. I'm the guy who's going to find the Show Game for him. He thinks I'm his man, his sellout. Just like all the rest. So I'll tell him I want to meet him alone. I'll say I have a lead, but it's tricky. I'll imply it involves someone close to him, meaning Viktoria, her mother even, but I don't say it. Only when we meet. Alone. I'll tell him where to meet me."

Now I'm shaking my head. We're standing face-to-face in the middle of the living area, with just a harsh overhead light, like we're in the climax of a stage play. "Uhhh," I mutter, because I'm still trying to fathom what he's telling me. "But that means," I say finally, "that you'll be the one revealing yourself to him. Our plan has you staying in disguise. This other way? You might as well be turning yourself in."

"You better believe it," he says, borrowing one of my favorite lines.

WEDNESDAY, NOVEMBER 29
OWEN

He couldn't help thinking that maybe his efforts would win Molly back someday, just like Lucy had guessed. Even so, what then? He wouldn't be able to see her. He would likely be in prison or worse. But he had no choice. Molly herself had given him no choice.

Lucy had agreed to his plan, in the end. Everything would have to go perfectly, including his alibi. No best-laid plans ever worked, he knew. This would be like going into combat, but without actual training. Owen would be relying mostly on what Lucy advised him and, with any luck, what Berta told them. Yet he couldn't help imagining how it could turn out. It would give him an excuse to leave *FreeChain News*, provided it even existed once Mason Snead was exposed. Maybe he could move to the West Coast, start over in a smaller town with a good paper. Or he could just freelance. Maybe he could finally muster the guts to see Molly in person again.

Owen was contemplating all this inside his neat apartment, back at his small desk, facing the wall. It was the very next day after he and Lucy had come up with a plan in her Meatpacking District hideout (*let's call it what it is*, he thought), not that many blocks from here. It was also just hours after he'd emailed Mason Snead that he would like to meet one-on-one to discuss his latest findings about the Show Game. It was "sensitive." He had to come alone. He couldn't tell anyone, not "a single soul."

Snead had emailed him back: *Sure, name the time and place.*

And so Owen had. He could only hope that Viktoria wasn't scanning Snead's emails, or writing them even.

Another email appeared on Owen's laptop. It wasn't exactly an email—it came delivered via a web-based message service. Owen didn't recognize it at first. He recoiled inside a moment, fearing it might be Mason Snead or Viktoria bringing the hammer down once and for all. And then realized—it was the email-like messaging service that Shane Bagley's lawyer had told him about.

Dear Owen,

I forgive you. I always had. I was the one who fucked up; if I hadn't, you wouldn't have. You should've written earlier—I could've used the company!

It's good to hear you get it, though. You're just a cog like me. The trick for all you cogs is to get the hell free of the machine.

Good luck with that!

Shane

PS: I finally finished my novel, all thanks to you :)

Owen stared at the screen, a smile stuck on his face, cradling his ukulele like a puppy. He wondered if he could write Shane again from prison himself, if that was where he was going to end up. The thought didn't scare him now.

Of all his few possessions, he was going to miss this instrument the most. Of all his few loved ones, he was still going to miss Molly the most. He wanted to text her, too, but he could not implicate her in any way.

Even if he did get away with it, everything would be different after. He thought about all those people living double or secret lives in all those investigative stories he'd written. They had just been objects to him. Nuts to crack. Onions to be peeled. Now he was cracking and peeling his own self.

His phone beeped.

Molly: *Are you okay? Should I be worried about you?*

He wanted to tell her about Shane Bagley, but it was too much to tell in such little time. The thought of possibly surprising her with it one day gave him even more of that warmth he felt just now staring at the screen smiling and cradling his uke.

I will be okay, he texted back. *You will see soon . . .* He closed his eyes a moment. Took a deep breath. *I love you*, he added.

I love you, too, Owen. Stay safe.

In his career he had met his share of deep-background sources, informants, whistleblowers, the perpetrators themselves even. Now Owen knew how they felt, crossing the Rubicon. He didn't feel fear. He was surprised to feel relief. It was the others he was concerned about. Would Molly worry about him once he'd done the deed? Change her mind even? Public perception was shifting about the Show Game, and fast. What bothered him most was the growing antagonism online. It sounded very much to Owen like astroturfing—secretly cooking up a sponsored movement that appeared to be grassroots. The Ultimates? What complete fools and tools. People like that now let themselves be tricked into seeing the Show Game as a cowardly trap, as un-American (whatever that was), as a terrorist act. People now truly wanted to find the perpetrators. Kill them even. It wasn't

STEVE ANDERSON

just those shadowy enforcers who beat up Berta, sent by who knew who, perhaps by Viktoria. It wasn't just the rich and powerful loyal to Mason Snead, or even the authorities, who could also be looking for them by now. It was people in general, all over. The hate was being orchestrated, fueled, and it could only be coming from Mason Snead. He had all the tools to do so, all the connections, and certainly the will. Snead was dividing the people. It was the oldest deceit.

So be it. Owen's only hope was that Snead really would meet him alone. Owen had proposed the place where he'd first met Snead: that aging coffee joint with the shutter rolled down. It was only blocks from here, and close to Lucy's hideout. It was now afternoon, pushing three p.m. By this evening, if all goes well, they will have Mason Snead duct-taped and ready for the Show Game of all Show Games. Showtime.

He picked up his ukulele, and he played and he played.

Eight thirty p.m. Darkness had descended on West Sixteenth between Seventh and Eighth Avenues, and the crisp, clear-sky cold made their breath catch that always looming glow of city light. So much for Lucy's alternate scenario—they were going for broke, together. Owen watched the corners at one intersection and Lucy had the other end, both in their disguises. Owen wore what he had on before, looking like a standard NYC construction guy in his hoodie and dusty jeans, and Lucy had completed the look by giving Owen work boots that made him taller, a fake beard, and a cigarette he waved around a lot to distract. Just another Joe looking for a lift. The burner phone in his pocket was his walkie-talkie, and he kept his finger on it in case he sighted Snead. Lucy on the other end had her homeless gal outfit on, with lots of baggy shapeless clothing, multiple bandannas and sweats and a hoodie under a grimy football starter jacket (NY Jets), and stocking cap pulled down low, complete with bags (one of which held her tactical pack) on her back and in a large shopping cart, but with a twist: she wore a surgical mask to better conceal her face.

They couldn't control how Snead would arrive. Owen simply had to take Snead's word that he'd be coming alone.

Eight thirty was the time arranged. Owen still saw nothing, no one, and Lucy was texting the same on her end.

Owen's lungs started tightening from the stress, so he shifted up and down on one foot, then the other, and ended up taking an actual drag of his menthol cigarette, which only made him cough and his chest tighter.

His regular phone beeped. A text, from an anonymous number: *You coming? I'm here.—MS*

Owen now remembered that when he first met Mason Snead, the man had appeared from a room he had assumed was the bathroom. But it had been dim in there then, still morning. That door must've led to an alternate entrance, he now realized.

His heart racing, Owen dumped the cigarette, ground it down, and called Lucy on the burner phone.

"He's already inside. Looks like he had another way in."

"No turning back," Lucy said, and her voice sounded thinner from fear. "Let's proceed, me from my end, you from yours." The abandoned coffee joint was closer to Owen's end. "We'll pass the doorway, you first, to get a look, then me. Then I'll loiter a bit, see if I can lure him out. You hang around. I know: if he asks, I'll say I saw a guy who fits your description. So maybe you're lost."

"I'll text him right now that I had the wrong street and am coming soon."

"Good, that'll gain us a few minutes," she said.

Owen was already texting Snead, to which Snead only replied: *Hurry up.*

They had surveilled the location, of course. It now had scaffolding out front, which was even better—thank god for all the NYC scaffolding. And good timing, too: one of the signs on the scaffolding revealed that the aging spot was soon to be transformed into an #AllGood drop-off point and smoothie/juice bar. The closest parking spot for their rental van was one street over, and it had taken Lucy half the day to get that.

They advanced toward the location. Owen spotted no one outside. He passed by, glancing from the side of one eye. The place was dark inside, even more so under the scaffolding. Lucy was coming fast from the other direction, her cart luckily not rattling since she, always the pro, had been wise enough to oil it. He passed her then, whispered, "Can't tell anything," and she continued on. Owen gave it a ten count, then turned. Lucy was now under the scaffolding directly outside, pretending to go through the bags in her cart, playing the part well, though Owen could tell she was using the activity to glance inside. Owen was about fifteen yards away; his cigarette had gone out and he relit it to maintain his disguise. He got close to the building wall. Moved along it. Creeping closer.

A figured appeared from inside. In the doorway. Lucy froze, midmotion.

Mason Snead.

He barked at her, as if she were a child, asking her something. Owen could tell he was now describing Owen Tanaka, investigative reporter. Lucy was shaking her head, then nodding.

Snead glanced at Owen down the sidewalk but didn't seem to give him a second thought.

Owen crept closer. He eyed the street, both ways. It looked all clear.

Five yards now. Under the scaffolding Lucy was pleading

with Snead through her surgical mask, pleading for money in a crazy voice. Snead snapped, "Leave me alone," turned his back to her, facing the opposite end of the street. Lucy backed up. She pulled the stun gun from her hoodie and fired into Snead's back. He twitched and jerked and flopped forward. Lucy scrambled on top of him, jabbed the syringe into his neck. Owen rushed over and zip-tied his wrists.

"How you like your roofie now?" Lucy growled as they lifted Snead, surprisingly light, into the shopping cart. Lucy handed Owen the duct tape and he slapped it tight over Snead's mouth while Lucy frisked Snead from head to toe. As she did, Owen pulled tarp over the shopping cart, covering Snead up as she worked on. Like this they looked like two homeless people rifling through their stuff, a common sight.

She pulled out from under the tarp finally and muttered, "Nothing, just his phone," which she handed to Owen. It was already turned off. She added a shake of her head. They couldn't truly know what he had on him, somewhere, something beyond Tiles or AirTags. Implants even. They couldn't. All they could do was push on.

They headed down the street toward the van, glancing every which way, looking like a meth-fueled pair now. Owen couldn't believe he was doing this. It was like watching himself act from outside his body. He was too worked up to be scared. They were two small wild animals in the deepest and darkest of woods, protecting their bounty from a million predators, everywhere, all around, all those windows, stoops, cars. He kept expecting someone to shout at them but no one did.

They reached the corner, Seventh Avenue, four lanes of one-way traffic. They waited at the corner with others, a dude with earbuds in, a woman staring straight ahead, focused. Them with a body under tarp. Surreal. Owen was puffing away to keep people clear.

He and Lucy both marching in place. The light changed. They pushed off, across the crosswalk, all hands on the cart handle, just another homeless couple looking for a spot for the night.

They turned for Fifteenth, for the van, a narrow street again.

"Hey!" they heard.

They kept going.

"Hey, you two!"

Lucy jabbed Owen. They halted. Turned around.

A man faced them. Midfifties, lean, T-shirt and jeans, tattoos on his arms, seemingly not fazed by the cold at all.

Owen stood tall. "What?" Lucy said.

"You two need help?" the man said. "I know of a place."

Owen noticed a cross tattoo among the others. Oh shit—a good Samaritan.

"No, we're fine," Lucy was saying. Owen noticed a black town car cruising slowly past on Seventh, then another, and told himself they weren't Viktoria or worse.

"I've been there, believe me," the man told them. "Come on. I'll take you there. Get you something to eat. Talk about what's keeping you out here."

"No," Lucy snapped, but the man only smiled a sad smile. His feet planted. He was not budging.

The adrenaline had surged up Owen's chest and throat like a fire hose and into his brain. He might as well be on meth. His shoulders squared. He got in the guy's face.

"She said no fucking way, man. What part don't you understand. Huh, motherfucker?"

The man sighed. He nodded. He backed away. They watched him. He finally turned and strolled off down Seventh Avenue with his head down.

They pushed on. Owen was now expecting to hear sirens, but there were none. They reached the van. Snead might have groaned under the tarp but they couldn't worry about that now. Lucy had told Owen there wasn't CCTV on this street or the one where they nabbed Snead, but they couldn't be sure. They just had to keep going. They reached their panel van, a silver Dodge. Owen kept watch while Lucy opened the side door. Then, together, they heaved the cart up into the van.

THURSDAY, NOVEMBER 30
ALEX / LUCY

I really hope Mason Snead liked his roofie. All right, it's technically not a roofie, but the same deal. It's ketamine, otherwise
known as Special K, vitamin K, cat Valium, kitty. Detaches you
from reality. We're inside my Show Game studio. Our way in is
an old delivery door on the side street, perfect for this. We had
frisked Snead while he was still out, as best as we could, then
searched him again later. It's now pushing six a.m. We've had to
hold Snead overnight because this good kitty got up on top of
him and kept him groggy, delirious even. He's been muttering
in different languages I don't know. I ended up slapping duct
tape back over his mouth, it was freaking me out so much.

It's a huge risk keeping him so long, but I want him to be lucid.
I want him to be lucid because I'm doing this, my final Show
Game, a little bit differently. We're doing it live. The live stream
will go out to the world via multiple platforms, FreeChain,
YouTube, TikTok, WhatsApp, you name it, platforms I forgot as
soon as we signed up for them while anonymous and encrypted.
We're doing it live for full effect.

And now Snead is finally conscious. Come hell or high water. We have him in a chair in the middle of the grim space, just one caged light on above him, all the lights off in the new living room corner so he doesn't identify any details, just in case we ever get away with this. But that is not the point.

Snead stares at us. We're standing back in the half darkness. Ever since he woke again, about twenty minutes ago, he's been peering into the darkness all around him as if to confirm how many people are holding him. We don't have the tripod up yet or the metal briefcase, not until we're ready. I want him lucid, but also scared if that's possible. Holding off on what we're planning will hopefully keep him guessing, sweating, despairing.

"Want that duct tape off?" I say. "If you try to yell, we'll tape your eyes shut too."

He mutters and nods.

I step into the light and rip off the tape, then jump back like he's a wild bear who might take a swat at me with his big paw claws. Even though he still has those zip ties restraining his wrists, resting in his lap.

He takes a couple deep breaths, then nods at us, not smiling but not frowning either. "Thanks."

"It wasn't a favor," I say.

"What did you give me?" he says. "You really know your stuff. That wasn't bad. I feel almost no ill effects. Let me know if you're so inclined to—"

I lunge forward and slap him across the face. He doesn't even grimace. He just stretches out his face to lose the pain and looks like he's yawning. I want to slap him again but I don't. I just step back.

Owen is staring at me in shock.

"Where's my phone?" Snead says.

Owen has it in his pocket. I glance at him, and he shakes his head. Our eyes are widening at the same time, and I can tell he's thinking the same as me: What if Snead has some kind of tracking device on his phone? Technically it can't be tracked when it's turned off, but there could be ways. That, or he's just trying to make us anxious.

"Tossed it in a garbage can," I say.

My answer doesn't seem to worry Snead, but it does make him cock his head at me. I'm using my regular voice.

He smiles. "You're Lucy, right?" he says.

I shrink up inside, the worst cramping I've ever known, like I've eaten toxic oysters, and I have chills all over. I can't speak. I can feel Owen staring at me, stepping closer, ready to hold me up.

"I have to admit, you got me with that homeless bit," Snead says. "You really played the part."

"Shut up," I say, like some stupid kid, like that young woman he'd raped twice.

"Now, I suspected it might be you, but I didn't know how you were going to do it."

Does he really know it's me? Or is he just fucking with me? "How would you know?" I say. "There's been too many victims for that, you sick fuck."

He ignores the comment. "I have to say, you caught me off guard going on offense like you're doing now. I wasn't sure if I was a target. Yet here I am." He adds a grin. He shakes his head. "Man, you nearly got old Gerry Hartwell to spill my name. Bravo." He adds a little clapping gesture, but with his wrists bound he looks like a trained seal, which he definitely is not.

I wanted him lucid, and now I've got the whole deal.

"And now it's your turn," I say.

"Still, you couldn't have done this alone. Even I would've

needed help—a Viktoria type at the least." He swivels his head toward Owen in the darkness. "Is that your helper? The one who's been abetting you all along? He's back, huh?"

"Shut up," I say.

"Chip?" Snead says. "Chip, is that you?"

My mouth drops open. I might have gasped. I want to slap Snead again, but my feet are rooted to the spot.

"Or should I say, Reggie Dinkins?" he adds.

I step back farther into the darkness. How could he know? For a moment I consider Berta having tipped him off, but that's impossible. No, it's just the same old, all-powerful Mason Snead. His tentacles everywhere.

"What, you didn't think I wouldn't have my own investigators on the case?" Snead says. "Oh sure, I had my *FreeChain News* team, guy by the name of Owen Tanaka, but he was just there to legitimize discoveries as they transpired. If need be. Though he was getting nowhere, despite my high hopes for him. Not his fault. Too many victims, so too many leads. No, see, I had my own private investigators, good people much like you."

I don't say anything. I just stand there, inside the darkness.

"They said you might've gone underground. I knew you were here in the city somewhere, I just knew it. I could just feel you," he says, drawing out the *es* in *feel*.

I feel like my feet are barefoot, and in icy cold water.

He snickers. "Now, don't go thinking I'd remember you by your face or name or any of that. Body. Ha! You're right. Lucy Holden? Who cares. There've been too many. But one of my investigators brought up your name as a possible perpetrator. He reminded me that you'd worked for me back at UnVest." He adds a chuckle. "I even gave you a ride."

"Fuck you. Go fuck yourself." I'm fumbling for the stun gun on my belt, but Owen rushes over and holds me by the shoulders.

"Don't," he whispers. "He's just trying to get to you. Don't let him. Don't let him win."

"Hey, who's that other one there?" Snead says. "Is that really Chip?"

I don't answer, and neither does Owen. But I can feel his body go rigid. He seems to have gained inches in height. He releases me. He walks into the light.

He pulls off his sunglasses, hat, beard.

"Oh shit," Snead says with an exaggeratedly amused look, his eyebrows arched and his mouth a drastic curl, like an emoji of himself. "Viktoria is not going to like this, not at all. She never did trust you."

"Too bad," Owen says.

Snead is still holding his amused face. He does a slight clap for both of us, just his fingertips, and mutters "bravo" again, but I can see his doll-like skin stretching on his face, away from his eyes and teeth, baring them as if with worry.

"I'm going to help Lucy make sure that you do not get away with it," Owen tells him. "That none of you do."

"Come on, Owen. We always get away with it. Do I have to confirm it for you? We wanted you to find this Show Game perpetrator so we could go after them, him, her, whoever. Our investigators weren't finding enough. So we put you up to it. You are the tool. You find, for us, the truth that we have ordered. You even sounded like you were thinking the same, or at least you told me such when you pitched me your plans, but now I see that was just to throw me off. No matter. After we had the story, we were going to squash it. The Show Game perp would soon vanish forever. If you ended up finding anything out about me meanwhile, then we would squash that, too, with the proverbial, but verified, iron boot. And if you tried pursuing it, we would sue the shit out of you, forever. Press charges. That's what my father taught me. His lawyers too. It's a war of attrition, and money always wins. We always win. That's what we're here for. You know. You studied history, I'm guessing."

"I don't care," Owen says.

"Yes, you do," Snead says. "And you're only making it worse. If you don't let me go, even more people will get hurt. Viktoria, she doesn't fuck around, unlike you two amateurs. Show Game? How quaint."

What's that mean? I wonder. *That even more people will get hurt?*

I have to shut this bastard up. He's just making up the truth, and making us believe it. That's been his MO all along. It's not just the lying, it's getting others to believe it. My chest is heaving with rage, and my hands clench. For the first time, I'm thinking of using violence. We could film his death. We could leave the bastard's body in one of those tubs. Who cares what happens to me. My one elbow's cocked. I've stopped blinking and can feel the air on my steeled eyeballs. I start walking toward Snead, my fists tight, ready.

But then Owen's next to me again. He cradles my elbow. He murmurs so Snead can't hear us. "Remember what I said? Do not let him get to you. That's exactly what he wants. You don't want to use violence, remember? Don't let him compromise you. Ever."

I nod, my elbow lowering. We stand in silence a moment, inside the darkness. Watching Snead. He can't see us. I'm not positive, but I think we really do have him worried. He raises his bound hands and tugs at his nose with one. He's glancing around, and his eyes are bulging, and his waxy skin now has drops of sweat on it.

"Hey!" he shouts finally. "I got bad news for you."

That gives me a jolt inside. Owen lets me go. I walk over to Snead, my arms crossed. "What?"

"I've been here a few hours at least, right? Possibly overnight. Which means a lot could have happened, could be underway. I always have contingency plans. So, if I haven't returned? And if Chip isn't here? Then I hate to break it to you. We were tracking him, just in case. So he's been targeted by now. And he's been found dead."

"I don't believe you."

"You better start." Snead adds a sick little chuckle. "Suicide, brought on by PTSD. You see, I have my own helpers."

"No," Owen blurts.

"Don't listen to him," I tell Owen. "He's fucking with me—with us."

But Owen's staring at me with eyes wide, because he can tell that it must be true.

I pull the stun gun and release the safety and fire into Snead's chest, making him grimace and fling his bound wrists out and kick his feet around in pain, for at least five seconds like I'm not supposed to because of valuable organs, and I don't care if it kills him or not.

Snead would've flopped right out of his seat and onto the concrete floor but his waist is duct-taped to the chair. He sits there slumped, in a daze that should be uncomfortable, but he's still got a little smirk on his face. He probably likes it, the freak. I remind myself, as I stare at Snead rolling his head around, drooling a little, that you can't just violate these fuckers like they had done to so many. No, you had to take away that thing that gives them such disgusting self-worth. Making them reveal the truth themselves is my way. I'm betting Mason Snead's biggest fear is being exposed to the world for what he truly is, despite all his bluffing to the contrary right now. He acts like he has no rules, no limits. So we're going to test that. We're standing there staring at him with our arms cocked, like two moving guys about ready to lift a big piece of furniture.

Owen's looking at me like he doesn't like this at all. He looks a little pale. "I hope I didn't inadvertently tip them off to you somehow. To your man Chip. Good god . . ."

I won't give it a second thought. "I don't care," I tell him, "but thank you."

Owen is still eyeing me, as if to gauge how well I'm doing. I stare back at him. I wonder how pale I must look.

"I'm okay," I say eventually.

"We've come this far," he replies, and I'm impressed by how much grit this dude has. He's really surprised me. He's that rare person who has recognized the major challenge of his life and is rising to meet it. There's a poise there, a focus, like an Olympic athlete. He's the best locker-room teammate ever. It gives me strength to be on his team.

"You can do this," he adds as if reading my mind.

"Thank you."

"Wheeewww," Snead warbles and throws his head back as if he's just snorted poppers, and the thought of him using amyl nitrite on me or any other victim makes me reach for the stun gun again—

My burner phone beeps. So does Owen's.

We stare at each other. We read:

Freebird. I'm at the door. Open up.

It's Berta Gonzales. Owen looks up from his phone at me. We had decided to let her know our basic plan and our location. She'd promised not to contact us unless she had urgent news. Her only goal has remained getting at Viktoria on her own. But now here she is at our door?

Owen steps over to me. "I can go," he whispers.

"No, you watch him," I whisper back. "If I have to stare at him any longer, I might just shock him again."

I navigate the dark former workshop, all purples and blacks and blues at dawn, using my burner phone as a light. As I climb the few steps and approach the door, my chest fills with the tightness of dread. What if it's some kind of ruse? What if Berta has been working us all along? I never did take a deep look at her relationship with her daughter. There could be a team of thugs outside. Berta could be waiting to torture me in this very same room even—

Stop! I tell myself. That's just what Mason Snead and all the Mason Sneads of the world want. They want us to be scared. Me. So that we will never truly act. They want us to be scared of the fear itself.

I listen at the door for a moment, but all I can hear is Snead chuckling far off at the other end of the workshop. He finally shuts up. I keep listening. I even cup my ear to the door like a kid. I unlock one dead bolt. I listen. Hear nothing. I unlock the other. Listen, nothing. I crack the door open, which brings in the crisp air. I peek around through the slight gap.

We've removed the exterior light by the door and it's still dim out, and she only appears in silhouette. But it's her. I've seen Berta like this before. I open the door farther and she slips inside. I lock the dead bolts. I flash my phone on her as she peers through the dark at Snead under the light across the long room. She's wearing a disguise, too: hair up under a trucker hat, boxy peacoat, and large, thick-framed glasses like New Yorkers can pull off. I breathe a sigh of relief. I mostly wish no one would carry guns, but I'm hoping she's packing under that coat.

"What's going on?" I say, and as soon as I do, my eyes, now readjusting to the dimmer light, see how drawn her face looks. Her chin might even be quivering. She pulls off her glasses. Her eyes are wet.

We hear Snead warble from afar. "Whooo is it?"

We ignore him. My eyes are wet now. They burn.

"Chip," I say.

"How did you know?"

I nod toward Snead in his chair. "He said he knows we have a helper. Even called him by name. Said he'd been found dead. I was telling myself he was just fucking with us."

Berta's shoulders slump. She shakes her head. "It'll be reported as suicide, and there will be no way to prove it otherwise. Plenty of factors can be seen as driving him to it. His wife had even left him for good. He tried getting in touch with her. But she'd taken his daughter away, once and for all I imagine."

"Oh god."

"I knew they'd had their own investigators on this, ones like you. They've always had. But she, they, were clearly making more progress than I'd thought."

I don't reply. By "she" Berta means her Hayley—of course she would've been in charge of that. All the more reason for her to distrust Owen. Me, all I can think of is Chip. Would they have tortured him? Probably not, since it had to look like a suicide. But who knew what they might have told him, might have implanted in his psyche for him to carry with him forever right before he died. I can only hope he didn't believe it, that he still recognized truth. And I forgive him already if he might've told them things about me, about this, that he didn't want to. I don't say this to Berta. She's surely considered that possibility, which she promptly confirms.

"I had to warn you," Berta adds. "I came personally, in case . . ."

"In case what?"

Suddenly my phone's like a cancerous and germ-ridden organ in my bare fingers. "Maybe these burners aren't even safe."

"We need to get rid of them. Who really knows? We can't really trust any of it."

"Right," I say and grab Bertha's burner from her hand. I go over to Owen who, already reaching the same conclusions, hands me his. It's like the guy can see us over in the dark, like he even has night-vision now. I toss the burners into one of the tubs and start smashing them with a mallet that the last tenant so conveniently left for me. I'm bashing them into bits.

In between the crunching and cracking blows, I can hear Snead chuckling again over in his seat. I imagine that I'm pounding his skull into bits, all that's missing is the blood and brain.

And I hate myself for it. I don't, cannot, want to become that.

Berta has meanwhile wandered over to the edge of the darkness. I go back to her and stand by her side. She has put her glasses back on. She nods at Mason Snead squinting at us, trying to make us out. Berta's nodding at him, her chin high. I realize now that they might've met before. Maybe she'd even tried to warn him or his people off Hayley before, years ago, when she thought there was still a chance.

"Goddamnit, Chip," Berta whispers in a trill that's close to sobbing, not caring if Snead can hear or not. We're yards away from him, but who knows what the bastard can hear. For all we know, he has some kind of bionic ear device.

Berta turns to me. Her chin is definitely quivering now. "What if it was my Hayley who did it?"

"It wasn't," I say. "You have to believe that."

Owen comes over and stands on the other side of Berta. We stare at the target, all three of us. I wait for Berta to compose herself, to start breathing normal again.

I turn to her eventually. "Without those burners, how are we going to stay in contact with you?"

"You're not. Because I'm going to be right here with you two the whole time. Right by your side."

OWEN

He wasn't getting cold feet. But fifteen minutes after Berta Gonzalez had arrived to join them, the reality of what they were doing started hitting Owen hard. The thought that he might have inadvertently led them to Lucy—and to her previous helper, a guy named Chip—should only have steeled him more. But he could practically feel the blood receding from his skin, surely blanching his face. His bowels wanted to empty, even though he didn't need to go. He felt heavy. Every move deliberate. Every action they took from here on out especially was going to shape their fates and those of many others forever.

Owen took a spare moment to compose himself inside the darkness of the IKEA living area, where he'd been plugging in an extension strip for Lucy's Show Game gear. He, for the hundredth time, recalled that last text he and Molly had shared.

I love you, too, Owen. Stay safe.

It would have to do. If that were the last time they ever communicated, it would wear well. He reminded himself that this was all about truth. Anything he did from here on out was to save it. He wasn't a hero. He simply had no choice. He took stock, looking around the room. He was seeing how this worked for the first time, on the inside. The sheer simplicity of it inspired him further. Beyond Snead sitting under the glaring light bulb, Lucy was setting up the tripod with red tactical light and burner phone ready to shoot video—for streaming the Show Game live on FreeChain and wherever else online that wouldn't block it. She already had the metal briefcase ready. It stood on a pedestal, this time just an old office chair jacked up to its highest.

279

Berta had set it there on Lucy's instruction and, feeling its light weight, still didn't ask Lucy what was inside. She had them huddle in the corner while Snead dozed again, that welcome side effect of the tranquilizer and repeated stun guns blasts, and Berta asked them good questions about the premises. They had good and bad news for Berta. There was one main door out— the one Berta had come in. It was located on a stoop with a platform that may have served as a small loading dock at one point in its long history, but any loading doors once there had long since been covered over. Their space had no windows and no other floors, so there was no good way to observe what was happening outside. But there were stairs down to a basement storage room. That room then had a few steps that led up to a rusty metal cellar double door opening to the sidewalk, once used for deliveries many ages ago. It still opened. They could bolt it if they wanted. But Lucy considered it more harm than help, because they were not escaping this. If anything, it would help whoever came to take them out. By the time anyone detected them, they would have those double metal access doors covered for sure.

"Don't be so sure," Berta had said. "We have to keep all options open. Remember that." And she made eye contact with both of them until both of them nodded.

Owen was glancing at Lucy, slightly nodding at her to urge her on.

Berta noticed immediately. "What? You forgot something? Or more bad news?"

"The latter," Lucy said. "He knows who we are. He figured out it was me. Then Owen revealed himself." She smiled at Owen. "He didn't want me to be alone."

Berta gave Owen a smile, but hers was sad and bitter.

"Maybe not the best move," he said.

"Doesn't matter," Berta said. "And Owen didn't give you away. Or Chip either. You got that, Owen? They would've figured it out anyway. They would've found you eventually. Even after."

Lucy nodded to that, solemnly, like listening to a funeral sermon. Then she devoted herself to the tripod. Berta meanwhile probed the ceiling with a high-grade penlight she'd magically produced, searching for any other access routes.

When Berta returned, she called them to another huddle off in the darkness of the kitchenette. "No other access," she said. "There's an old ventilation shaft but there's no getting up that. Now, downstairs? That's another story. We should be listening for that."

"I have to urinate," Snead blurted into the glaring light surrounding him.

Berta registered it with barely the twitch of one eyelid. And Owen wondered just what kind of operations she'd been on. Maybe it had been forced interrogations even, in locations vulnerable to attack and their supplies low. Just because she was FBI overtly didn't mean she had not become some other being covertly. But then she paused, as if having lost her train of thought, and she released a sigh that made her sound tired for the first time. Owen handed her a water from the fridge, and some nuts, both of which she declined. "No. We'll need to conserve," she continued mechanically, staring into the darkest corner of the room.

Owen now observed Lucy watching them. She had been looking more worried, with her brow pinched, and he could spot the concern in her eyes. Now Lucy kept glancing over at him. She was practically shouting it at him. She wanted him to do what they were both thinking.

Berta snapped out of it. She glared at him, at Lucy. "What? Out with it, you two."

Owen cleared his throat. "Do you feel up to this?" he said. "I mean, it's all right if you're not. We understand."

Berta showed him a grimace that made him wince inside, like she was a kid with a new mousetrap and he the mouse just stepping into it. "You mean, can I hack it, right? That what you mean? What, from my age, or maybe it's my sex?" She pointed at him, stabbing with the finger. She grimaced at Lucy, too, like she was Owen's identical male twin. "Let me tell you two something, just for the record. You know how I know Chip? I trained the damn guy. Me. I did." She added a couple pats to her chest.

"Point taken," Owen muttered. But he and Lucy did share an amused glance. And it relieved the tightening in his bowels for a time.

Berta waved Lucy over to them, around the sofa.

"Listen," Berta said. "You, Lucy—you come first now. My daughter second. Maybe I can get her detained somehow. Maybe I can still divert somehow. I don't know. We'll play it by ear. But I will not interfere in your operation. I'll give suggestions. I might object to things. But you're calling the shots. Just so that's crystal clear, to both of you."

Lucy's brow had stopped pinching. Her eyes had widened with respect, maybe awe. "Thank you," she said.

She and Owen shared an optimistic nod.

Owen glanced at the back of Snead. Snead kept twitching, kept trying to spin in the chair, but the wheels had a lock, luckily. In the light, in silhouette, the combination of chair and hunched man and bound limbs made him look like part beast, part weapon. Berta, meanwhile, was eyeing Snead like he was only a piñata and someone had just handed her the big stick. Owen even noticed the hint of a smile.

Minutes later, they set up the shot. They were all still in disguise despite Snead knowing identities, more in respect for

Berta than anything. She had her trucker hat pulled down tight over her pulled-up hair and her collar up. Snead watched her, his eyes scanning.

"Not very polite of you not to introduce yourself," he said to her.

Berta ignored him. She was positioning the chair that held the metal briefcase to the side of Snead while Lucy directed from her spot looking at the phone's video camera. Then Lucy switched on the red tactical light mounted to the multifunction tripod, illuminating the corrugated silver case.

She'd already told Owen earlier: *This time? It's empty, a prop. I don't have anything inside.*

She didn't have any smoking-gun evidence implicating Snead in all his exponentially sick crimes, besides her own body and mind and memory of course. Even if she did, it would require a briefcase bigger than the five boroughs put together. No, Lucy was still betting that Mason Snead's biggest fear was being exposed to the world for what he truly was. And that this would destroy him.

Snead's eyes widened, but sparkled with delight. "Oooh, here we go," he said. "When are you posting on FreeChain? I want to see."

Lucy had decided not to tell Snead they were doing it live this time. It would probably give him an actual erection. All their eyes had long adjusted to the dark majority of the room and all of them were instinctively moving on tiptoes, like an actual film crew right before an interview. They couldn't see outside, but Owen knew the morning light would soon be finding the spaces between the buildings, the purples and blacks out there becoming grays and blues.

Sunrise meant the morning news. Owen again checked the portable shortwave radio and TV they had, set well behind the tripod on a dinged-up, oil-paint-encrusted metal table, both working only by antenna and neither with good reception. The screen was tiny, and black and white. It might as well have been 1978. The few stations they got on the TV were showing no damning news, to his semi-relief. Nor was the radio. Certainly nothing about another lowly deserter who had committed suicide; the country was full of them.

So that Snead couldn't hear any developments, Owen was using the single-ear earphone that came with the set. Owen's job was to help monitor the outside world just in case the news got out. Berta, meanwhile, was standing nearby in their darkness behind Lucy. She had the programmable digital radio scanner, which she kept checking with headphones as well, but she could walk and talk and listen like the pro she was. She kept giving Owen little shakes of her head, as if reading his mind that he wanted updates, even though she'd told them she didn't put much stock in the scanner. Their location would likely be compromised. They'd never know who found them—FreeChain's back-end feelers, YouTube/Google's, Snead's henchmen, local law enforcement, feds, NSA, anyone. And, from Berta's experience, their arrival wouldn't likely be announced even over a scanner. Yet it was all they had. It was a crapshoot.

And that didn't even take into account the public out there, Owen knew. Popular sentiment about the Show Game was rising, if not exploding via social media, and dividing rapidly. The harsh opposition to the Show Game as fueled by astroturfing was all too easy to engineer, and Owen figured that Snead was somehow behind that, too—the only MO of a narcissistic socio-path being chaos, with a clear eye toward sowing mistrust, division, violence even.

Snead had raised his chin and was glaring at Lucy, who was still standing behind the tripod, ready to roll. She turned to

Owen and Berta and gave them that look that said, quiet on the set.

"Ask whatever you want," Snead said. "Ask away."

Owen felt a hard ball forming in his gut, and his mouth felt dry. He suddenly wondered if Snead would not just simply lie. They might unintentionally be playing into his hands, falling right into his trap even. He could better own the big lie this way, and all would believe. Who knew what Snead would say. He could even blame his own crimes on them—they were trying to cover it up! Such was the mark of a true sociopath.

Owen's TV was on low volume in his ear, but he now heard a drumroll-like sound. He peered at the screen:

BREAKING NEWS: Master Entrepreneur Mason Snead Reported Missing

ALEX / LUCY

Me, I'm more than ready to get this started, but I turn to Owen and Berta and they both have earphones in and Owen's glancing at Berta like someone just stabbed him, and Berta's clearly deducing something from the look on his face. Berta shakes her head back at him as if to say, *whatever it was you just saw or heard, it was not on my digital scanner.*

Now my heart is thumping, wanting to burst right out of my chest. I take a couple deep breaths, and do not let Snead see me.

He's holding his bound hands up to block the light.

"What are you waiting for?" he says. "Let's do this. I'm ready to crush it."

The three of us meet halfway, in a dark huddle. Owen gives me the news. It's all over the media. All that is known is that Mason Snead has been reported missing. There's likely more to that, as Owen clearly knows all too well, but it's currently being withheld. Berta confirms that she's hearing little activity on the scanner, at least locally. None of us should be surprised, but it doesn't exactly help the pit in my stomach and dry swelling in my throat.

"We should now assume that the gears are in motion," Berta tells us.

I can finally see the strain on her. Her face looks drawn and her mouth stays parted a little, as if she, too, needs more air for her thumping heart and racing blood.

"Which one of you two women is talking?" Snead barks at us. "You all sound the same."

We ignore him. But it does make Berta raise her chin, and her eyes light up like she's just realized something she hadn't before.

"We go anyway," I tell her and Owen. "Let's see how far we get."

"Only option," Owen says mechanically, and Berta nods even more assertively.

I turn to Snead. I stride up to behind the tripod.

"Here we go!" I begin. "To win, you have to earn one hundred fifty points. You get fifty for admitting that you did it. You get another fifty for saying who helped you directly. Then, you get that final fifty for saying that you are sorry. To the world. To all those you hurt, devastated, let die thinking they're worthless. If you do all that, you win, and you're set free—"

"Yes, yes, I know, I know," Snead says, grinning now.

And as soon as I've said this, it already sounds inadequate, like a child's description of the universe. How is our little show supposed to capture it all, even if he does admit anything? We'll need a good hour at least. The truth is so damn messy.

I also can't help noticing that Snead hasn't even glanced at the metal briefcase on the chair.

"Just remember," I continue, "we have proof of it all, plus we have that briefcase there as your handy little glowing red reminder, so we'll just release it all, anyway, if you don't admit it, or don't say who helped you, or that you're sorry."

Snead loses the grin. Opens his mouth to speak. He only moves his lips, but I'm a pretty good lip-reader. "I'm ready," he says.

I'm ready too. Because the briefcase is me.

I'm going to tell the world everything. About him. About what they did to me. What they do to so many others, every day, in both the tiny and even horribly larger ways.

I take a deep breath. I push the red button, turning on the video. This time we're live to the world, and Snead still doesn't know. I'm doing it as *Jane Doe* this time. I hold up the voice changer.

"Hello, world," I say into it. "The first thing you the audience should know is that, yours truly, the creator of the Show Game, is a woman. She has been all along. Now, with that out of the way . . ."

Mason Snead isn't grinning now, but he's still holding his chin high, the very picture of pride and even honor. *There will be people who see him as having the latter no matter what he says*, I remind myself, swallowing hard.

I say, "For the first fifty points, do you admit to the following—"

"Pssst!"

It's Owen, behind me. I whip around, rush over to him. Letting the live feed run, showing just Snead waiting, shifting, peering from his bound position in his chair.

Owen shows me the screen. More Breaking News: they're reporting that the approximate location of where Snead is being held has "now been revealed."

Berta has rushed over too. "It's all over the scanner," she says in a staccato whisper. "It's this area, this block sounds like, but they don't know the exact address."

"Oh shit," Owen mutters.

"Cool your jets. If they knew the exact location, they'd probably be bashing the door down by now."

Not unless Mason Snead wants his own Show Game, I think in horror. Such is the narcissist. I don't tell them that.

"Jesus, look," Owen then says. He shows us the little TV screen.

Now I couldn't even speak if I wanted.

Owen switches channels. More of the same.

"Seriously?" I mutter eventually.

People. Crowds. They know the location too. They're descending on the area, some in support and others against according to the news ticker. Some even have signs. TV helicopters and drones are capturing it from above. There are hundreds of them, but swelling into thousands by the second, like waters surging into streets from a nearby river flood.

"What? Come on," Snead says.

We ignore him.

"It'll be chaos," I say.

"This might work in our favor," Berta says. "His people might've alerted supporters and protesters somehow first via FreeChain, the dark web, who knows. That ridiculous Ultimates group. But now it could get out of control. His own henchmen can't get in here. And the authorities? They'll have trouble clearing a path."

"Come on, you guys!" Snead shouts.

I glance over. He's rocking and tilting like a toddler on too much sugar, trying to get the chair moving again.

Owen takes a deep breath. Berta gives me a hard stare. "It's your show," she says.

"We're doing it anyway," I hear myself say, and it sounds so gloomy, like the doomed sergeant in a war movie.

I walk up to the tripod, make sure the stream screen is still showing *Live*.

"You can't handle this!" Snead blurts, practically singing it before I can even bring the charges.

"Wait for the question—"

"No! This is my show, I'm the guest. Let me talk. Don't bother with that briefcase."

"Oh, we'll bother," I say. "That's exactly what we're going to do."

"No, you're not. You can't. You can't handle me."

"I said wait—"

"No!" Snead tries stomping his feet. His head jerks around, back and forth.

"Yes. I repeat: For the first fifty points, do you admit to the following—"

"I was abused," Snead says.

My mouth hangs open.

"From a very young age," he says. "Mentally, physically, sexually."

"What?" I mutter.

"I can confirm that I was given up for adoption," he continues. "I technically ended up in a foster home, sure, but it wasn't a regular one, oh no no, so let's not be giving regular foster homes a bad rap or adoptive parents for that matter."

Oh no, you're not—you don't get to play the victim. Not you. Do you? I glance at Owen and Berta, who shrug back. We'll let him talk, see where this goes.

Snead had pause, as if letting us digest this a moment. "This so-called foster home," he continues, "was secret, part of a trafficking ring. For abusing. All ages, as long as you weren't full adult. Those involved were, are, rich and powerful, and friends of my father's. My parents, Myron and Clarice Snead, were likely part of the ring, too—part of the same ring that I run now. Not that I will ever know for sure, because his death can never be explained. Not even I know. But I assure you it was not natural. Because I once heard that he was having second thoughts." Snead's face hardened, more like bone than skin. "And you know what? That is what you get . . . but only if you have second thoughts."

My throat clears, releasing the heat behind my eyes. They probably owned that building I once escaped, the so-called private club. This is Rosebud straight from hell. I want to abort but something deep inside me just lets it roll. The Truth is still the truth, and I asked for it.

Snead is sitting straight up, as best he can. His chin still high.

"No, no," I mutter, my heart racing, jumping.

"You must listen," he says. "I am not a victim! Hell no."

"Stop."

Snead sneers at me. "You see, I am above all that. I learned from all of it. This was my true education. Skipping high school for college, traveling the world with a backpack? It was all part of my broadening. My first investor? I was basically his pimp . . ."

Snead stops talking, tilting his head. He's listening for something. I listen, and I hear it too. It's a low rumble, punctuated by sirens in the distance. Berta sends Owen to the door, to check on it. He peeks out, bringing a shaft of fresh daylight, freezes there a moment, then slams the door and rushes over to me and Berta.

"Holy shit!" he whispers, "there are tons of people out there. Can't tell whose side they're on. No police getting through that any time quick."

"What's that sound?" Snead says.

No one answers him.

"Keep rolling," he shouts. "I want my time. This is my time! I want to tell the whole world."

Live streaming is still rolling. So I let it roll. I nod at Snead to keep talking.

"I am nothing new," he says. "My father taught me that. Nor was he. I've existed all throughout history. Rome, Middle Ages, Inquisition, Enlightenment, revolutions, you name it. Modern times, too, sure. And you can guess where. Always a man, always with great means and taste. Call it what you like. Stealing many men's souls. Robbing their faith. But in the end they always thanked me. Compromise them once, you compromise them forever . . ."

I'm shaking my head. This is starting to sound more than crazed. I would laugh out loud if it weren't so horrific. Snead is owning it, like he's launching some bold new start-up, another fucking TED Talk. He actually wants to make it legitimate, make him the victim and perpetrator and master all in one. He's that sick, that narcissistic, the ultimate product of his environment.

"Don't shake your head at me!" he shouts at me, but with a half-smile. "UnVest was how you found out about Dwayne Specklin, am I right?"

I mute the audio. The video's still live.

Owen and Berta step forward, surely glaring at me, but they let me do it.

Snead is right. I was able to leverage our research on pedophile priests to confirm that it was Specklin who had abused my brother—so much so that my brother killed himself.

"So you were using me, too, in your way," Snead continues. "But that's okay. Because you never would've found out without me!"

That jolts me. I'd considered that he might call me into this, but I didn't know it would feel like touching an electric cattle fence.

"No," I blurt.

"Yes," Snead says. "See? I told you that you can't handle this. Me. If you follow this logically. This truth? It means that I am practically your own brother."

"Fuck you." I back away from the camera, into the darkness. The audio's still on mute. A bad dream silent movie. The whole world must wonder what they're seeing. It's just Snead in his chair.

Berta grabs me by a shoulder.

What happens next happens in sheer seconds.

"You have to go, now," Berta says. "Both of you."

Owen's standing on the other side of me now. "What about you?" he says to Berta.

"I'm going to create a diversion."

"No!" I bark at her. "You were going to come with us."

"I never was, Lucy, and you know that. This, it's my way of reaching my little Hayley, and it always was."

"Don't go!" Snead shouts from his chair. He then groans in half frustration, half pleasure, and it reminds me of things sexual that I don't want to know. I'm just thankful I can't remember my two nights with him. "Please," he moans, "please . . ."

"All right," I tell Berta. "We'll go."

OWEN

The corroded old metal cellar double door wasn't bolted now, but Owen and Lucy could feel and hear the people trampling on it as they passed. They waited for the bang-rumble to end, both of them on the rickety steel steps, all four hands on the handle in case it stuck somehow.

They had discussed this as an escape plan, but Owen hadn't thought Lucy would go for it. Then Snead opened his mouth, and Berta made too much sense, and here they were, back in their disguises. It was the only chance, really. They'd let the camera roll, the video still streaming, with Berta behind the tripod. As they rushed down into the cellar, quietly so that Snead couldn't hear them, they heard Berta promising Snead that Lucy was still here—she just didn't want him to see her now. Not yet.

Berta had turned the audio back on. Snead was talking. But Owen and Lucy could barely hear now. The rumbling above was too great.

"Ready?" Owen said.

Lucy had frozen. "What if they're not on our side?" They could be torn apart alive, she really meant.

The rumbling above returned, vibrating in their knuckles and wrists on the handle.

"We have to take the chance," Owen said. "Come on. All right? You wanted him to talk. He's talking. I wanted the truth. The real truth. Forever. I got it. We both got it. So now we at least try to survive."

"But he hasn't said he's sorry."

"He never will either. You know that. His kind never will."

Lucy nodded at that. She listened. The rumbling stopped again.

"Let's go," she said.

They pushed and charged up the steps at the same time as they turned the handle and they rushed out of the doors and Owen pushed them shut again so no one would head down there, not yet. The sunlight blinded them a second. People were rushing by them, but a few stopped. Owen and Lucy moved in a circle, watching those few become a larger circle around them.

Two athletic-looking women in rain gear smiled at them. One whispered, "Wait, are you them?"

Owen and Lucy exchanged glances. Then Owen spotted a protest sign passing: LONG LIVE THE TRUTH.

"Yes," he blurted.

"Good for you. Come on." The women hooked their arms onto Owen's and Lucy's and dragged them along and they moved within the crowd, concealed by it, all in a blur of people bundled up, the people shouting chants that pumped steam into the cold air and raising their gloved fists now, and more and more signs. Owen heard sirens, but they were still off in the distance.

They turned a corner of the block, then another. The women had moved on. He and Lucy were now locked with another group, young men and women on Owen's side and old hippies on Lucy's side. She nudged him as they passed a side street and Owen saw the police and riot teams forming blocks away. They had no choice but to let the crowd carry them.

They turned another corner and were suddenly in a massive crowd facing the little platform up the short steps leading to their hideout. All were jostling for position, and he now saw that protesters from the other side were starting to argue with the opposing groups Owen and Lucy were now inside. The Ultimates were there with their silly masks and homemade flags and wannabe military gear, of course. He then noticed that people had phones and devices with the live stream on. They could see Snead on-screen, ranting away, but Berta must've said something to bring all these people to this door.

The Ultimates had signs with slogans like MIGHT MAKES RIGHT, POWER IS THE KING GOD, and SINNERS = SAINTS; some arguments were descending into pushing, shoving, worse. Owen spotted a few men with open carry weapons and gritted his teeth, bracing himself for shots at any moment. Who knew what else they were lugging under all those parkas and overcoats.

Yet lines of riot police were moving in from all sides, separating groups into sections. But that was behind them. Hundreds, possibly thousands, filled this street before the platform, and it would take the police time. Owen glanced at someone's screen and saw what looked like Snead shouting for Berta, looking around still bound to his chair, all alone.

The door at the top of the steps parted. Slowly. People calmed, hushed.

Berta emerged. She had removed her disguise hat and glasses. The platform had a little pipe railing. Berta grasped it with white knuckles as if prepared to be shot any moment.

Owen and Lucy grasped at each other's sleeves. Owen watched the faces around him. Some were beaming at her like pilgrims at the Vatican on Easter, while others glared at her like she was a serial killer who'd just been acquitted on a technicality.

All seemed to calm even more. All stopped moving, even the police.

Through the heads, Owen spotted a shock of jet-black hair, a severe bob cut.

It was Viktoria Jett.

He nudged Lucy, who stood on tiptoes to spot her.

Two thuggish-looking men were about ready to charge up the stairs, but Viktoria gestured at them, shouting. They turned to her, listened to her, and guarded the steps instead.

The morning sun was just now finding its way through side streets and between rooftops, building spires, twinkling metal and glass and glowing the stone and plaster.

Berta and Viktoria had made eye contact. Berta stared down at her.

"Who are you?" someone shouted at Berta.

Berta nodded, then released her hands from the railing and held her arms up high, partly in surrender, partly in exhortation. "Who am I? I am Alex. And I am Jane Doe. And so are all of you."

LUCY

I want to run to Berta, to stop her, but then I see Viktoria Jett's face. It's suddenly Hayley's again. That hard face of Viktoria's softens and opens and the new sun glows on it and the difference couldn't be more striking than if Viktoria aka Hayley had grabbed at her severe hair and pulled off a wig and face mask.

Berta still stands at the top of those steps, having just made her declaration that she herself is me. Berta keeps her arms up high. Her daughter walks up the steps to her, slowly, and I'm sure she's starting to cry.

The last thing I see before Owen and I move out is the two of them hugging.

Owen drags me along through the crowd. It closes ranks after us and there's no way back. I keep glancing over my shoulder, keep hopping up on tiptoes for another look.

Up on the steps, Berta is now talking to the police moving in on her. It makes sense what she did. She has the perfect reason—her little girl. She wanted to save Hayley from Viktoria forever. Plus, her voice is also female. That was why her eyes had lit up when Snead remarked that our voices all sounded the same—she realized she had a plan. And Snead himself, he probably had no idea who the mastermind was, apart from a woman. I want to slap her and hug her tight at the same time. My eyes grow warm with tears of utmost awe and respect. All I can think is, I hope Berta can finally take those vacations with her husband one day.

Meanwhile the police are letting some of the crowd retreat and flee. They have no choice—it's the only way to release the pressure of the crowds and get at Berta and inside to Snead. As Owen and I move on, we merge into that flow of people looking for a way out.

Someone dropped a phone, I see. I pick it up in midstride, look at the screen. FreeChain app. Snead's still there on our streaming video, speechifying away from inside. I hold it to my ear as we move on, aiming for the end of the throng and open street.

"The tech economy, and libertarian this or that, and the sharing economy, digital blah blah, it's all just a sham," Snead says. "Just another religion. As are the leaders. Bishops, politicians, tycoons, so-called tech geniuses. You all bought it! And you should. Because you need us. And you know why? Because you can't manage yourselves. None of you. Or at least you don't believe you can and never will."

As we pass others staring at Snead on their FreeChain, I hear a guy say, "We're just lucky he never ran for president." And that guy looks like a supporter to me.

The police are waving us through and out along with others. We jog, keep going, a couple streets, around a corner.

"Good job," I tell Owen as we catch our breath. "You sensed it, you acted on it. You should be proud. Your Molly should be proud." And I think that's the only time I ever see his eyes well up. Then again, it's been a long fucking day already.

"I hope so," is all he says.

We can hear Mason Snead's rant coming from passing phones and out of cars and apartment windows. The guy sounds completely nuts. It's narcissism fully exposed. I stop listening. We pass a bar. They have a TV on. We stand in the window and watch like regular New Yorkers. The news is showing the scene outside our hideout. The police are standing back, giving everyone room. They're listening too. I can see that some people who were fighting before are now talking, smiling even. Some are laughing, showing each other Snead on their phones. Some start hugging. Others just walk away shaking their heads, which I'll take as a win.

I can't see Berta or Viktoria now, but I assume they're still talking, hugging, crying despite the police. I hope so. I tell myself they are.

I can tell you how some of this plays out. Once we're in the clear, I will make a statement to the press: I was the mastermind. I, Lucy Holden, am Jane Doe. Berta Gonzalez was only trying to save her daughter. Owen wants me to do it too. Because, as he later tells me, "the full Truth can't be partial, or contradictory, and it can never be turned on its head. Otherwise, people will be deceived or self-deceived into believing the opposite."

Plus, I don't ever want Mason Snead beating me to it.

I will do my time. I might even write a book about it.

We might never know if Mason Snead had even identified me. As for the man himself, he will vanish from public life. As part of a controversial plea deal, it will be rumored that he "retired" to an ultraexclusive private mental institution where he remains very much the same person, repeating to a select few fellow inmates, over and over, that monologue he'd unleashed on the final Show Game.

In one of the stranger twists, Anne Blade will make a slight career pivot. She'll get a job as communications director of the very same private institution housing Mason Snead. Both Owen and I can imagine the rest. Anne Blade could gain full access. Maybe she'll cut off Snead's balls, one at a time. Maybe she'll slowly torture or poison him. Whatever the plan, Anne Blade will have a rock-solid alibi. Or, maybe she'll simply exist there, as a reminder to the man. Do not hinder us, and sure as hell do not abuse us. Not anymore. Because we will persist.

Viktoria will face multiple charges. She will become Hayley Gonzalez again, awaiting trial. She will claim that she was trying to rein in Mason Snead and his people, not help run them as I and Owen had assumed, especially considering her outward behavior. Her mother's ultimate sacrifice convinced her to finally end her masquerade.

But Owen and I don't know any of that yet. We're still staring into the window of that bar with a TV on inside. The news has switched back to Snead, still on my streaming video. I hold the phone to my ear.

Inside the final hideout, Mason Snead is still raving away in his chair. The room is not as dim—someone has turned on a light somewhere. I can make out figures moving toward Snead, slowly, as if they're game wardens about to handle a crocodile, but they're all in silhouette and it's unclear who they may be. Are they his own powerful backers' henchmen? Or cops and feds? His many victims? Maybe it's Viktoria herself.

Before the video stream is cut forever, the last expression we see on Snead is one I've never seen on him, and I expect no one else has, either, apart from his own very first abuser. It's naked fear. Ashen face. Eyes wide. Tears even. He rears back in horror. He speaks.

"No, please, don't . . . don't make me . . . please, don't hurt me."

Snead screams, a screech like a siren on high, distorting, cracking—

The screen goes black, blank.

Owen, next to me, has a tear running down his cheek. I wipe the tear. Hold him by the shoulders until his eyes find mine.

"Stop texting your wife, and call her," I tell him, and he nods.

And I walk off with my head high, with Owen in tow.

WEDNESDAY, DECEMBER 20
OWEN

He wanted to start running now that he'd finally made it into the terminal of Seattle-Tacoma International Airport. But he didn't want to attract attention, or scare anyone, so he fast-walked, which probably made him look even crazier or desperate since he was heading for the exits and not for a departing flight. He didn't care, not anymore. He was almost past security, to as far as nonpassengers could get.

He saw her first. Or did she see him? It was such a blur, all the feelings, the grin spreading across his face, his feet practically floating along.

Molly took careful steps toward him like along rocks in a stream, but she had the same grin, the same blurred look. It had been so long since they'd seen each other, too many months. They still hadn't talked on the phone, let alone by video. Their texting had been working for them so they had stuck to it, until now.

He took her all in at once, and she him. Her soft chin-length hair and her bangs, round glasses. Her compact body. She sparkled. That curl at one side of her mouth now, that twinkle in her eyes. Drawing him in. She stopped before him, with both feet. He grabbed her, held her, his eyes burning hot.

Later, they sat with nearly untouched beers at a corner booth in a little pub in her neighborhood, Queen Anne. They kept staring at each other like two kids who'd just decided to elope, wanting to giggle, wanting to touch each other. Then their faces opened up and stretched tight. Serious now. Questioning. Why did they used to fight?

"It was because I'd wanted to keep my job away from you," he told her. "I thought it would wreck what we had."

"I wanted more, not less," she said. "Don't you get it? The problem was the distance. You wouldn't let me in. But then you started to, and now look at us."

Molly was right again. In an instant, one warm and lovely moment graced by the sunlight from clouds breaking, and magnified by the old pub windowpane, he imagined them working together as an investigative team, not just him working away despite her. Maybe they even teamed up with Lucy Holden.

Then Owen got a little tug in his gut. He now had to tell Molly about Lucy Holden, before it was too late. As promised, Lucy was going to give herself in soon, in the days between Christmas and New Year's. There would be a trial. He would be implicated. He knew that. For now, he had a job still in NYC, but it wasn't anything to go back to. FreeChain was losing so many users it was rumored to be up for sale, just like AltaVista back in the day. Buyers would circle FreeChain with sharpened teeth, and the carnage wouldn't be any prettier than every other journalism buyout. And there might be other, far more sinister threats. Maybe Mason Snead's tentacles could still catch up with him one day—the man would always have his true believers.

But for now, Owen felt grateful. In his own screwed-up way, Mason Snead, via Lucy Holden, had gotten him and Molly back together.

The clouds shifted. The light glowed on Molly's lovely round face now.

Molly reached out. He gave her his hand.

"I'm ready," she said.

ACKNOWLEDGMENTS

I'd like to thank my stalwart agent Peter Riva as well as Mara Anastas, Emma Chapnick, Laurie McGee, Sidney Rioux, and the whole fantastic team at Open Road Integrated Media. Editor Anna Bierhaus and beta readers Carie Ageneau, Cheryl Isaac, Lauren Lanier, and Peter Pappas provided invaluable editorial feedback. My wife, first reader and proofer René, supported me every step of the way—she even gave me the idea for this story.

ABOUT THE AUTHOR

Steve Anderson is the author of the Kaspar Brothers novels: *The Losing Role*, *Liberated*, *Lost Kin,* and *Lines of Deception*. *Under False Flags* is the prequel to his novel *The Preserve*. Anderson was a Fulbright Fellow in Germany and is a literary translator of bestselling German fiction as well as a freelance editor. He lives in Portland, Oregon.

stephenfanderson.com
stephenfanderson.com/mailing-list

STEVE ANDERSON

FROM OPEN ROAD MEDIA

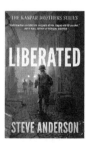

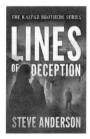

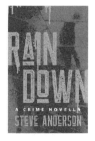

OPEN ROAD

INTEGRATED MEDIA

INTEGRATED MEDIA

Find a full list of our authors and titles at www.openroadmedia.com

FOLLOW US
@OpenRoadMedia